More Beautiful Than Before

McNally Men #3

MOLLY McCARTHY

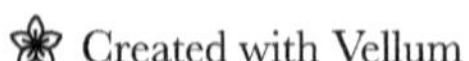 Created with Vellum

CONTENT NOTE

This book contains contains strong language, sexual content,
and mentions of domestic violence.

For everyone who's had to wait longer than they would have liked for their happily ever after, and for everyone who is still waiting. Your time will come.

1

———

It should have been the best day of his life. Twelve hours ago, Fletcher had received the promotion he'd been working toward his entire career—an event that would have most people jumping for joy. After dedicating almost twenty years of his life to teaching, he had just been named the brand-new principal of Harper Elementary School.

Though his promotion was unfortunately due to the current principal's bad health, leading to Fletcher being promoted mid-year, he was beyond proud of his accomplishment. Principalship had been a goal of his for as long as he could remember, not because he cared about climbing some career ladder, but because he cared so deeply about his students' welfare. He'd always longed to be in charge of hiring the best teachers, providing them with top-of-the-line materials and resources, and ensuring that the school environment primed students to learn and thrive.

Having accomplished his greatest goal, Fletcher should have been sitting in Paddy's Pub celebrating. Instead, he was drowning his sorrows because the day that should have been the best of his life was also the day he'd been dumped by his longtime girlfriend.

The one he'd *thought* would be forever.

The single shot of whiskey and foamy beer sitting before Fletcher mocked him. After almost ten years with Christa, she had broken things off during the same conversation in which he'd announced his promotion. Sure, they'd been growing apart for a while, both putting extra hours into their careers and spending less and less time together. He had thought they were working toward having the financial stability to start a family. Apparently, Christa had been on a completely different page.

Fletcher knocked back the shot of whiskey as her parting words echoed through his mind: "*If I had a baby with you, you'd never give me the time of day again. You can't even step away from the kids at your job for a single moment.*"

He slammed the shot glass down a little too hard, catching a nasty glare from the bartender. Shooting her an apologetic nod, he picked up his pint glass with the pads of his fingertips.

What level of insecurity did it take to imply that having a baby would take too much of his attention away from her? Christa had always been a little…high maintenance…but *that* was over the top. As he started in on his beer, Fletcher realized he wasn't so much mourning the loss of Christa as he was the loss of the future they could have had together.

Having helped raise his two younger brothers, Jack and Beau, then spending so many years educating and caring for other people's children, Fletcher was beyond ready for kids of his own. He simply couldn't believe that, at the ripe old age of forty-two, he was single and back to square one. Ten years had gone down the drain that day with nothing to show for it.

Maybe it was for the best. Maybe it was time to move on and embrace the present. He had a brand-spankin'-new job to celebrate, and now that he was free from Christa's clutches, he could explore what other options may be out there. Hell, he hadn't even considered another option in a decade. It was high time he widened his horizons.

Fletcher was halfway through his beer when he spied a radiant redhead over the rim of his glass. She had just entered the building and was making her way toward the bar, her lush hips swaying as she walked. The black skirt and gray blouse she wore were modest but did nothing to hide the curves of her body. A mane of red hair spilled over her shoulders like a copper waterfall.

As she got closer, her emerald-green eyes met his brown ones, and Fletcher almost choked on his beer. She was stunning. The smattering of freckles running across the bridge of her nose gave her a youthful air, but her soft curves were all woman. Her dress didn't reveal much, but the creamy skin he could see looked soft, smooth, and oh-so touchable.

Settling down one stool away from him, the woman sent Fletcher a look that was half-greeting, half-smirk. He wondered if she'd caught his near-blunder, though he'd eventually managed to swallow his beer without issue. He struggled to tear his gaze away as the bartender approached.

"Vodka soda," the woman ordered in a slightly raspy voice that only added to her appeal.

Fletcher took another sip of his beer as he tried—and failed—not to watch her. Crossing her legs beneath the bar, she adjusted her skirt over her lush thighs as she quickly surveyed the rest of the bar. Her shoulders seemed to relax infinitesimally when her gaze returned to him.

She nodded toward the empty shot glass and now half-empty beer. "One-person pity party or solo celebration?"

Fletcher rolled the glass in his hand. "Little bit of both."

The bartender returned with her vodka soda, fixing a wedge of lime to the rim of the glass before sliding it across the bar. The woman accepted her drink with a demure grin. Taking the lime wedge, she squeezed it into her drink with long, thin fingers. Her nails were short and unpainted, yet still feminine. The small detail meant she must have been practical —more concerned with the functionality of her fingers than with how they looked. The opposite of Christa, who had always been more preoccupied with appearances.

Laying the wrung-out lime on the counter, the woman sucked a bit of juice from the pad of her thumb before turning toward Fletcher. Her smile turned sultry when she caught his gaze on her lips.

Fletcher cleared his throat. "How about you?" He gestured to her drink. "Celebrating something or drowning your sorrows?"

She cocked her head to the side as she took a sip. "Little bit of both."

One side of his mouth quirked up in a grin that quickly became an open-mouthed stare as her pillowy lips met the rim of the glass for another sip. He compulsively swallowed before composing himself, settling his lips into an approachable smile.

"I'm Fletcher."

"That's an unusual name," she remarked, uncrossing her legs and hooking her feet onto the rim around the bottom of the barstool. She swiveled a little more in his direction.

"It was my mother's maiden name. She was an only child and took my father's name, so she wanted to pass down her family name in some way."

The woman nodded and drummed her fingers on the bar. "My mother's maiden name was O'Shaughnessy. That would be a mouthful for a first name."

"Yes." Fletcher chuckled. "It would. So, what should I call you?"

She hesitated before reaching out her hand. "You can call me Maeve."

He shook her slender hand, appreciating her firm grip. Some people were barely even active participants in a handshake. They just dangled their hands out like dead fish and let them be pumped up and down. A firm grip like Maeve's exuded a certain amount of confidence and self-assuredness.

"It's nice to meet you, Maeve."

She retracted her hand and wrapped it around her glass. "You too, Fletcher."

"So," he said, grabbing hold of his own glass. "It seems we're both experiencing some conflicting feelings tonight. Why don't we focus on the good stuff and have a toast to whatever it is we're celebrating?"

Her lips curved into a tantalizing grin as she lifted her glass into the air. "To new beginnings."

"I'll drink to that." Fletcher tapped her glass with his, their fingers brushing together ever so slightly. The contact sent a tingling sensation up his arm, threatening to make him choke on his beer again.

"So, what's your new beginning, if you don't mind my asking?" His voice came out scratchier than he would have liked, and he resisted the urge to clear his throat again.

Maeve pursed her lips. "I just moved to town, so it's a fresh start for me."

"That's cool," he said. "Welcome to Boston. We're aggressive drivers, and the winters can be hell with all the snow, but you won't find better clam chowder or more dedicated sports fans."

Maeve scrunched her nose in distaste. "I don't like seafood or sports, but I'm sure I'll be able to find some redeeming qualities in this city."

Fletcher chuckled into his beer. "I hope so."

"What about you? You have a new beginning happening, too?

"Actually, yeah. I just got a promotion. I'm the new——"

"Wait!" she said, cutting him off. "Don't tell me. Let's… let's not talk about that stuff tonight—where we work, where we're from, what our families are like. Let's stay away from personal details." Shifting on her stool, she added, "If you want to keep talking, that is."

The hint of vulnerability revealed that she wasn't quite as self-confident as Fletcher may have originally suspected.

"I do," he replied. As if he *wouldn't* want to continue flirting with such an alluring woman.

Maeve's eyes took on a faraway look as she continued. "For tonight, let's just be…Fletcher and Maeve at a bar. No responsibilities. No obligations. Let's forget about our problems and the problems of the world and just be two people at a bar."

Fletcher took a long pull of his beer. "Fletcher and Maeve at a bar. I like the sound of that." He also liked the sound of forgetting about his problems. He was already so sick of over-analyzing the past ten years with Christa. Eager for a distraction, he asked, "If we're not sharing any personal details, then what do you want to talk about?"

Maeve's lips tilted into a wry smile as she considered his question. "Do you believe aliens exist?"

Fletcher's eyebrows lifted at the out-of-the-box question. "I do, actually. Our universe is so vast, and we've only been able to explore a small amount of it. I'd be willing to bet there are forms of life on other planets. I don't know if they'd look like the little green aliens you see in the movies, but I think they probably exist."

Maeve's eyes lit up as he spoke, her body turning a fraction more in his direction. "Exactly! It's so self-absorbed to think we humans on Earth are the only intelligent life forms in the entire universe. There are probably aliens on other planets, making fun of us for being so pompous."

Fletcher snickered at the thought. "Do you think we make good entertainment?"

"Oh, definitely," she said around sips of her drink. "Humans are so weird."

"I wonder if they're just waiting for us to destroy the planet so they can swoop in and take it over for their own alien usage."

"Probably. Hey, if aliens could exist on a planet like Venus or Mercury, then they could definitely withstand Earth post global warming."

Fletcher nodded at the sad fact. When Maeve placed her glass back down, he noticed it was nearly empty.

"Can I buy you another drink?"

She frowned down at her glass, as if just realizing she'd consumed the whole thing. Glancing from the glass to him, she did another visual sweep of the bar before replying, "Sure."

Fletcher flagged down the bartender and got them another round, this time going for a whiskey on the rocks for himself. Three drinks would mellow him out without removing any of his faculties. He didn't know how much of a lightweight Maeve was, but she seemed equally as composed and relaxed as he was.

Once the bartender set down their fresh drinks, he continued the conversation.

"What about ghosts? Do you believe in them?"

Maeve nodded with a look that said *duh.* "Once again, I believe it's arrogant to think that our spirits only have one life within our bodies. I think they must keep bopping around in some parallel universe after we die. They probably watch us to amuse themselves just like the aliens do." She rolled her eyes as she squeezed a fresh lime wedge into her drink. "What about you?"

"I definitely think they could be real," Fletcher said. "The law of conservation states that energy can neither be created nor destroyed—only converted from one form to another. So, when someone dies, where does all that energy go? It has to be transferred somewhere. Why not to a ghost?"

Maeve blinked hard at his explanation. "You're pretty smart, huh?"

He smirked. "One might call me nerdy. I read a lot, and I really enjoy science fiction, so this stuff is kind of my jam."

"That's cool," she replied. "I don't have much time to read these days, but I used to enjoy fantasy."

Fletcher added that to the scant arsenal of things he knew about Maeve. Though she wasn't giving him personal details, he could tell a lot about her from just their interaction and conversation. She was bold, but some of that was a mask to hide the vulnerability lurking underneath. She was open-minded and curious. She was possibly trying to avoid something…or someone? And she was so, *so* sexy.

Her tongue darted out to catch an excess drop of liquid beneath her bottom lip. Fletcher tracked the movement with his gaze, and his jeans instantly felt tighter. He wracked his brain for something to keep the conversation going without giving away the fact that his fly was probably leaving an imprint on his cock.

Thinking of her favorite fantasy genre, he asked, "How about mythical creatures, like vampires, and werewolves, and stuff? Where do you stand on those?"

She wrinkled her nose. "I think they're fun to read about, but I don't think they exist in the real world. You?"

He shrugged and sipped his beer. "I don't know. I think anything's possible."

Maeve wagged her head and smiled playfully. "Next you'll tell me you believe the Earth is flat."

Straight-faced, Fletcher met her gaze. "It is."

Her smile dropped.

He couldn't hold on to his mock seriousness for long, though, and laughter burst from his throat at her horrified expression. "I'm kidding, Maeve."

Her cheeks pinked, and she reached out to swat his shoulder. "That wasn't funny. I thought I was going to have to cut and run for a second there."

Fletcher worked to control his laughter as well as his reaction to her casual touch. That third drink must have loosened his inhibitions *just* enough, because before he knew it, he was saying, "Not alone, I hope."

Maeve's gaze shot to his, and her nostrils flared. For a moment, he couldn't tell whether her reaction was lust or anger that he dared to imply they may leave the bar together. When her pupils widened and her breathing sped up, he knew it was the former.

"Do you want to get out of here?" he asked. Though his radar may have been a bit rusty, he was sure he hadn't misread her interest.

Maeve threw back the rest of her vodka soda and wiped her lips with the back of her hand.

"Yes."

2

───────

After ordering an Uber, Fletcher took Maeve's hand to help her off the barstool. They walked hand in hand out of the bar, mutually agreeing to wait for the car out on the sidewalk so they could enjoy the crisp, early spring air. It had been an unseasonably warm late-April day, but the sun had long since set, and the temperature was dropping rapidly.

A cool breeze caressed them, and Fletcher wasn't sure whether the goosebumps that crawled up his arms were from that or from the feel of Maeve's warm, delicate hand in his.

"My place or yours?" he asked, realizing they had never decided on a destination.

"Yours," she replied quickly.

Glancing down at Maeve, he found her chewing her bottom lip. All appearances of bravado seemed to have seeped from her as soon as they stepped out of the bar.

He brushed her hand with his thumb. "Are you sure you want to do this? If you want, I can order a second Uber, and you can go home."

"No." She shook her head. "I want to go back to your place."

pulled her other hand into his, turning her so ce to face. "Are you sure? We don't have to rush or g you're not ready for. If you want to just give me er so we can meet up again sometime, we can do that."

"I'm sure," Maeve answered, but she must have seen the uncertainty written on his face, because when he didn't immediately respond, she grabbed two fistfuls of his jacket and pulled his face down to hers.

At the first touch of their lips, Fletcher froze, shock chilling him even more than the spring breeze had. But then, Maeve's soft lips registered, and he began kissing her back. Not having been adequately prepared for the kiss, he pulled back to suck in a ragged breath before retuning his lips to hers. They were silky, and supple, and *perfect*.

Apparently, her tongue was just as curious as her mind, because it began exploring the curve of his lips almost immediately, seeking entrance. Fletcher granted it, opening and deepening the kiss. Their movements were frenzied, frantic. And while the passion was exhilarating, he didn't want her to think his promise of not rushing was empty.

Gently removing her hands from his jacket and placing them on his waist, Fletcher framed her face with his hands as he eased back.

"What's wrong?" she asked, her brow furrowing as she caught her breath.

"Nothing." He brushed a chunk of her lustrous red hair behind her shoulders. "I just want to slow down a little. We can take our time."

Surprise, or maybe confusion, swept over Maeve's face before she acquiesced with a nod.

Cradling her jaw, Fletcher lowered his lips to hers and gently caressed them. This kiss was sweeter, lacking the desperation of their earlier one, but equally full of longing and promise.

The beep of a car horn had Maeve jerking backward. Fletcher reached out to catch her hand so she didn't wind up on her ass in the flowerbed outside the bar.

Wearing a sheepish grin, she squeezed his hand. "Thanks."

He pointed to the source of her scare. "I think that's our car."

Maeve's gaze followed his finger, and she appeared to take a deep breath.

"Let's go."

~

The ride back to his place was torturous. Shortly after he slid into the seat beside Maeve, she placed her hand on his thigh, dangerously close to the bulge in his pants, and began rubbing a rhythmic pattern. The contact was natural, almost mindless, and Fletcher wondered if it was a sign of nerves or excitement. Even through the thick denim of his jeans, he felt her touch like a hot brand.

They didn't share many words in the car, but they didn't have to. Maeve's hands were communicating plenty on their own. Her fingers stroked a little higher, heading toward forbidden territory—at least while they were in the car with another person.

Fletcher shifted in his seat, though trying to find a comfortable position with a raging hard-on was an impossible task. He snaked an arm around Maeve's waist, giving her hip a squeeze. She turned her gaze from the window, her sharp green eyes blazing into his.

"How far?" she asked, her eyes filled with need.

"We're almost there," he rasped, lust and yearning clogging his throat.

"Good," she breathed, her hold tightening on his thigh.

Moments later, the car pulled up to Clear Ridge Apartments. Fletcher puffed out a breath of relief, thanked the driver, and jogged around to open Maeve's door. She took his outstretched hand with a shy smile and allowed him to lead her into apartment 34. Inside, Fletcher offered to take her jacket and hung it on a coat hook in the entryway, then they strolled into the kitchen.

"Do you want a drink?" he asked, unsure what exactly was supposed to come next. It had been a long time since he'd wooed someone, and he'd never moved quite this quickly. What was the protocol for taking home someone that you'd just met and desperately wanted to sleep with but also didn't want to put pressure on?

Maeve hugged her arms loosely around herself. "No, thanks. But I'd love a tour." Her gaze roamed the kitchen, taking in the exposed brick and stainless-steel appliances.

"Sure." Fletcher opened his arms wide. "This is the kitchen, obviously. There's the living room." He motioned across the open floor plan to the black leather couch and chairs, flat-screen TV, and fully stocked bookcases. "And down here," he said as he began down the short hallway, "are the bedrooms and bathroom."

He stopped outside one room and gestured through the open doorway. "This is the guest room. My brother, Beau, used to live here with me, but he moved out to live with his girlfriend a few months ago." Fletcher led Maeve to the other bedroom doorway. "And this is my room."

She wandered in and gave his room a thorough visual inspection, not unlike she'd done at the bar. Fletcher got the feeling this woman didn't miss a trick. He crossed his arms and leaned against the doorframe, watching as she inspected his most private space.

She ran her finger down his mahogany dresser. "This is gorgeous."

"Thanks," he said, watching with amusement as she not-so-subtly scanned the items atop his dresser. He was confident there was nothing damning there—he liked to keep things clean and orderly—but it was fun to watch her snoop.

"Would you like to head back out to the living room, or…" He trailed off.

Maeve shook her head as she walked toward where he was propped in the doorway. "No, I think I'd rather stay in here."

Fletcher's breath hitched when she stopped just inches away from him. "O-okay," he sputtered. Apparently, her bold streak was back with a vengeance.

Maeve pressed her palms to his chest and tipped her head back to meet his gaze. "Kiss me, Fletcher," she whispered, her eager hands pawing at his chest.

Determined not to rush, he cradled her head, lacing his fingers through her thick hair. Tipping her neck back to just the angle he wanted, he slanted his mouth over hers and granted her wish.

Maeve let out a throaty moan as their lips met. Her fingers tangled into the fabric of his shirt, clutching to him like the end of a rope. Once again, her insistent tongue sought entrance into his mouth, and Fletcher did nothing to fight it. Rapidly losing his grip on his self-control, he slid his tongue along hers as he pressed her back against his dresser, caging her in with his arms.

Maeve pulled back to suck in a breath, so Fletcher lowered his lips to her neck, pressing kisses to her fair skin. She let out a soft, sweet sigh and tipped her head further to the side, giving him greater access to her neck.

So caught up in trying to get her to make that sound again, it took Fletcher a few moments to register her small hands fumbling with the buttons of his shirt. Keeping his lips glued to her neck, he tilted his torso away to help her out. He chuckled under his breath when she released a disgruntled squawk, but she finally managed to pry his shirt open.

Fletcher took a step back, allowing his shirt to drop from his shoulders to the floor. Maeve stared at his chest with a hunger in her eyes that made him stumble back another step. When was the last time someone had looked at him like that? With such longing, as if she would perish if she couldn't have him.

Her gaze devoured his contoured chest coated in light-brown hair. Fletcher knew he kept in good shape by going to the gym and going for the occasional run, but he wasn't ripped like his little brother, Beau. His body was nothing special. Yet, Maeve looked at him like a starving woman at a buffet.

Unable to bear her scrutiny any longer without touching her, he tugged her into his arms and brought his lips back to hers. Her hands returned to his chest, this time gliding over his bare skin. Fletcher groaned when her fingernail scraped over his nipple, and she playfully nipped at his bottom lip.

Keeping her secure in his arms, Fletcher backed Maeve across the room until the backs of her knees met the edge of the bed, and she collapsed onto it. Sitting on the edge put her at eye level with his stomach, and her wandering hands reached for the button of his fly.

"Maeve, wait," he blurted.

Her eyes shot to his just as she achieved her goal of unbuttoning his pants.

"Hmm?"

"Are you… Are you sure you want to do this?" he asked. She was obviously eager, but Fletcher wanted to be absolutely sure he wasn't taking advantage of the situation. She *had* had a few drinks, though she seemed perfectly capable of decision-making.

"I am," she said. "Are you?"

He responded by bringing her hand to rest on the growing bulge in the crotch of his pants.

"I guess you are," she quipped as she brushed her fingers along his rigid erection.

"But you can change your mind at any time," he reminded her.

Maeve maintained eye contact as she drew his jeans down his legs. "Okay."

Fletcher stepped out of his jeans and reached for the hem of her shirt to pull it off.

"Wait!" she cried, grabbing hold of the bottom of her shirt. "Actually, I'd like to keep this on."

A frown creased his brow. "Oh, okay."

"It's just…" She hesitated, fiddling with the fabric in her fingers. "I've had babies. I have scars, and stretch marks, and…"

"I don't care about any of that," Fletcher said honestly. A few scars or stretch marks didn't bother him. Hell, a bunch of scars and stretch marks wouldn't bother him. He was dying to see Maeve in full. Would her nipples be a soft pink or a dusty rose? Did she have freckles in other places besides the bridge of her nose? These were the questions that plagued him, but he would take Maeve however he could get her.

"I just…I'd be more comfortable keeping it on." She shrugged, then wrapped her arms around her torso.

"No problem." He tucked a lock of hair behind her ear. "Can I take this off?" he asked, fingering the fabric of her skirt.

Biting her lip, Maeve nodded.

"Lie back and lift your hips," he instructed.

She obeyed, her teeth still sunk into her pillowy bottom lip. Lying before him on his bed, eyes wide with excitement, Maeve looked like temptation personified.

Fletcher appreciated her in the pose for a moment before dragging the skirt slowly down her legs, revealing lacy white panties that sported a suspicious damp spot. A guttural groan rang from his throat at the sight.

Normally, he would have left the panties on for a bit and gotten to work on foreplay elsewhere, but without being able to access any of her upper half, he was forced to get creative. Gliding a single finger up one leg and down the other, he was pleased when Maeve squirmed slightly beneath his touch. He repeated the motion, this time grazing his fingernail slightly over the sensitive skin of her inner thighs. When she lifted her hips toward his touch, Fletcher knew it was time to lose the barrier.

He slid a finger beneath the elastic waistband of her panties. "Can these go, too?" As sexy as the underwear was, he'd much rather have her naked.

Maeve gulped as she nodded, lifting her hips again to make it easier for him to slide her panties off.

Fletcher's breath whooshed from his lungs when he discovered that the hair between her legs was the same stunning auburn as the hair currently spread out over his pillow.

"You're so beautiful," he murmured as he lay on his side beside Maeve, his fingers dancing over her thighs. "I can't get over how much I love your red hair." He skimmed his palm over the neatly trimmed triangle at the apex of her thighs.

A shy smile flirted with Maeve's lips. "Thank you." She ran her hand over his pectorals. "I can't get over how much I love your chest hair. I never knew I found it so sexy."

Fletcher's chest puffed with pride that she found him as attractive as he found her. He leaned down until their lips met, and she rolled toward him, hitching a leg over both of his as she deepened the kiss. His erection, still caged in his boxers, jutted against her soft belly. Maeve rubbed against it, teasing him.

Fletcher's hand found itself in the perfect position to explore between her legs, so he did. With no panties left to soak up her excitement, his finger grew damp as he dragged it through her folds. Maeve's eyelids drooped with pleasure as he repeated the gesture once, twice, three times before moving higher to find the tight bud of nerves that would really set her off.

"*Yes*," Maeve sighed when he reached his target. Fletcher circled one way and then the other before gently pressing on her clit, testing her responses to each touch. Her hips bucked into his hand, and he memorized the amount of pressure that had incited the response. He began moving his fingers in a rhythm, bouncing between exerting that perfect amount of pressure on her clit and trailing his touch over her slit, never quite slipping inside.

"Fletcher." She arched into his touch, greedy for more.

"Hmm?" he teased, knowing exactly what she craved.

She tried to push his hand lower. "Fletcher, please."

He parted her folds and tucked a finger just inside her opening. "Is this what you want?"

Maeve let out a gasp as he slid his finger in just a little farther.

"Yes!" she cried as she clenched around him.

"You're so responsive," Fletcher mumbled as he worked his finger in and out slowly.

"I… It feels so good," Maeve managed between moans of pleasure.

He placed a kiss on her forehead. "Good."

He was focusing intently on his task when her hand snaked between them to find his erection. He grunted at her touch but tried to return to his mission: Maeve's orgasm. That proved impossible when she slipped her hand into his boxers and skin met skin.

"Fuck," Fletcher growled, instinctively thrusting into her grip.

Maeve stilled as she fisted his erection, her focus shifting from her own pleasure to his.

"Not yet," he chided, circling her wrist and tugging her hand from his boxers. "Let me do this for you first."

Her lips turned down as her hand dropped to the mattress.

Fletcher kissed the frown right off her mouth. "Just relax and enjoy."

Maeve's brows drew together in confusion, as if that was an unfamiliar concept. "But what about you?"

"Don't worry about me," he said, his finger sliding in and out of her easily. "We'll get to me later." He slipped a second finger in, giving Maeve a moment to acclimate to the feeling before pressing his palm against her clit.

"Oh!" Her surprised exclamation gave away her growing excitement as much as her bucking hips did.

"That's it," Fletcher murmured when she cried out and clamped around his fingers. A shiver wracked her body, and he knew she was close. "Give it to me, Maeve."

Her eyes snapped shut at the sound of her name, and then she was coming, spasming around his fingers as he held the heel of his hand firmly on her clit. He stopped moving so as not to overstimulate her, but he kept his hand in place as she enjoyed every last ounce of pleasure.

Maeve's eyes opened slowly as she came out from under the spell of her orgasm. "Whoa," was all she said.

Fletcher chuckled under his breath. "That's a good thing, I hope?"

She blinked a few times before answering with a whispered, "Yes."

He stroked his fingers lightly over her thighs, enjoying her soft skin. "You're so sexy." He kissed a beauty mark on her neck.

Maeve blushed and averted her gaze. "I think it's time to lose these," she said, pulling down one side of the waistband of his boxers.

"I couldn't agree with you more," he said as he yanked them off, tossing them to the floor beside the bed. His erection had grown rock hard in response to Maeve's pleasure.

She practically purred when she caught sight of his length, her hand immediately encircling it.

Fletcher hissed when she squeezed just the right amount.

"Lie back," he said because she had come up onto one

elbow to touch him.

"But I want to return the favor."

Fletcher removed her hand from his erection. "I don't want to come in your hand. Lie back," he repeated.

Maeve complied, dropping back onto the mattress with a sigh. Fletcher leaned over to rip open the bedside table drawer and grab a condom. Her gaze followed him as he rolled it over his length, sheathing himself so he could come where he really wanted to.

Once again, Maeve looked absolutely edible as she lay before him. He was tempted to use his mouth on her, but he didn't know how much longer he could last. Nudging her legs apart with his knee, Fletcher found her glistening with the evidence of her excitement. The sight was intoxicating.

"Grab onto the headboard," he rasped.

A look of confusion crossed over Maeve's features, but she obeyed, reaching back and feeling for the curve of his mahogany headboard. He wished like hell he could see the way the movement would inevitably lift her breasts, but as it was, the pose gave her a look of openness and obedience that almost had Fletcher coming on the spot.

"Good girl." He settled himself between her thighs. "Keep your hands there while I make you come again."

She inhaled sharply, her grip tightening on the headboard.

Satisfied by her reaction, Fletcher notched himself at her entrance and slowly thrusted inside of her. She was tight but pliant from her orgasm, and he worked himself in and out smoothly.

She let out a sound of pure pleasure that he utterly delighted in. "You like that, huh?" he asked, pumping his hips a little faster.

Maeve's response was to wrap her legs around him and dig her heels into the backs of his thighs, spurring him on. "Harder," she whispered.

Fletcher let out a feral grunt. He appreciated a little

submissiveness in the bedroom—he always had—but he was also more than willing to comply with his partner's demands.

"Hold on tight," he warned as he slammed into her.

She cried out and clutched the headboard, her knuckles turning white with the effort. Fletcher paused for a moment, assessing to make sure it was a cry of pleasure and not pain. When her strangled voice wailed, "More!" he finally let loose, pumping his hips hard again, then again, and again, and again.

Soon, Maeve was screaming his name, and he couldn't hold back any longer. With one final thrust, he filled the condom as she quivered around him. Her feet dropped from the backs of his thighs to the mattress as her whole body softened. Relief, pleasure, and warmth flooded Fletcher's body as he dropped to the mattress beside her. He rolled off the condom before collecting Maeve into his arms and pressing his lips to her hair.

"That was…" He couldn't find the words to describe the pure bliss that had permeated the entire night. Maeve was a complete curveball, coming into his life at the most adventitious time and completely beguiling him with her beauty, grace, and hint of mystery. Not to mention, that was easily the best sex he'd ever had.

"Amazing," she finished his sentence for him.

Fletcher stroked up and down her side over her shirt, lowering his lips to hers for a long, slow, lingering kiss.

"Will you sleep here tonight?" he asked. He wasn't ready to end this just yet. Maeve felt a bit like a mirage—wondrous and more than welcome, but apt to disappear at any moment. As long as he had her in his arms, though, he could ensure himself that she was real.

Maeve cocked her head to the side, uncertainty tainting her features.

"At least stay for a bit. Let me hold you."

"Okay," she acquiesced as she cuddled into his chest.

3

The clock on the bedside table read 2:25 a.m. Fletcher had begun snoring softly about a half hour ago, right about the time his arm around her waist had gone limp. Holding her breath, Maeve gently disentangled herself from his grasp and slid out of the bed. Gathering her clothing from where it was scattered on the floor, she quickly and silently dressed. Her blouse was wrinkled beyond repair, but she had no one left to impress.

As she retreated through the doorway of Fletcher's bedroom, Maeve allowed herself one final glance at him. Studying his wavy blond hair, strong shoulders, and muscular torso tangled up in the sheets, she couldn't help but try to memorize every detail of his appearance. He was *so* handsome. Perhaps she'd been watching too many Disney movies, but her first thought upon spotting him was that he had Prince Charming hair. Between that and his deep, kind, brown eyes, she was a goner.

She'd gone to Paddy's Pub with every intention of flirting the night away, and she had promised herself that if she felt the urge to do something more, she would go with the flow and see where the night took her. It had taken all day to psych herself up, thinking it would take every ounce of her courage just to approach a man. But Fletcher had made it so easy. So natural. It was a shame she would never see him again.

While her night with Fletcher had felt like a fantasy, it was just that—a fantasy. Flirting with sexy men in bars, allowing them to take her home and make love to her, sneaking out in the middle of the night… That wasn't Maeve's real life. She was heading home to that now.

Tiptoeing from the bedroom, she headed out to the kitchen and ordered an Uber. It didn't take long to arrive, and she discovered that it also didn't take long to get home. Fletcher didn't live far from her. Hopefully, that wouldn't prove to be an issue. Then again, Boston was a big city. What were the chances of them running into each other again?

Maeve was just climbing the stairs to her unit of the two-family home when a soft mewling sound caught her attention. She froze, her gaze scanning the hedges and flowers shrouded in darkness until she caught sight of the culprit. Rushing down the stairs, she flew into the flowerbed where a skinny, shivering, gray cat was halfway lodged in the gutter. Its yellow eyes pierced the darkness like head beams in the night. It let out a disgruntled *meow* as Maeve knelt in the dirt beside it.

"Come here, baby," she cooed as she wiggled the cat out of the gutter. It came into her arms easily, and she wrapped it as best she could in the fabric of her shirt. If she hadn't been worried about wrinkles before, she would have been now. The creature's claws dug into her skin as it clutched at anything it could reach.

"Oh, honey," she said, her heart breaking for the small animal. It quivered in her arms as she ran a thumb over its slick head. "You just need a safe place to land, don't you?"

As quietly as she could while cradling the crying cat, Maeve entered the front door to her home. *Her* home. Though the new space didn't quite feel like it yet, the knowledge that it belonged to her filled her with pride. Her very own safe place to land—and now the cat's, too.

She was heading for her bedroom to figure out what to do when Connie's head popped up from the couch.

"Mae!" she cried, hurrying to rise from her reclined position.

Maeve paused, instinctively swaying from side to side as if she was soothing a baby in her arms. "Hey, Con."

Connie Robinson was her best friend, landlord, and guardian angel all wrapped into one. In her mid-fifties, Connie still had a youthful look that made her seem like a comrade rather than an elder to Maeve. Her rich, deep-brown skin held a luster that could only be achieved through a meticulous moisturizing routine. Her graying box braids may have hinted at her age if she didn't tend to wear them in a variety of funky styles. Tonight, they were wrapped up on top of her head in a gingham-patterned silk scarf.

"What the hell is that?" Connie squawked as she approached.

"It's a cat," Maeve said, unwrapping the cocoon she'd created with her shirt to reveal a glimpse of the poor creature.

Connie let out a noise of disgust, shrinking back from it.

"Be nice, Connie," Maeve chided as she stroked a finger over the animal's bony spine. It *was* a rather unseemly sight with its matted gray fur and protruding skeleton. "It just needs a little TLC. Sound familiar?"

Connie's face softened into a warm grin. It brought out the faint wrinkles around her eyes that proved she wore a smile more often than not. After what that woman had been through, it was no small miracle she kept such a positive attitude.

"I think you're the perfect person to give it that," she said quietly.

The sentiment struck Maeve right in the chest. Before she could allow emotion to overcome her, she lifted the bundle in her arms slightly. "Will you help me give it a bath? I'm not entirely sure what to do."

"Neither am I." Connie eyed the cat skeptically. "But I'll do what I can to help."

And that was Connie—willing to help even if she wasn't so thrilled about what it would entail. As they climbed the stairs to the second-floor bathroom, a thought dawned on Maeve.

"What were you still doing here?" she asked. "You could have gone back over to your place once the kids were asleep."

Connie lived in the other half of the two-family home. She had inherited it from her father when he passed away a few years prior but had remained in her home in California, leaving this house idle until she decided what to do with it. When Maeve needed a fresh start fast, Connie had decided to move across the country with her and was allowing her to live here rent-free until she got back on her feet. Guardian angel, indeed.

"I was getting a little worried about you," Connie admitted. "I know you said not to wait up, but… Did you have a good night?"

Maeve shrugged as she reached the top of the staircase. "Sure."

Connie stopped in the threshold to the bathroom, crossing her arms. "That's a bit of an evasive answer, don't you think?"

Maeve sat on the closed lid of the toilet, still cradling the cat in her arms. "I had a good night," she said as she slid her palm rhythmically over the cat's back. It had stopped shaking and now provided a surprisingly calming presence.

Connie remained silent. Maeve glanced up to find her friend watching her with a brow raised.

"That's awfully cryptic."

Maeve continued patting the cat. "What's cryptic about saying I had a good night?"

Connie's eyes narrowed. "What made it so good? Did you

do anything interesting? *Meet* anyone interesting?"

Maeve's hand stuttered in its rhythm. She let out a half-sigh, half-groan but figured she owed Connie an answer. Her friend *had* babysat both of her children for the night and was now helping her rescue a stray cat, after all.

"I went to a bar," she said, focusing her attention on a spot at the base of the cat's spine that it seemed to enjoy the most. "And I met a nice man."

Connie's eyes narrowed further. "And?"

Maeve released another annoyed sound. Might as well just get it all out there. Connie wasn't known to let her get away with anything. She began speaking quickly. "We talked and flirted, and then he invited me back to his place. We slept together, and it was unbelievably good, and he wanted me to stay, so I did for a while, and then I snuck out when he was asleep."

Connie blinked a few times. "Wow." She seemed to process the story for a few moments before a wide smile bloomed on her face. "I'm so proud of you, Mae."

Her heartfelt words were as sweet as they were unexpected. Maeve swallowed past the emotion clogging her throat. "You're not disappointed in me for being reckless or moving too quickly?"

Connie uncrossed her arms and knelt beside the toilet. Surprisingly, it wasn't their first heart-to-heart to take place in a bathroom, and the location didn't seem to bother her one bit.

"Maeve," she said, placing a gentle hand on her shoulder. "I'm not disappointed in the least. You have a good head on your shoulders, and I trust you to make the right decisions for yourself. I'm proud of you for putting yourself out there. I can't imagine how difficult that was."

Tears pricked the backs of Maeve's eyes. Connie's trust and pride in her never ceased to amaze her, and she was even more stunned to find that she was proud of herself as well.

"Thanks, Con," she said, choking back tears.

Connie gave her shoulder a rub before standing up and perching herself on the side of the sink. "So, are you going to see him again?"

Maeve shook her head fiercely. "No. I think I got men out of my system for a while. I just needed to prove to myself that I wasn't…broken, you know? Now, I can focus on getting the house in shape, getting the kids settled, and finding a job."

Connie cocked her head to the side. "Why can't you do those things *and* see this man again?"

"Because," Maeve said on a sigh. "My life is complicated enough as it is. I have so many more important things to focus on right now."

Connie shook her head slightly. "What about your happiness? When do you get to focus on that?"

Maeve's hand stilled on the cat's back. "I'll be happy when the house is in good shape, the kids are settled, and I have a job."

Connie opened her mouth to release a no-doubt sarcastic yet frustratingly logical retort, but the cat cut her off with a yowl.

Maeve resumed patting him, thankful for the opportunity to change the course of the conversation. "I want to give him a bath, but I don't know what kind of soap is safe to use on his fur. What do you think?"

Connie watched her for a moment, possibly thinking about her question but probably deciding whether or not to call her out about avoiding the real matter at hand. "How about dish soap?" she suggested. "I always see them using it to wash oil off birds in the commercials."

Maeve nodded. "Good thinking. Would you mind grabbing some from the kitchen, and I'll fill the tub with warm water?"

Connie shot her a thumbs up on her way out.

"Here we go, little guy." Maeve lifted the cat so she could

inspect his underside and confirmed that he was, in fact, a boy. "Let's get you clean."

She filled the tub with a couple of inches of lukewarm water and gently placed the cat into it. He immediately let out a hiss that seemed far too ferocious to come from his emaciated body. A moment later, he jumped from the water, back into her lap. Maeve groaned as her skirt soaked through almost instantly. This outfit had been doomed from the start.

"This is going to be harder than I thought," she muttered. Without thinking, she dropped into the tub herself with the cat still in her lap. It was the middle of the night, she was already wet, and this cat needed to get cleaned.

Connie returned to find Maeve sitting in the water, fully clothed.

"Huh," she clucked. "He's already got you wrapped around his little paw."

"He didn't like the water," Maeve explained. "Just bring the soap over here, and let's get him washed."

Connie handed her the bottle of dish soap with a mocking grin. "People get far too attached to their pets these days. Pretty soon, you'll be buying a specialty stroller to take it for walks."

"Ha ha," Maeve deadpanned as she squirted some soap into her palm and began lightly working it into the cat's wet fur. The sudsy foam was soon tinged with brown as it removed dirt and grime. She wouldn't know until he was dry, but she suspected that, without the coating of filth, the cat was probably a lighter gray than she had originally thought.

"Can you scoop up some of the water and pour it onto him while he stays in my lap? I think it'll keep him more comfortable than submerging him."

Connie dutifully knelt beside the tub and did as she was asked, despite the look on her face that said she couldn't quite believe she was doing it. Soon, the cat was sopping wet but clean. He had even begun purring, as if he realized the two women were there to help him, not torture him with water.

"I think he likes you," Connie noted as Maeve wrapped the cat in a towel. The little thing was purring like a tractor now.

Maeve frowned at how small he felt in her arms. "He's probably hungry. I should feed him something before I go to bed."

"There are some leftover chicken fingers from the kids' dinner in the fridge," Connie said. "Just wipe the breading off and give him the chicken part."

"Good idea. Are you sure you've never rehabbed a cat before?" Maeve asked. "You seem to know an awful lot about how to care for one in an emergency. Dish soap and chicken nuggets and all."

"Nope. I just rehab people," Connie said with a wink.

Maeve sobered. "Thank you for helping me tonight. It's late. Why don't you go home? I'll get those chicken nuggets ready and then go to bed myself."

"You never need to thank me for my help," Connie said, wrapping Maeve in a side hug as she held the cat to her chest. "I'll see you in the morning. Goodnight."

Maeve wished her goodnight, and the cat devoured a few chicken nuggets before she locked him in her bathroom with a water bowl and a makeshift litter box made out of a cardboard box for the night. She wasn't sure if he would use it, but at least if he chose not to, the bathroom was small, and it would be easy enough to clean. If she let him have free rein of the house, who knew where his excrement could end up.

With the cat tucked in for the night, Maeve checked on her other two charges. The kids were sharing a room—a fact they were not thrilled about, but it was necessary, given their current circumstances. She certainly couldn't afford a bigger place. Hell, she couldn't even afford the place they were in. Thank God for Connie.

The door to the kids' room squeaked slightly as it opened, and Maeve held her breath. To her relief, both kids remained sound asleep. She crept over to Allie first. Her tenacious, feisty, eldest daughter. The seven-year-old proved the stereotype about redheads being hot-tempered to be true. Honestly, she reminded Maeve far too much of herself—at least, how she used to be.

Maeve feathered a light kiss on her daughter's forehead before checking on Andy. A year younger than Allie, he was the sweet, mellow counterpart to her spirited self. Where Allie led, Andy followed, but he had his own thoughts, ideas, and desires as well. He was Maeve's snuggle bug, her wide-eyed, innocent little cherub. With a barely there kiss to his hair, she exited the bedroom for her own down on the ground floor.

As she scooted into the bundle of covers atop her air mattress, Maeve couldn't help but remember how comfortable Fletcher's bed had been. Perhaps it was her current lack of a real bed, or perhaps it had been the strong arms that held her as she rested in Fletcher's, but either way, she couldn't help but miss the warmth and sense of safety that had enveloped her there.

What if she *had* stayed in his bed? Would they have woken up together? Made love again? Would he have put her pleasure first again, or had that been just a one-time courtesy? Would he use those magical fingers again? Or even his mouth? She could only imagine how magical *that* would be.

These were questions she would never have any answers to, but just pondering the possibilities fulfilled some lonely, aching part of her. Some day, she would be ready to actually pursue something with a man. Something more than a one-night stand to remind her of her womanhood. Something that could blossom into a real relationship. Into forever. And she hoped when she was ready for that, she would find a man as good as Fletcher.

4

———

She hadn't left her number. He hadn't even gotten her last name. Fletcher wasn't past internet stalking to try and figure out who she was, but he didn't even have any personal details to go off of. If you knew someone's workplace or where they had gone to school, you could usually find them on Facebook or at least LinkedIn, but he knew nothing about Maeve other than that she was new to town, believed in aliens and ghosts, and enjoyed fantasy books. Oh, and she had kids. She *had* mentioned that.

Sipping his coffee at the kitchen island the next morning, Fletcher lamented the fact that he hadn't pushed Maeve for more information about herself. Then again, he hadn't expected her to sneak out in the middle of the night. She'd never agreed to sleep over, but when she'd curled up in his arms, he had kind of assumed that she would.

Dropping his head into his hands, Fletcher rubbed his palms over his eye sockets. *Shit.* The first new woman he'd been attracted to in years, and he'd let her get away. It may have seemed a bit quick to get over the long relationship he had with Christa, but there had been so much distance in the past few months. They hadn't slept together in at least twelve weeks. For all intents and purposes, he and Christa hadn't been together for a while.

Fletcher hadn't been looking for anything at the bar other than a drink to take the edge off. Maeve had been a pleasant —no, more than pleasant—surprise. And now, she was just gone.

A light knock on the front door had him leaping from his stool, thinking it could be Maeve. Maybe she had just gone out to get them breakfast or something, and now she was returning. He longed to pull her back into his arms, into his apartment, into his *bed*.

Fletcher's heart sank when he opened the door to find Emma, his brother Beau's girlfriend, standing outside. It wasn't that hers was an unwelcome face; it just wasn't the one he'd been hoping to see. The containers that filled her arms, though, he would gladly accept.

Emma peeked at him over the tower of food-prep containers. "Hi, Fletcher."

"Hey, Em," he greeted her as he took the bulk of the containers before she could drop them. "What's all this?"

Emma followed him into the kitchen with the rest of the food. "I made chili. And then I made cornbread to go with it. Then, I figured I should just round out the meal with dessert, so I made chocolate chip cookies, too." She plunked the containers she was holding on the island. "I've been stress cooking."

"What's wrong, sweetheart?" Fletcher asked, his brow creased with worry as he relieved himself of his own haul. Beau had rescued Emma from human traffickers about a year prior, and her life hadn't exactly been easy before that. Fletcher hated to see her upset in any way. She deserved to live a life full of rainbows, butterflies, and unicorns after what she'd been through.

They'd grown close during the time that Emma and Beau still lived with Fletcher. He and Emma shared a love of literature, and she was just so damn endearing that it was hard not to love her. She was the perfect complement to Beau's rough edges.

Emma let out a soft sigh as she sat in the stool Fletcher had recently vacated. "I'm worried about Beau. He started that new job—the private security one? Today was his first assignment. I know his shoulder is all better, and he's highly trained, but I still can't stop thinking about him getting hurt again."

Beau had been shot in the shoulder the second time he rescued Emma from the human traffickers—yeah, it had happened twice. But he had since healed and gotten antsy to do something in his field again. Beau had told Fletcher about the freelance job doing private security gigs for high-profile clients, but he'd forgotten that it started today.

He'd been a bit distracted.

"Don't worry, Emma. He'll be fine. It's just security. It's not like he's going after bad guys anymore."

"I know." She chewed on the edge of her thumbnail. "Anyway, let's talk about you. Get my mind off it. Congratulations on the new job!"

Fletcher beamed, unable to hide his joy and pride at finally being a principal. "Thank you. I can't wait to get started. I already have a list of things I want to get done right away."

"I'm sure you do. You'll be amazing at it," Emma said.

He sure hoped so.

"I am nervous, though. It's a lot of responsibility. A lot of people looking to me for guidance—children and adults. I hope I can fulfill everyone's expectations."

"You will." She nodded as if it was a sure thing and returned to chewing on that thumbnail. "I also wanted to say that I was so sorry to hear about your breakup with Christa."

Fletcher ran a hand over his head. "Thanks. It was the right move for us."

"You two were together a long time," Emma said.

"Yes." *Too long, probably*, he thought to himself. "I think it's more of a blow to my pride than anything else."

Emma shot him a pitying glance. "Well, hopefully this food cheers you up a bit."

"Will you stay and have some with me?" he asked. They hadn't gotten a chance to catch up about their latest reads in a while. It would be nice to have a little distraction from his current woes.

"Sure!" she replied.

~

As it turned out, Fletcher's worries about not living up to expectations as the new principal of Harper Elementary had been unwarranted. He fell into the role naturally, and everyone had been showing him a great deal of respect so far. As his first week as principal came to a close, he found himself feeling better than ever.

It was Friday morning, he'd surprised the office staff with donuts, and he had just finished orienting a couple of new students. Anderson and Alina Walsh were two very sweet siblings—a boy and a girl, the former in kindergarten and the latter in first grade. Fletcher would meet their parents when they came to pick the kids up. It was odd timing to have new students starting as the school year was wrapping up, but apparently, they were new to town.

All in all, Fletcher couldn't be happier with how his first week on the job had gone. And as a bonus, he'd been so busy that he had barely had time to feel bad about not being able to get in touch with Maeve.

His secretary, Bethany, popped her head into his open office door. "Your brother Beau is here."

"What?" Fletcher asked, surprised by his brother's arrival. "Send him in."

"Hey, bro!" Beau hollered as he sauntered into the office. His presence in any room was larger than life, and that included Fletcher's previously quiet inner sanctum. "I knew I'd find myself in the principal's office again someday." Beau snickered. "I spent so much time here as a kid."

Fletcher rolled his eyes. "I know. I was the one constantly bailing you out, remember?"

He'd helped raise his two brothers after his father had died. At fourteen, Fletcher became partially responsible for Jack, who'd been four, and Beau, who had only been two. As the eldest, Fletcher was tasked with things like making their meals, helping them with homework, and yes, picking them up from school when they got in trouble—which had happened a lot.

Beau came around Fletcher's desk to wrap him in a bear hug. "Congrats, man. You look so good in this office."

Fletcher grinned and adjusted his glasses on his nose where they'd been jostled by Beau's exuberant embrace. "Thanks, man. Means a lot." His earlier train of thought came rushing back to him. "Is everything okay?"

"Oh, yeah. Everything's great," Beau replied, holding up a greasy brown paper bag. "I brought you lunch."

Fletcher recognized the logo from Maria's, their favorite taqueria in the city. "Did you get me a burrito bowl?"

"Of course I did," Beau scoffed as he unpacked the food from the bag, setting the complimentary chips and salsa in the center of the desk. They sat down with their own meals on either side.

"I'm glad everything's good with you," Fletcher said. "I know Emma was worried about you at your new job."

A tender grin grew on Beau's face as he unwrapped his burrito. "She's cute when she's worried about me. I wish she wouldn't worry, though."

"She's always going to worry. She loves you."

Beau's grin widened. Lovesick bastard.

Fletcher groaned as he swallowed the first bite of his burrito bowl. "This is incredible. Way better than cafeteria food. Thanks for bringing me lunch. That was really thoughtful."

"I actually wanted to talk to you about something," Beau said around bites of his burrito. "I feel a little shitty because of your recent breakup and all, but…"

Fletcher swallowed the chip he'd been chewing and wiped his mouth with the back of his hand. "Just spit it out, Beau. I'm a big boy. I can handle whatever it is."

"I want to propose to Emma," his brother blurted.

Fletcher's eyebrows shot up. It wasn't all that surprising that Beau wanted to marry Emma—he'd fallen head over ass for her—but Fletcher had always assumed he would be the first McNally man to get married. Jack had already made that impossible by marrying his wife, Natalie. But now his youngest brother would be beating him to the altar as well.

"Beau, that's great," Fletcher said sincerely, pushing away his own unsettled feelings.

"Do you think it's a good idea?" Beau asked.

"Of course I do," Fletcher said. "Emma is sickeningly in love with you, man. I'm sure she can't wait for you to propose. And selfishly, I'd love to have her as a sister-in-law."

Beau flashed him an uncharacteristically shy smile. "She would be my wife," he said with awe.

"And you'd be her husband," Fletcher said, hardly able to believe the words. His clown of a baby brother was going to get married before him, the man who had spent his whole life wanting a wife and kids.

"What if she says no?"

Fletcher reached across and flicked his brother's nose. "She won't say no."

Beau's lips pulled into a goofy grin. "Yeah, I don't think so either."

After Beau left, Fletcher responded to some emails, did a classroom observation on one of the newly hired teachers, and finalized a form he'd composed for gathering feedback from staff about current protocols and any changes they'd like to see.

It was almost time for school to be let out, and the two new students were meeting him back in his office where they would be picked up. He was hoping to make it customary for new parents to pick their children up from the principal's office on their first day so he could meet them. Fletcher wanted to be a hands-on principal, to get to know his students and parents—not just when they were in trouble, but all the time.

Bethany popped into his office, accompanied by the two tiny humans Fletcher had briefly met earlier. The female first-grader brushed her strawberry-blonde curls from her face as she bounced into the doorway.

"Hi, Mr. McNally!" she exclaimed.

Her kindergartner brother entered a little more timidly, slipping his hand into his sister's as he sidled up next to her. His cropped copper hair shone beneath the fluorescent lighting.

"Hi, Allie," Fletcher said to the girl. She had promptly corrected him when he'd used their full names that morning. "Andy." He shot a kind smile at the shy boy. "Thanks for coming back to see me again. I can't wait to meet your parents."

"We only have a mommy now," Allie announced, her gaze darting around his office with interest, as if that statement left her totally unaffected.

Fletcher silently cursed himself for his ignorance. He knew better than to assume every child had two parents.

"Well, I can't wait to meet your mommy," he corrected. "Did you two have a good first day?"

"Yes!" Allie replied. "I made four new friends, and we built a pyramid out of tissue boxes. Did you know the ancient Egyptians built pyramids? They filled them with treasure!"

Fletcher chuckled at the little girl's exuberance. "Wow," he said. "It sounds like you learned a lot today."

Allie beamed at him, showing off her missing front tooth.

"And how about you, Andy? How was your day?" Fletcher crouched down beside the boy to make himself more approachable.

"Good," Andy said, tightening his hold on his sister's hand. "Mrs. Sullivan read us a book about a naughty cat. He reminded me of Peeve."

"Peeve is our cat," Allie chimed in. "My mommy found him in the gutter. She says he's fresh because he likes to steal our socks, and last night, he jumped on the counter and ate a whole muffin. She named him Peeve because he's our pet. Get it, pet peeve? My mommy is so funny."

Fletcher's head spun with the stream-of-consciousness story, but he managed to catch the gist. "She sounds very funny," he said. A flash of red hair entering the outer office caught his eye. "And I think she might be here."

Both kids swung their gazes toward Bethany's desk, where their mother was signing a form.

"Mommy!" Allie squealed, dropping her brother's hand to run toward her mom. He followed right behind her and wrapped his arms around his mother's leg, clinging to her like a barnacle.

"Hi, babies," came a familiar smoky voice. Though Fletcher had only heard it for one night, he would never forget that voice. His breath caught when he finally looked at the woman's face and registered those shocking, emerald-green eyes.

"Maeve?" he rasped, his throat clogged with a complex

mixture of confusion and elation. He'd been wracking his brain for ways to find her again, and now, here she was, presented to him like a gift.

Maeve's smile fell as she lifted her gaze to his. "Fletcher," she whispered.

"That's Mr. McNally," Allie corrected her mother matter-of-factly. "He's our new principal."

Maeve stared at him. Fletcher, unable to produce a coherent thought, stared right back.

After a prolonged moment, Andy tugged at Maeve's hand. "Mommy, what's wrong?"

Maeve recovered quickly. "Nothing's wrong, honey," she said. Then, she reached out her hand to shake Fletcher's. "It's nice to meet you, Mr. McNally."

Fletcher shook her hand, remembering how that same hand had felt against his skin, gliding along his chest, squeezing his cock…

"Nice to meet you," he responded, his voice appallingly husky.

Maeve dropped his hand like a hot coal, using hers to ruffle Andy's hair. Sobered by the reminder that they were in the presence of her children, Fletcher cleared his throat and crouched down to their level.

"Allie, Andy…would you mind if I chatted with your mom in my office for a few minutes? I think Bethany has some markers behind her desk that you can color with."

Allie's face lit up. "I love coloring!"

"Great." Fletcher shepherded the kids over to Bethany, then motioned for Maeve to enter his office. She did so with a glare.

Fletcher clenched his teeth as he shut the door behind them, realizing this may not be the happy reunion he'd been hoping for. After a tense, silent moment, he was still facing the door and had his hand clamped on the doorknob, so he took a deep breath and turned toward Maeve.

"You…you wear glasses," she blurted before he had a chance to speak.

He frowned and reached up to touch the wire frames where they rested against his temple. "Yes."

"You didn't have them on the night we met."

Though he couldn't figure out why this was relevant, he explained, "I was wearing contacts. My allergies have been bugging my eyes, so I wore my glasses today."

She frowned slightly as she studied his face, but she didn't seem to have anything more to say, so he took over.

"You didn't leave your number. You didn't leave me any way to contact you."

Maeve chewed on her lip and studied the closed door as if plotting an escape route.

Fletcher's voice dropped. "I *wanted* to contact you."

Her gaze flew to his. "Fletcher, I…"

When she trailed off without an explanation, he moved around to the other side of his desk. "Sit, please." He motioned to one of the empty chairs as he sank into his own.

Maeve crossed her arms and remained unmoved. "I'll stand."

Fletcher sifted his fingers through his hair. Dammit. Now she was looking down at him like he might one of his students. She had totally shifted the power differential, and he wasn't sure he liked that.

He folded his hands in front of him on the desk. "Fine. I'm sorry if you're unhappy to see me again."

Maeve's scowl softened a touch. "I'm not unhappy. I'm just…surprised."

Fletcher crossed his arms over his chest in a mirror of her pose. "I'm surprised, too. I know you mentioned having had babies, but I never expected…"

She winced. "Me either."

Another silent moment passed before Fletcher relaxed

back into his chair. "I haven't been able to stop thinking about you," he confessed.

Maeve seemed to deflate, uncrossing her arms and finally sinking into a chair. "Me either," she repeated.

Fletcher waited until her gaze met his. "I want to see you again."

One red eyebrow arched up her forehead. "You're seeing me right now."

"That's not what I meant, and you know it."

Maeve released a sigh that sounded halfway between defeated and annoyed. "We can't see each other again."

Fletcher huffed out a breath. "Look, Maeve, I know it's a little complicated that I'm your kids' principal, but it's not like I'm their direct teacher. I don't assign or influence grades, so it's not like I could give them any special treatment. It shouldn't be a problem if we have a relationship."

Maeve was shaking her head before he even finished speaking. "It was one night, Fletcher. One amazing, mind-blowing night. But it's over now. Let's just keep it in the past."

"What if I don't want to keep it in the past?" he challenged. He would never pressure a woman to do something she didn't want to do, but Maeve had admitted that she couldn't stop thinking about him. It clearly wasn't a lack of attraction that was making her hesitant to pursue a relationship.

She stood, once again on the defensive. "Then, you'll have to just get over it. I'm not looking for a relationship right now."

Fletcher stood as well. "I'm sorry. I shouldn't have used that word. No rushing into things, right? All I'm asking for is another date."

Maeve shook her head. "I can't."

"Can't or won't?"

Fire flashed in her eyes as she responded, "Both."

A knock on the door interrupted their stalemate.

"Yes?" Fletcher barked, not breaking eye contact with Maeve.

The door flew open, and Allie sprang in, a brightly colored piece of paper flapping from her hand. "Look, Mommy! I drew an Egyptian pyramid. It's full of treasure!"

Maeve stroked her daughter's hair as she studied the drawing. "Wow, baby. It came out so good."

Andy came trudging in with his own picture dangling between two fingers.

"What did you make, sweetheart?" Maeve asked.

He held up his picture in both hands so everyone could see. Fletcher could make out three humans—two small ones and a taller one, all with red hair—and a gray creature that must have been the cat he spoke of earlier.

"I drew our family," Andy said quietly. "Even Peeve. At our new house."

Maeve regarded the drawing quietly, her eyes soaking in the figures and the house behind them. Something about the picture had her almost choked up, and Fletcher was tempted to sling a supportive arm around her shoulders. But no—she didn't want that. Didn't want *him*.

"I love it," she finally murmured, bending to kiss the crown of Andy's head. "We'll have to hang these pictures up on the fridge."

"Can we stop and get magnets on the way home?" Allie asked.

Maeve squeezed her daughter's shoulder. "You bet." Turning to Fletcher, she said, "Nice chatting with you, Mr. McNally."

He couldn't help but smirk at her obvious dismissal. "You too, Ms. Walsh."

5

———

Maeve was getting the kids ready for school a couple days later when she got the texts.

Where are you?

I know this is you, Mae.

Answer me.

Cold fear swept through her as the texts flooded in. How the hell had he gotten her new number? As quickly as her fingers could move in her jittery state, she blocked the number. It was a temporary solution to a much bigger problem, but it was the best she could do in the moment.

A clatter across the room made her jump. "Shit! Peeve."

The cat had knocked over one of the only decorations in the still-sparse room—a frame housing a photo of Allie and Andy together as toddlers.

Ever since his first night there, Peeve had grown increasingly bold. As he'd started gaining weight—and therefore energy—he had begun showing off a mischievous streak a mile wide. He was living up to his name by constantly doing irritating things like stealing socks and other soft items, knocking objects over, and eating human food any chance he got.

The name had actually been Connie's idea. After her comment about taking animals for walks in strollers, she'd gone on to share a multitude of other pet peeves with Maeve. Apparently, Connie had strong opinions against homemade pet food, letting pets sleep in bed with you, and, perhaps most staunchly, putting clothing on them. When she'd walked in on Maeve wrestling the skinny cat into one of the kids' old onesies the morning after rescuing him, she'd simply raised a brow and said, "Pet peeve." And thus, Peeve was named.

Maeve hurried to pick up the knocked-over frame, relieved to find the glass hadn't broken. The last thing she needed this morning was another catastrophe. A text—or, in this case, texts—from Jason was enough trouble for the entire week, if not more.

"What was that?" came Allie's voice as she trotted into the kitchen for breakfast.

"Nothing," Maeve said. "Peeve just knocked something over."

Allie gave the cat a scratch behind his ears. "Silly boy."

The animal pushed his furry little head into her touch, rubbing against her hand as a satisfied purr rumbled from his chest. Peeve may have become an increasingly aggravating presence, but he sure was cute when he wanted to be.

"Come on," Maeve prodded. "We've got to eat quickly if you're going to make it to school on time."

Allie hopped up onto one of the mismatched kitchen chairs as Maeve poured her a bowl of cereal. Peeve plopped onto the floor by her feet, content to lick his paws and wait for any scraps of food to drop. He would be disappointed to find that the only thing being served was cereal, not his favorite— bacon or breakfast sausages.

Andy entered the kitchen a moment later, rubbing his eyes.

"Oh, honey, did you have trouble sleeping again?" Maeve asked.

Andy nodded as he climbed onto a chair next to Allie.

"You know you can always come get me when that happens," Maeve reminded him.

"I know," Andy replied, "but I'm a big boy. I can fall asleep on my own."

Maeve released a sigh as she poured his cereal. Jason had always pushed the "big boy" language and made Andy feel like he needed to be tougher when, in reality, he was just a sensitive six-year-old. Despite her attempts to counteract that toxic masculinity, Maeve found that Andy had internalized some of it. Hopefully, she could correct some of those thoughts now that Jason was out of the picture—if he stayed out of the picture, that is.

"Hurry up," she urged as she threw together two bagged lunches for the kids. She mentally added *buy lunch boxes* to her to-do list. While she hated to go the wasteful route of brown paper bags, she hadn't yet purchased lunch boxes. There were just too many things you had to remember to buy when you were starting from scratch.

"Done!" Allie announced as she finished her last bite of cereal and raced to the front door to put on her shoes and jacket.

"Done!" Andy echoed as he did the same.

Maeve followed close behind, slipping into her faux-shearling jacket and booties. The spring mornings were still chilly, and it was the type of weather where you had to wear layers in the morning and shed them as the hours went by. By afternoon, you could usually get away with a simple t-shirt and pants.

"Race you to the car," Allie challenged her brother, and they both took off, their backpacks bumping against their bodies as they ran.

Maeve managed to get them to school just in the nick of

time. She mentally patted herself on the back, then took a leisurely ride home, thinking of which errands she would plan to tackle today. She felt like she was finally falling into a decent routine. Her feelings of victory turned to defeat when she returned home to find the two brown bags still sitting on the kitchen counter. In her haste, she'd forgotten to grab the kids' environmentally unfriendly lunches.

Today was just not her day.

After a few deep breaths to try and center herself—Connie had taught her about square breathing, a technique in which you inhale, hold, and then exhale your breath for equal amounts of time—she got back in the car to drive to the school again.

Having managed to successfully avoid Fletcher at drop-off and pick-up all week, and with the day she was having, Maeve should have known her luck had run out.

She was just setting the brown bags on Bethany's desk when Fletcher emerged from his office, looking luscious in fitted gray slacks and a light-blue button-up shirt. Women liked to rave about gray sweatpants, but really, one shouldn't sleep on gray slacks. They stretched over Fletcher's thighs in such an enticing way that Maeve had to hold herself back from licking her lips.

Forcing her gaze away from his pants, she looked up, but as it turned out, that view was equally appealing. Fletcher's overlong, wavy, blond hair just brushed his collar, making her think of how it had felt when his hair tickled her skin. The thin, wire-framed glasses perched on his nose gave him a studious look that was perfect for his principal role but also inexplicably turned her on. He hadn't been wearing them the night they'd hooked up, and she almost wished he had been just so she could have ripped them off while they were kissing to get closer to him.

"Maeve," Fletcher said, jerking to a halt halfway to

Bethany's desk. His secretary wisely made herself busy at the copy machine.

"Hi." Maeve pointed to the brown bags. "Forgot the kids' lunches."

"Oh." He nodded, running a hand down his jaw. "Thanks for bringing them by. I was just—"

Her phone buzzed in her jacket pocket, and she blocked out the rest of Fletcher's sentence as alarm shot through her. Was Jason texting her again? Had he somehow found a way around being blocked?

She held up a finger. "Sorry, I have to check this." She unlocked her phone with slightly shaking hands, but it wasn't a text that had caused the vibration. It was a notification from Facebook Marketplace.

"Argh," Maeve grunted as she read the message.

"Everything okay?"

She sighed. "No. I mean, yes, but I just got a notification that the bedroom set I was trying to buy got purchased by someone else. It was a great deal. I should have known it was too good to be true."

Fletcher scratched his chin. "You need a bedroom set?"

Maeve looked up at him through narrowed eyes, her thumb hovering over the phone, where she'd been preparing to type a strongly worded message about not stringing people along when you were just going to pull the rug out from under them and sell the furniture they desperately needed to someone else. "Yes. Why?"

Fletcher shrugged and stuffed his hands in his pockets. "I have one you can have."

Maeve stared at him. "You have an extra bedroom set I can have."

"Yep."

She rested her hand on her hip, cocking it out to the side. "How much?"

Fletcher shook his head. "No charge."

Her eyes tightened further. "No, thanks. I don't need your charity." No matter how desperate she was for a real bed to sleep in, there was no way she would allow herself to be in debt to Fletcher.

He scratched the back of his neck as he studied her. "Fine. You can repay me for it."

"With what?"

Fletcher's brown eyes blazed as they bore into hers. "Dinner."

Her breath caught. *Dammit.* Not only was it beyond tempting to agree to dinner with him, but Maeve also yearned for a more comfortable place to sleep. She was still working out a kink in her neck from a couple nights ago when the air mattress had begun deflating, leaving her all cock-eyed as she slept. She'd gradually sunken lower all night, too exhausted to get up and re-inflate it until morning. The resulting crick in her neck wasn't worth the extra few minutes of sleep.

Maybe she could do dinner—*just* dinner—with Fletcher if it meant getting free furniture. Besides, dinner didn't have to mean anything fancy, right? He hadn't specified that they had to go out, or get dressed up, or anything like that. She was already cooking up a plan in her head.

Maeve dawned her best scowl as she replied, "Fine. Bring the furniture over on Saturday, and I'll make you dinner."

Fletcher's lips curved into a smile as if he thought he'd won that round. "That sounds great. I'll borrow my brother's truck and bring the furniture over on Saturday, then. You'll need to give me your address. Oh, and your phone number, too, in case we need to make any changes to the plan." He grinned like the cat that got the cream.

Maeve resisted the urge to roll her eyes. "Hand me your phone."

Fletcher eagerly fished his phone from his pocket, unlocked it, and handed it to her.

Plugging in her number, Maeve held back a chuckle as she

named her contact. "All set," she said as she locked the phone and handed it back. "See you Saturday."

"Looking forward to it."

Fletcher laughed out loud when he received a text from *Ravishing Redhead* a few minutes later. He couldn't have come up with a better description of Maeve if he'd tried. Despite all her claims of not wanting a relationship or even a date, Maeve couldn't seem to hold back her flirtatious side.

RAVISHING REDHEAD

Any food allergies I should know about?

FLETCHER

Nope. I'll eat anything you make me.

RAVISHING REDHEAD

Good.

The brief exchange felt like a win in itself. Fletcher hadn't known how he was going to finally get Maeve's number. Multiple times, he'd been tempted to log into the school's registry and search for her information, but that would have been a huge breach of ethics. If he wanted Maeve in his personal life, he had to pursue her purely in his personal life, not allow his position of power as her kids' principal to play into things.

His phone buzzed again, and a burst of excitement tore through his chest as he anticipated seeing *Ravishing Redhead* again, but the name *Baby Brother* popped up instead. Fletcher wasn't one for cutesy names in his contacts list—he would prefer everyone to be listed under their legal names—but Jack had messed with his phone at one point, naming himself

Awesome Brother and Beau *Baby Brother,* and Fletcher had never bothered to change them. Now, though, he was starting to see the value in the fun nicknames.

As he opened Beau's text, Fletcher was greeted with a photo of a stunning, shiny engagement ring. The thin, simple gold band housed a gorgeous oval-shaped diamond. It was classy without being ostentatious. His brother had picked well, especially for his modest girlfriend.

His phone buzzed with a second text.

BABY BROTHER

Ring secured.

Fletcher sat back in his office chair, surging with pride. Previously an immature, wise-cracking lady-killer, Beau had grown up a lot in the past few months. Sure, he was still fond of sexual innuendos and was too competitive for his own good, but being with Emma had made him a better man.

FLETCHER

Good pick. She'll love it.

BABY BROTHER

Thanks, man. I'll let you know when the deed's done.

And by deed I mean proposing to her.

Though I'm sure we'll be doing the deed after that as well.

Fletcher shook his head silently to himself, even as his shoulders shook with laughter.

FLETCHER:

Goodbye, Beau.

As he pocketed his phone, Fletcher's thoughts turned to the engagement ring burning a hole in his sock drawer. It had been his mother, June's, ring, given to her by his late father,

Noah. She'd worn it for two decades after he died before deciding to pass it down to Fletcher, her eldest son and the one everyone assumed would get married first. He knew she'd always assumed he would give it to Christa—so had he.

Now, the beautiful diamond ring sat untouched at the bottom of his drawer, leaving him wondering if he'd ever get a chance to use it.

6

Fletcher arrived around three p.m. on Saturday, pulling the large black truck full of furniture into Maeve's driveway.

"He's here!" Allie cried as she watched his arrival through the window. Maeve had thought about sending the kids over to Connie's half of the house but figured that wouldn't do much to hide the fact that Fletcher was there. He would be going in and out of the house as he delivered the furniture, so the kids would definitely have caught sight of him at some point or another.

Andy tugged on her hand. "Can we go say hi to him, Mommy?"

"Sure," Maeve answered as she rustled Andy's copper hair.

Allie flew to the front door, swinging it open so fast it banged against the wall. Maeve cringed, hoping it hadn't left a mark. *Buy doorstops*, she thought, adding it to her seemingly never-ending list of to-dos.

Andy trotted out the door behind Allie, doing his darnedest to keep up.

"Hi, Mr. McNally!" their voices chimed in unison as Fletcher climbed out of the truck.

"Hey, kiddos!" He stooped down to give them quick hugs.

Fletcher had quickly become her kids' favorite person at Harper Elementary. They liked their teachers, but they *loved* their principal. He routinely visited each classroom, made himself visible at pick-up and drop-off times, and sometimes ate his lunch in the cafeteria surrounded by students. Plus, rumor had it that he kept a stash of lollipops in his desk drawer, taking them out only when a "star student" came to visit him. As far as Maeve could tell, every student was treated as a star student—a fact she found incredibly endearing.

"Hi, Maeve," Fletcher said as he righted himself and took the few steps to reach her.

She crossed her arms and leaned against the porch railing. "Hi, Fletcher."

He gestured to the overflowing bed of the truck. "I've got a dresser, a bedside table, and a bed frame broken down into four pieces, plus the box spring and mattress. I brought a lamp and mirror, too, because I have no use for them."

Maeve's eyebrows inched up. "Wow. Did you load all that up yourself?"

Fletcher cast a glance at the mountain of furniture. "No. My brother Beau helped me get it all out of my place and into the truck. I should be able to carry most of it by myself, but I was hoping you could help guide me and keep things steady. I brought a dolly, too, which should help me move the dresser."

Maeve uncrossed her arms and followed Fletcher over to the truck. She tucked her hands into her back pockets as she watched him pull a steel dolly from the back. "Of course I'll help you. I'm not afraid of a little hard work. I like to exert myself every once in a while."

Fletcher eyed her with a raised brow. "Good to know."

Her cheeks warmed, and she quickly changed the subject.

"Luckily, my bedroom is on the first floor, so the biggest struggle will just be getting everything up the porch steps."

"I think we can handle it," Fletcher said as he flipped the back of the truck bed open.

Andy and Allie were bouncing up and down beside the driveway, so Maeve went over to tell them to play in the yard and be careful while the grown-ups moved the furniture. By the time she returned to Fletcher's side, he'd already unloaded all four pieces of the bed frame onto the driveway.

"Why don't we each grab one of these pieces. The headboard shouldn't be too difficult to carry, if you want to handle that one. Then, you can show me to your bedroom," Fletcher suggested.

Maeve gulped at the connotation that sentence could hold, even less subtle than her earlier remark. She fastened her grip on the headboard, which only served to remind her of holding onto *Fletcher's* headboard.

The man had been there for less than five minutes, and she was already turning everything into a sexual innuendo. *Snap out of it,* she hissed silently to herself.

"Right this way," she said, her tone deceptively casual as she led Fletcher to her bedroom. Together, they brought all four pieces of the bed frame as well as the nightstand, lamp, and mirror to her room. Peeve had gotten spooked at the first loud noise and was watching their progress from beneath the couch.

Maeve's shoulder had started aching at some point, but she did her best to power through without letting on that she was in any pain. They decided to leave the box spring and mattress in the truck until the bed frame was put together, which just left the frighteningly cumbersome dresser.

"How are we possibly going to get this out of the truck and into the house?" Maeve asked as she inspected the dresser in the bed of the truck.

Fletcher shot her a smirk as he answered, "Very carefully."

Maeve wrung her hands together. "What can I do to help?"

He hopped into the bed of the truck and pointed to the dolly in front of it. "I'm going to lower it down slowly. I need you to hold the dolly steady and guide the dresser so it's centered on top of it."

Maeve nodded and brought the dolly as close as she could to the back of the truck.

"Here we go," Fletcher said as he pushed the large piece of furniture forward. His arm muscles bunched and bulged as he lowered the dresser. The plain white t-shirt he wore stretched over his chest and abdomen while presenting a glorious view of his muscular arms.

Maeve was so distracted that she completely forgot about her task until Fletcher called, "Is it centered?"

Shit. She quickly turned her gaze to where the dresser met the dolly and was relieved to find that it was, in fact, centered. "Uh, yeah," she called back.

Fletcher grunted as he released the dresser from his grip. "Good." He wiped a few beads of sweat from his brow with the back of his hand, then glanced over at her. "We make a good team."

Maeve gulped and turned away from his intense gaze. "Yeah."

Silence reigned for a moment until Fletcher hopped out of the truck bed. "I'll pull the dolly. Can you please follow behind and just make sure that the dresser stays steady and centered?"

"Sure," Maeve said. "But what about the porch stairs?"

"I can bump the dolly up the steps," he said confidently. "It would be helpful if you pushed as I pull, but my main worry is just that it doesn't fall and hurt someone or break."

Maeve nodded and took her position behind the dolly, bracing her palms on the large wooden dresser and doing her best to ignore the twinge in her bad shoulder. Fletcher grabbed the handle and tilted it until he could efficiently pull the heavy load. "Ready?" he asked.

"Ready."

They began the slow journey across the driveway, with Fletcher constantly checking in to make sure she was doing alright. When they reached the porch steps, he narrated each time he was going to go up another step, giving Maeve countdowns so she would know when to push. They communicated efficiently and got the dresser up the stairs much more easily than she had expected them to.

When they got to the center of the room, Fletcher lowered the dolly and looked around at all the empty space. "Where do you want it?"

Not a sexual remark, she screamed in her brain. *Not a sexual remark!*

She pointed to a lonely wall to one side of where her bed would go. "Let's put it here."

"You've got it." Fletcher used the dolly to move the dresser over to the wall, then slowly and carefully shifted it onto the floor. Stepping back, he wiped his hands together. "Looks great." He turned to find her rubbing her sore shoulder and frowned. "Are you okay?"

"Yeah." Maeve dropped her hand to her side. "Just not used to working this hard, I guess."

Her attempt at humor didn't deter him. He took a step closer, then stopped short, as if he'd received a zap at their proximity. "I could massage it for you if you'd like."

The sincere look in his eyes melted a bit of the ice that encased Maeve's heart. He was genuinely distressed to see her hurting, and the foreignness of that was both alarming and refreshing.

"It's fine," she said, but he was already moving closer.

"I learned how to give really good shoulder massages after my brother got a shoulder injury last year. Let me see if I can help work out the kinks."

Fletcher placed a hand on her shoulder and waited for her response.

"O-okay," Maeve replied when she built up enough breath to speak.

His thumb began digging in gentle circles around her trapezius muscle, working it in exactly the right way. Without permission, her neck rolled a bit to the side, a whimper escaping her throat.

"Does that feel good?" Fletcher asked, his mouth much closer to her ear than she would have expected. His breath danced over her skin, almost making her shiver.

"Uh-huh," Maeve replied, working diligently to contain any more whimpers or moans. The care with which he treated her shoulder almost had her tearing up. Between the relief she felt in her muscles and the intimacy of having him so close and caring, she was in the danger zone. Much more of this and she'd be apt to jump his bones.

"Okay, I think that's good," she said as she slipped out from his grip. "Thanks."

Fletcher tucked his hand into his pocket. "Happy to help."

Maeve turned toward the door. "So, how are we going to put the pieces of the bed frame together?"

He watched her for a moment before waving for her to follow him back out to the truck. "I've got tools."

Outside, he opened the passenger side door and bent to retrieve a toolbox from beneath the passenger seat. Maeve tried and failed not to gawk at how his jeans strained against his ass when he bent forward.

"Here." He straightened to stand with a red, steel toolbox dangling from his grip.

Trying to school her expression, Maeve grasped for something to say other than *nice ass*. "I didn't know you were such a handyman."

Fletcher's brown eyes pierced hers. "There's a lot you don't know about me."

She heard the words he'd left unsaid: *but you could if you'd give me a chance.* She swallowed, unsure how to respond to that, when Andy came running over, eyeing the toolbox in Fletcher's hand.

"Are you going to use tools, Mr. McNally?" he asked.

"I sure am, buddy," Fletcher said. "Want to help me?"

Andy beamed up at him. "Sure!"

Fletcher glanced at Maeve. "If that's okay?"

She smiled softly, grateful he thought to ask her permission. "Of course."

Maeve called for Allie to follow them inside, and they all headed for the master bedroom. The kids began exploring, opening the dresser drawers and flicking the lamp on the bedside table on and off. Peeve even got brave enough to join them, hopping up onto the bedside table and giving them a show by lifting his hind leg and licking his nether regions.

Fletcher placed the toolbox on the ground and took a look around. "You know, it's a shame I didn't have a second bedside table to give you," he said, scratching at his jaw. "Now you only have *one nightstand*." His words were serious, but the way he emphasized the last two and the smirk he wore said he knew exactly what he was doing.

Maeve wagged her head at him. She'd definitely been reading too much into some of his comments, but he *had* been making lots of thinly veiled remarks about their one night together, how they'd make a good couple, how she hadn't given him a chance… She had to hand it to him—the man was determined.

Crossing her arms, Maeve turned to Allie. "Honey, want to help me make dinner? We're going to make something *extra* special for Mr. McNally."

Allie squealed and clapped her hands. "Yay! I'll help you, Mommy."

Maeve led her daughter out to the kitchen to prepare the "special" meal she had in mind. Granted, it was what her kids considered a special meal. It was the one they got on nights when Maeve didn't have the capacity to cook a real meal, when they were sick, or when she wanted to cheer them up. It was also the least date-like meal she could fathom.

It was macaroni and cheese and chicken nuggets.

Maeve pulled over a chair for Allie to stand on by the stove. "We're going to preheat the oven to 350 degrees," she said.

Allie punched in the numbers. "Now what?"

Maeve placed a pot of water on the stove. "Now, we boil this water. Then, we cook the nuggets and the mac and cheese. Hopefully, Andy and Mr. McNally will be done putting the bed together by then."

About a half hour later, the boys came tromping into the kitchen. Andy wore a look of pride on his face, and Maeve hoped a little male time with Fletcher had served him well. Lord knew he could use a good male role model in his life.

Not that Fletcher was going to be in his life as anything other than his principal.

"Mommy, come see your new bed!" Andy said, his toothy grin melting her heart.

"I'd love to, baby. Allie, will you watch our meal?" Maeve asked with a wink. Allie shot her a thumbs up and attempted to wink back but ended up just closing both eyes in a slow blink.

Fletcher led them back to the bedroom, where he spread his arms out wide in a *ta-da* gesture.

"Wow," Maeve breathed as she took in the room, which was far less sparse than it had been that morning. The bed frame dominated the center of the room, its wooden spindles reminding her of Fletcher's own bed. A shiver ran through her as she recalled his gravelly voice. *Grab onto the headboard.*

Trying her best to ignore the memory, Maeve moved her gaze over the rest of the room. The dresser and mirror decorated the wall to the left of the bed, while two windows adorned the one to the right. The lone bedside table—or, as Fletcher liked to call it, the one nightstand—sat between the bed and the windowed wall. Atop it, the lamp cast a warm glow on the space, making it feel cozy and homey, exactly as Maeve wanted it to.

"This is perfect," she whispered, holding back tears as she took in her new haven.

Fletcher cleared his throat. "The furniture really fills up the space nicely, and the paint looks fairly new, so you should be good on that for a while."

Andy chimed in with a comically dramatic sigh. "I wish we could paint *my* room. Yellow is so bleh."

Maeve looked at Fletcher over Andy's head. "He and Allie are sharing a room. It was yellow when we moved in. Allie loves it, but Andy says it's too bright."

"It feels like I'm staring at the sun," the little boy complained.

Fletcher cocked his head to the side. He studied Maeve for a moment, as if testing her mood, then spoke. "I could help paint your room, Andy. I have all the tools at home."

Maeve froze, her brain zinging with conflicting signals. On the one hand, it would be a good excuse to see Fletcher platonically again. Allowing him to paint her child's room didn't exactly seem like it would send him the wrong message, and it would make Andy happy. Two birds, one stone.

But on the other hand, this furniture-delivery situation was supposed to be a one-time thing. She couldn't let Fletcher think his presence in her home was going to be a regular occurrence. Especially not if he was going to show up in jeans that hugged his ass and t-shirts that molded to his muscles.

"Oh, you don't have to do that, Fletcher—"

Andy latched onto her hand. "Please, Mommy?"

Maeve looked down into his earnest hazel eyes. They held such hope that she was unable to deny him. With a sigh, she relented. "Okay, baby. But only if Mr. McNally is sure it won't be any trouble."

Fletcher was nodding when she looked back at him. "No trouble at all. Like I said, I have all the tools at home. Maybe I could come by again next weekend?"

Andy dropped Maeve's hand to fling his arms around Fletcher's leg. "Thanks, Mr. McNally!"

The sight of her son hugging Fletcher did things to her stomach and her chest—warm, fluttery things—so she immediately pivoted. "I think our dinner is about ready. Let's head back to the kitchen."

The three of them joined Allie in the kitchen, where Maeve doled out the less-than-gourmet meal onto plates.

Fletcher cast her a wry smile as she set his plate before him. "Mac and cheese? Chicken nuggets?"

She raised a brow. "Do you have a problem with that?"

He looked like he was trying to hold back a smile as he scooped up some macaroni onto his fork. "No problem at all. In fact, this is my favorite meal."

Of freaking course it was. Maeve couldn't be sure if Fletcher was just saying that, or if he truly adored kids' food, but either way, it seemed he had won yet another round.

"Well, enjoy, then."

The kids eagerly dug into their meals, and Maeve nibbled at a chicken nugget as she watched them interact with Fletcher. The conversation flowed so naturally between all three of them. Fletcher knew exactly how to talk to children— which should have been obvious, given his job—but Maeve had never met a man who had such a way with kids.

At one point, Fletcher let Allie know of their plans to paint the kids' bedroom.

"I want to keep the yellow," Allie announced in a voice that said she was not apt to change her mind.

"But you love blue," Maeve argued. "Remember your old

blue bike? And your favorite blue dress? It's always been one of your favorite colors."

Allie shook her head vehemently. "Blue is the color of blueberries, and I don't like blueberries, so I can't have a blue room."

"Well, *I* don't like yellow," Andy said, his little voice escalating.

Maeve was taking a deep breath to prepare to resolve the argument when Fletcher spoke.

"What if we paint two of the walls blue and keep two of them yellow? Then, you can each put your beds in the corner of your own color and have your own space." He glanced at Maeve. "If that's okay with you."

Once again, he was giving her the final say. He wasn't steamrolling her or making the kids promises he couldn't keep to get on their good sides. Sure, maybe he had overstepped a bit by suggesting alterations to *her* house, but she recognized that it was all in the name of keeping the peace.

"That sounds like a great plan," Maeve said, relieved by the agreeable looks on the kids' faces.

"Okay!" Andy exclaimed.

Allie was a little more reluctant to agree. "But then, when I'm lying in bed and I look across the room, I'm gonna see his ugly blue walls."

Fletcher only had to think for a split second before offering a solution. "We can turn your bed so the footboard is in the corner. That way, you'll be facing the yellow walls when you lie in bed."

Allie's eyes widened. "And I can put up posters of kittens to look at, too!"

"Sure," Fletcher replied, an amused smile crossing his lips.

The kids turned to each other and began chatting about what else they wanted in their room, and Maeve took the opportunity to quietly thank Fletcher.

"That was amazing," she whispered out of the side of her mouth.

He shrugged. "Conflict resolution between tiny humans. It's kind of my specialty."

When the kids were done eating, Maeve directed them to go brush their teeth and put on pajamas. When the whining and moaning and excuses as to why they couldn't possibly go get ready for bed now began, Fletcher once again stepped in with a solution.

"While you two are getting ready, your mom and I are going to carry in the mattress and box spring. What if, after that, you bring one book down to the kitchen, and I'll read it to you?"

He shot a questioning glance at Maeve, and she nodded her approval. There he went again, resolving tiny-human conflicts.

7

———————

Fletcher left Maeve's house feeling simultaneously triumphant at her willingness to see him again and melancholy because he was now heading home to an empty apartment. Her house had been so full of life with the two kids running around and Peeve generally wreaking havoc, while his apartment would be quiet enough to hear a pin drop.

He'd grown so used to living with Beau—and Emma, too, since she'd moved in last year. When the couple had moved out a few weeks prior, Fletcher found that he really missed having the extra bodies around. He and Christa had never lived together, which, looking back, was probably another red flag. She had always preferred to have her own space and insisted their relationship was better that way. Fletcher, on the other hand, was realizing just how much he craved company.

On the way home, he swung by a paint supply store because he most certainly did *not* have painting supplies at home. He'd only said that because painting the kids' room seemed like an excellent excuse to see Maeve again, and he knew she wouldn't go for it unless he made it seem like it wouldn't be an inconvenience in any way, shape, or form.

Arriving home to his empty apartment, Fletcher dropped his newly acquired painting supplies just inside the doorway, ready to be snatched up next weekend when he returned to Maeve's house. He'd gotten everything but the actual paint, which he figured Andy would want to pick out himself. Luckily, he had thought to grab some blue paint swatches from the store so Andy could do just that.

Without a second thought, he pulled out his phone to text Maeve.

FLETCHER

I found some paint swatches for Andy to look at. I'll give them to you on Monday so he can choose, then I can grab the paint before I come over next weekend.

The three little dots that indicated Maeve was typing popped up, then disappeared, then popped up again. His heart fluttered each time the dots appeared, revealing just how desperate he was to connect with this woman. He'd left her house no more than half an hour ago, and yet the thought of talking to her again had him feeling like a third-grader with a crush.

RAVISHING REDHEAD

Are you sure? I can probably find time to go to the paint store this week so he can pick out a color.

FLETCHER

It's no problem. I already have the swatches.

RAVISHING REDHEAD

Okay, if you're sure.

FLETCHER

I am. I'll catch you at drop-off to hand them over to you.

RAVISHING REDHEAD

thumbs up emoji

Relieved that Maeve had agreed to his plan, he tried to keep the conversation going by asking the first question that popped into his head.

FLETCHER

Did the kids go down okay?

The typing dots popped up, disappeared, popped up, disappeared, then popped up again, his heart flip flopping along with them.

RAVISHING REDHEAD

Yes.

Thanks again for your help today.

FLETCHER

It was my pleasure. I'm glad the furniture will work for you.

RAVISHING REDHEAD

I'm in the bed right now. It's very comfortable.

An image of Maeve in bed bombarded Fletcher's brain. Only, the bed she was in was his. And she wasn't wearing any pants. And she was gasping his name. He adjusted himself in his jeans.

FLETCHER

More comfortable than your air mattress?

RAVISHING REDHEAD

Much.

Grinning almost maniacally, Fletcher typed out his response.

FLETCHER

Glad you like the bed so much. You sure you don't want another nightstand?

RAVISHING REDHEAD

Goodnight, Fletcher.

FLETCHER

Goodnight, Maeve.

He was still smiling as he slid his phone into his pocket. All through his nighttime routine, he couldn't seem to wipe the goofy grin from his face. How was it that this woman he had just met, who seemed utterly determined not to give him the time of day, had him so totally charmed?

As he climbed into bed, Fletcher knew he would sleep soundly with the comforting thought that he would get to see Maeve again on Monday.

~

Monday morning came bright and early, and Maeve was appalled to find herself carefully considering her outfit for the day. She told herself it was because the other moms always looked so put together at drop-off, while she usually breezed in wearing leggings and a t-shirt. But deep down, she knew it was because she was going to see Fletcher.

After a few minutes of sifting through her wardrobe—which was considerably smaller than it used to be, since she'd only been able to pack so much—she chose dark jeans, a plain white top with some lace at the neckline, and her favorite brown leather bomber jacket. She looked put together without looking like she was trying too hard.

Allie came buzzing into the room and did a twirl to show off the frilly pink princess dress she'd picked for the day's outfit. It was actually an old Halloween costume, but Allie had adopted it into her everyday wardrobe. Maeve loved that her daughter was carefree enough to wear whatever she wanted, even if it was outside the norm. Allie was just so unafraid to be herself. Maeve hoped she never lost that.

Maeve clapped as Allie danced around before she came skidding to a stop.

"Mommy, you look so pretty!" Allie said, her eyes widening as she took in Maeve's drop-off outfit and the minimal make-up she'd applied, which was still much more than her usual bare-faced look.

"Thanks, baby." Maeve sent her daughter a grateful smile. A seven-year-old's opinion may not hold too much weight for some people, but Maeve appreciated that Allie had noticed her efforts. "Grab your brother so we can go. We don't want to be late."

Allie trotted off to find Andy, and Maeve gathered all their belongings by the front door. A fly was zipping around the foyer—a bunch of them had gotten in during the furniture-moving process—and she had been killing them non-stop for the past couple of days. One might have thought having a cat would help with the problem, but as it turned out, Peeve would rather play with the flies than kill them. Luckily, Connie had lent her the perfect solution: a bug zapper shaped like a tennis racket.

Maeve grabbed it now and promptly zapped the fly to its untimely death. It took a few tries to get the massive bugger down, but he eventually dropped to the floor. She felt a momentary pang of guilt when she saw his body lying limply on the ground, as she really hated to see any living creature suffer, but she simply couldn't stand the incessant buzzing the flies had subjected her to since the weekend.

Upon hearing the small *zaps* the instrument let out, Peeve trotted into the room, located the fly, and began batting it around.

"Enjoy, buddy," Maeve said. "Kids, let's go!"

They pulled up to Harper Elementary in record time, and the kids eagerly hopped out of the car to find their assigned liaisons. Parents volunteered as drop-off and pick-up liaisons, standing outside the school and waiting for groups of kids from the same class to arrive, then escorting them to their classrooms. Apparently, it was a new system under Fletcher's command, and parents were eager to help out—especially the single moms.

Maeve eased the car into one of the visitor parking spots so she could get out and meet Fletcher. She had just spotted him chatting with a parent across the walkway when a group of moms caught her attention.

"Hey!" called a tall blonde in skinny jeans and an immaculately ironed blouse. "It's Maeve, right?"

Maeve took in the huddle of women, all with immaculately styled hair and make-up, even at the early hour. "Yes," she answered warily, wondering what these women possibly wanted with her. Perhaps her slightly elevated outfit and make-up acted as some sort of bat signal, alerting them that she was ready to join the ranks of the PTA princesses.

"I'm Tiffany," said the blonde. She began pointing to each of her companions. "This is Jennifer, Rebecca, and Stephanie." The two brunettes and fake redhead all waved and widened their huddle to accommodate Maeve.

"Nice to meet you all," she said politely, wringing her hands down by her stomach.

Tiffany, their leader, continued the conversation. "We've been dying to meet you. Our kids are all in classes with either Andy or Allie, and they just adore them."

Maeve's heart warmed at the kind words about her children. "Oh, that's so nice. I know they're so fond of all their classmates as well."

Her words weren't entirely true—each of her kids had complaints about certain other students—but Maeve had no way of knowing whose parents these ladies were, and she didn't want to risk getting on anyone's bad side. It might be nice to get to know some of the other parents at the school. She could use some local friends besides Connie.

The fake redhead piped up then. "My little Timothy seems to get along so well with your Andy. They're both on the shyer side, but I think they really enjoy each other's company. We should get them together for a playdate sometime."

Maeve nodded. "Sure, that would be great."

As soon as the words left her mouth, she began wondering what these people's homes looked like compared to hers. Hopefully, Andy would be invited to their houses rather than the other way around. Maeve's was nowhere near ready for public consumption. She didn't want to think about why she'd had no reservations about allowing Fletcher to see her bare-bones home but dreaded the thought of one of these women setting eyes on it. Somehow, she just knew he wouldn't judge her.

One of the brunettes—Rebecca, she thought—smirked as she caught Maeve unconsciously looking toward Fletcher. "Mr. McNally is the best, don't you think?" she asked.

Heat painted Maeve's cheeks, and she hoped the ladies didn't notice. "He seems really good with the kids."

"Good with the parents, too," Jennifer said as she twirled a lock of her brown hair around her pointer finger. "Not that'd he'd give any of us the time of day, other than to discuss our kids."

Rebecca snorted in agreement. "Trust us, we've all tried."

Maeve's jaw tightened at the thought that each of these beautiful women had thrown themselves at Fletcher. She did find herself satisfied, though, that none of them had had any luck in their attempts. Perhaps she wouldn't have either if Fletcher had known he was her children's principal before they'd slept together.

"We're all single moms," Tiffany explained. "And Fletcher has got to be one of the most eligible bachelors around."

"He was in a relationship until not too long ago," Stephanie said in a dramatic whisper. "One of the moms here works at the library with his brother's girlfriend and found out from her. We were all thrilled when we heard it ended, because it meant we finally got a shot with him, but he hasn't shown interest in any of the moms here, even though there are so many single ones to choose from."

"How about you, Maeve? Are you married?" Stephanie asked.

Maeve caught Tiffany trying to glance at her ring finger, so she slid her hand into her jacket pocket. "Not anymore."

Jennifer clucked. "We're better off this way. Men are trash." She cast a sideways glance at Fletcher and let out a dramatic sigh. "Except him."

Rebecca put a hand on her friend's shoulder. "Give it up, Jen. He's never going to go for one of us."

Jennifer grimaced, and the other three women quickly matched her expression.

"Listen, Maeve," Tiffany said, breaking the tension. "We also called you over to ask if you were going to be making something for the bake sale next week. You do know about the bake sale, right?"

Maeve tensed because she did not, in fact, know about the bake sale. "Uh…remind me what it's for again?"

"We're raising money to fund field day. It's an annual end-of-the-school-year event. We need to fundraise for activities and refreshments. Last year, we had three different styles of bounce houses, and we want to top that this year."

"Oh," Maeve said. "That sounds like fun."

"It *will* be fun," Tiffany gushed. "But only if we raise enough money!"

"So, are you going to be able to help us out by baking something?" Rebecca pushed.

Maeve felt the weight of each woman's eyes on her, and the peer pressure was enough to have her blurting, "Sure! Of course."

Tiffany clapped her hands and squealed. "Perfect. I'll add you to our list of volunteers. If you give me your email, I can add you to our email list, too, so you'll get messages about all upcoming events, including field day."

Maeve reluctantly gave Tiffany her email, unable to think of a valid excuse for not doing so. Plus, she really did want to get the kids involved in field day. It seemed like a great opportunity for them to make friends.

After a few more moments of chit-chat, Maeve noticed that Fletcher had finished his conversation and was headed their way.

"Hey, everyone," he greeted the group. "Mind if I steal Maeve for a minute?"

Jennifer's jaw visibly dropped, and Rebecca's eyes widened comically.

Maeve pursed her lips to hold back a smile. "It was nice meeting you all," she said. "I'll talk to you later."

Fletcher took her by the elbow as he led her away from the group and across the walkway to a quieter spot. Maeve felt the school moms' eyes on her all the way over.

"Good morning," Fletcher said when they reached a low rock wall. He sat down and patted the seat beside him, indicating for Maeve to sit. She did, angling herself toward him so she didn't have to see the curious glances at her back.

"Morning." She let her hair fall in front of her shoulder to create a curtain that would really block out the rubbernecking moms.

Fletcher studied her for a moment, his eyes roving over her upgraded outfit, hair, and make-up. He cast an especially appreciative glance at the way her top hugged her breasts, and she was ever so grateful that she'd put a little more effort into her appearance.

8

———

Numerous gazes followed Maeve with interest as she walked back to her car. The school moms were still huddled together, glancing back and forth between her and Fletcher as they whispered to each other, likely making up outrageous stories about what they might be up to together. Maeve did her best to ignore them until she was safely back in her car.

Booking it out of the parking lot, she drove back to the house and found Connie lounging on the porch, two steaming mugs set on the table before her. She was wearing a thick knit sweater to protect herself from the morning chill.

"Hi," she called to Maeve, standing as she approached.

"Hey," Maeve replied.

"I want to show you something," Connie said, sounding far too excited for the early hour. She pointed to the hanging plant that had decorated the porch for weeks. "Look in the plant."

Maeve got up on her tiptoes to peek into the pot. At first, she didn't know what she was looking for, but then she noticed that there, nestled in amongst the leaves and flowers, was a small, intricately woven bird's nest full of tiny little off-white eggs. They were so dainty they almost didn't look real.

"Whoa!" she exclaimed.

"Isn't that something? I Googled it, and I think it's a sparrow's nest," Connie said.

"That's so cool. Do you think they'll hatch?"

Connie nodded. "I don't see why not. We should keep an eye on it for the next couple of weeks. My Google search said it could take ten to fourteen days for the eggs to hatch."

Maeve lowered her feet flat on the ground. "I can't wait to show the kids. They'll love it."

"Come sit." Connie ushered her into a vacant chair, pushing one of the mugs across the table. "Coffee for you."

"Thanks." Maeve took a sip of the toasty warm coffee and sighed happily.

"You were out early this morning," Connie noted, her shrewd eyes assessing Maeve.

"We were out on time," Maeve corrected her. She and the kids had gotten into a bad habit of running late to school, though they usually made it just in the nick of time, with Maeve screaming into the parking lot just as the drop-off liaisons were ready to go off-duty. Although it was simply due to a lack of planning on her part, it was also what had allowed her to avoid the school moms for so long.

"And you look like a million bucks," Connie added.

Maeve shrugged and sipped from her mug. "I'm trying to step it up a little, I guess."

Connie's eyes narrowed. "Are you sure there's nothing else going on?"

Maeve fiddled with the handle of the mug for a few moments before deciding she wouldn't get away with keeping secrets from Connie.

"Okay," she said with a sigh. "Remember that guy I told you about a couple weeks ago?"

"Then, go for it!" Connie said so loudly Maeve was sure the whole neighborhood heard.

She lowered her head to the table once more and left it there this time.

~

That evening, Fletcher received a text from Maeve.

RAVISHING REDHEAD

Andy likes "cloudless sky."

FLETCHER

I'll pick up a gallon tomorrow.

RAVISHING REDHEAD

hug emoji

Fletcher was amused that she used such an affectionate emoji when, this morning, he'd simply touched her hand, and she'd scurried off like a frightened gazelle. It was as if one part of her couldn't help but flirt with him while the other was determined to fight every ounce of chemistry they had.

He returned to the book he was reading but was interrupted again a few minutes later, this time with a text from Beau.

BABY BROTHER

SHE SAID YES!!!

The text came along with a string of photos of Beau down on one knee, Emma crying, a close-up of the ring on her finger, and a shot of the happy couple, looking more in love than ever before.

Fletcher was immediately flooded with pride and happiness for his brother, and he texted him back as such.

Fletcher rolled his eyes and decided not to entertain his brother with a response, instead scrolling through the joyful photos a few more times. As he did, sorrow began tugging at his heartstrings. They both looked so happy. So in love. Emma laid her hand on Beau's chest as if he was her rock. Her world. When would *he* finally get that? *Would* he ever get that?

As if his self-pity wasn't already climbing to intolerable levels, another text arrived a few moments later, this one from *Awesome Brother*, aka Jack. It contained a set of photos as well, mostly of Noah during his ten-month-old photoshoot. Natalie had painted a set of canvases with the numbers one through twelve, each decorated with a different nautical theme. The "1" was turned into an anchor, the "2" into a crab, and so on. Each month, they took a photo of Noah with the corresponding canvas to document his first year of life. It was sickeningly cute.

Fletcher responded how cute the photos were, but his heart wasn't in it. It wasn't that the photo's *weren't* cute. They were utterly adorable. Noah had developed the most delightfully chunky legs, and Fletcher longed to squeeze and kiss them and generally love on the baby. But even more than that, he longed for a child of his own to send photos of. He craved a milestone *he* could celebrate with his brothers via text.

He'd spent his whole life trying to live up to his father's legacy—taking over as the man of the house and helping raise his younger brothers. He'd been there through it all, from rescuing them from the principal's office as kids to giving them advice on everything from jobs to relationships as adults. He'd raised them into the men they were today, and in turn, he'd watched them both find the loves of their lives.

When would it finally be his turn for a happily ever after?

9

———

When the next weekend rolled round, Fletcher was more than ready to see Maeve again. He'd missed her at drop-off and pick-up every day since Monday—always busy with something else or tending to some emergency or another. One day, it was a jammed copy machine. The next, a disgruntled parent demanding a teacher change for their child. Fletcher missed Maeve's face, her husky voice, her sarcasm, and her wit. Her mere presence seemed to brighten up his day.

When he pulled into her driveway on Saturday, armed with a gallon of *cloudless blue* paint, he couldn't help the smile that stretched across his face.

Andy and Allie were playing on the porch while Maeve sat close by at a table along with another woman. Andy seemed to notice Fletcher's arrival first, and he sailed down the porch steps, skidding to a stop at the top of the driveway.

Fletcher gave him a wave through the windshield, then put his car into park and hopped out. "Hey, bud!"

"Hi, Mr. McNally! Where's your big black truck?"

"That was my brother's truck," Fletcher explained. "This is my car." He pointed to his sensible Honda Civic.

"Oh." Andy wore a little frown that creased his brow, but his face quickly brightened. "Did you bring the blue paint?"

Fletcher held the gallon aloft. "I sure did. Are you going to help me with your walls?"

Andy nodded vigorously. "Definitely. I love painting."

Allie came leaping down the steps then. "Me too! Can I help?"

"Of course," Fletcher replied. "I'll take all the help I can get." He shot a glance toward Maeve up on the porch, hoping she would be helping them, too. She raised her hand in a timid wave.

Fletcher looked back down at the kids. "Why don't I go chat with your mom for a few minutes, then we can get started?" Both kids seemed content with that plan, so Fletcher climbed the porch steps, dropped the paint and supplies by the front door, and joined Maeve and her friend at the table.

"Hey," he said with a wave.

"Hi, Fletcher," Maeve said. "This is Connie." She gestured to the other woman, who had long, gray braids cascading over her shoulders and kind, dark-brown eyes that matched her brown skin. "She's my best friend." A wry look passed between the women at that statement, but Fletcher wasn't brave enough to dig into that at the moment. "Connie owns the house and lives in the other half of it," Maeve added.

Connie extended her hand. "It's so nice to meet you, Fletcher."

He shook her hand. "Likewise. Beautiful house you've got here."

Connie grinned as she pulled her hand back. "It was my father's. I inherited it a few years ago. It's a great old house, but it definitely needs some work."

"Well, I'm happy to help out however I can," Fletcher said. He tossed a sly grin at Maeve. "Plus, Maeve thinks I'm handy."

Maeve's cheeks grew pink, making Fletcher mentally fist pump the air. He'd been at her house less than five minutes, and he was already getting to her. This day should be fun.

"That's so kind of you, Fletcher," Connie said. "I know Maeve appreciates your help with the furniture and the painting."

"Sure, talk about me like I'm not here," Maeve muttered, her arms crossed over her chest like a petulant child.

Connie pinched Maeve's upper arm. "Oh, hush. You know you're grateful."

Maeve rolled her eyes heavenward, but her tone was sincere when she said, "Of course I am. Starting from almost nothing, I can use all the help I can get."

The ladies shared another one of those indecipherable looks before Connie stood. "Well, I have some work to do today, so I'll leave you all to it. Can't wait to see the two-toned room when you're finished."

Maeve stood and gave her friend a hug. "See you later, Con."

Connie wished them well and retreated into her side of the house.

"Should we get started?" Maeve asked.

"Let's do it."

They gathered the kids and headed into their bedroom. They were delighted by the small, child-sized rollers Fletcher had purchased to go along with the two regular-sized ones for him and Maeve.

"We shouldn't need primer since these walls are already painted," Fletcher said as he inspected the current paint job. "We will need to wash the walls we want to paint, though, to ensure it'll stick." He turned to Andy and Allie. "That'll be a grown-up job because the cleaner I brought has some nasty chemicals in it. But then, you guys will get to help paint with those cool rollers."

The kids cheered and went about rolling the so far unused

rollers over every surface possible in their bedroom, including each other's bodies and Peeve, who was, well…peeved about it. He let out a yowl and darted beneath Allie's bed. Then, the children's game turned to "who can coax Peeve out first?" which involved them trying to lure him out with various objects, from a toy mouse to a crinkly ball.

Fletcher and Maeve set about cleaning the walls with the spray bottle of cleaner and rags he'd brought. While they waited for the walls to dry, he used painter's tape to tape off the floorboards and ceiling so they wouldn't end up blue as well. It was hard enough for adults to keep paint where it belonged, let alone overzealous kids. Meanwhile, Maeve entertained the kids by assembling some Legos that had already been strewn about the floor as if they'd been in the middle of the activity.

Fletcher loved watching Maeve interact with Andy and Allie. While he enjoyed the feisty, spirited side of her that often came out around him, the side she showed around her children was softer and gentler, but just as sexy.

When he declared the walls ready to go, each of the kids got a turn to stir the paint before they got to work. Fletcher offered to take on the task of cutting in the edges with a paintbrush, while the rest of them could go to town with the rollers. Andy and Allie got a kick out of making designs like smiley faces and stars. Fletcher took pleasure in Maeve's joy as she laughed with her children.

"Hey," he said, crooking his finger to beckon her over.

"What's up?" she asked, her face gorgeously flushed and her smile contagious.

"You've got a little something." He gestured to a streak of blue paint on her cupid's bow.

"Oh." She frowned and wiped her finger over it, which just smudged it further.

"Here," he said. "Let me." Taking her face in his hands, he used the pad of his thumb to swipe the paint away.

Maeve's gaze never faltered as she watched the process, and she gulped when he pulled his finger away. She'd been still as a statue, but now she blinked up at him.

"All set," Fletcher said with a smirk. She swallowed and licked her lips, which made him need to turn away. Sure, he enjoyed messing with her, but he wouldn't risk getting a hard-on in front of her kids. They returned to painting with Allie and Andy none the wiser.

Many hands made light work, and the first coat of paint was finished within a half hour. They all stepped back to take in the full effect of the blue walls.

"Now what?" Andy asked as he fiddled with the roller in his hands.

"Well, we're going to need to do a second coat," Fletcher said. "But we have to let this dry for a few hours first."

He could have sworn Maeve froze beside him. He guessed she hadn't thought about the fact that this would be an all-day affair.

"Aw, man. I hate waiting," Allie complained.

"I bet we can find something to keep us busy," Fletcher said. "Actually, we'll probably need lunch soon."

Maeve's face contorted into a grimace. "I'm sorry, I don't have much in the house right now, so we'll probably have to order take-out."

Fletcher considered that for a moment. They could either order food, or he could take the opportunity to try and impress her with his cooking skills. "I'm sure I can come up with something to cook. Would you mind me scrounging around your kitchen?"

He prided himself on being able to make something from very little—a skill he'd learned growing up. It wasn't that his family had been lacking food, but rather that his mother had been lacking the time to grocery shop and cook since she'd been so busy working and keeping them afloat. June was a potter in Fletcher's hometown of Nantucket and owned her own studio and shop. It did quite well in the touristy location, but not without her putting in a lot of hard work.

Maeve shrugged. "Sure, if you want to. But I'm telling you, there's not much there."

Fletcher flashed her a confident grin. "I'm sure I can make it work."

The kids had decided to continue working on their Lego set while Fletcher cooked, so Maeve found herself alone in the kitchen with him, sitting at the table and watching since he insisted on cooking *for* her instead of accepting her assistance. He'd really dug deep into the fridge, freezer, and cabinets and had foraged some frozen skirt steak, leftover broccoli from a couple nights ago, a couple of fresh peppers, rice, and canned pineapple. Maeve couldn't figure out how all those items went together until he explained that he was making a stir-fry.

While Fletcher gained control over each of the ingredients —it was a game of timing to figure out when to boil the water for rice, brown the frozen meat, and add the other ingredients, which were in various stages of rawness—they began chatting.

"Where did you learn to cook like this?" Maeve asked, watching as he diced a green pepper.

"I started cooking a lot as a teenager," he said, not taking his eyes off the cutting board. "My dad died when I was fourteen, and I had to help out with my little brothers."

Maeve's heart sank. "I'm so sorry, Fletcher."

He spared a glance up at her. "Thanks. It was a long time ago, but it was really hard. I actually enjoyed taking care of my brothers, Jack and Beau, though. They were huge troublemakers, but I love them."

"How old were they when…when you started caring for

them?" Maeve asked, reluctant to mention his father's death again.

"Jack was four, and Beau was two," Fletcher said as he went back to his chopping. "I was kind of an oops baby, born only seven months after my parents got married. You can do the math. Jack and Beau were planned."

"Wow, they were so young," she said.

Fletcher sighed. "Yeah. They never really got to know my dad, which is a shame because he was a great man. The early years were the hardest, not only because everyone was still grieving, but because the boys needed so much care. My favorite stage was when they were in elementary school. I loved how imaginative and curious they were."

Maeve detected the passion in his voice. "Is that why you decided to work with kids?"

Fletcher had finished chopping the second pepper and dumped it into a large frying pan. "Yeah. I knew after a few years of raising my brothers that I wanted to help do the same with other kids, too. I went to college for elementary education, then taught for twenty years before getting this promotion to principal."

Maeve mentally did the math. If Fletcher had started teaching right out of college, he'd probably been twenty-one or twenty-two, which put him in his early forties now. That was a lot of years of helping raise and teach other people's kids.

"Do you think you ever want kids of your own?" she asked.

A small smile crept onto his lips. "I definitely do. It's always been a dream of mine."

Her heart sank again because having more kids was not in the cards for her. *Not* that she was thinking of pursuing a relationship with Fletcher that would lead to him expecting her to have his children.

"I just haven't met the right person to start a family with

yet," he added. "I thought I had at one point, but…that didn't work out."

Maeve recalled one of the school moms saying something about a recent breakup. "I'm sorry. Breakups suck."

"Don't be," Fletcher said. "It was for the best. If I hadn't broken up with her, then I probably wouldn't be here with you right now." His gaze caught hers, and his eyes pooled with some unnamed emotion as he held her gaze. Her belly started pooling with that same nameless emotion, and she shifted in her seat. Maybe it was less that she couldn't name it and more that she didn't want to.

"So, are you still close with your brothers?" she asked.

"Yeah," Fletcher said. "Jack still lives on Nantucket, where I grew up, so I don't get to see him all the time, but we talk on the phone a lot. He's married with two kids. Carter is three-and-a-half, and Noah just turned ten months old. He named the baby after my father."

"That's so nice," Maeve said, not missing the wistfulness in his tone when Fletcher spoke about his brother's kids.

"My youngest brother, Beau, lives close by with his girl-friend, Emma—no, sorry, fiancée. They just got engaged last week."

"Oh, how exciting!"

"Yeah, it is." Fletcher sighed and dropped the spatula he was using to stir-fry the meat and veggies onto the counter. "It's just…"

"Just what?" she prodded.

"I always assumed I'd be the one to get married and start a family first. I'm the oldest, you know?"

"Just because you're the oldest doesn't mean you'll be the first to do anything," she pointed out.

"I know." He scrubbed a hand over his face. "I just never thought both my baby brothers would be living my dream before me."

Maeve gave him a sympathetic smile. As the food sizzled

in the pan, Fletcher began cleaning up what he could, placing dirty dishes in the sink, pepper stems in the trash, and so on. Her mind wandered to his anguish over being unmarried and childless. She loved her children and wouldn't give them up for the world, but as for her marriage… She wondered how her life would have been different if she'd gone a different route. Perhaps Fletcher not having married yet was actually a gift in disguise. Because, as Maeve knew, if you got married to the wrong person…

She must have jumped a foot in the air when a cabinet door slammed shut, startling her.

"Sorry," Fletcher said. "Just putting away the rice."

Maeve held a hand to her chest as her heart began pounding like a horse's hooves on a racetrack. "No worries," she choked out as she tried to catch her breath and remind herself that he wasn't angry. That hadn't been a violent cabinet slam. Just an overzealous one. He wasn't going to hurt her.

"Hey, are you okay?" Fletcher asked, a worried frown drawing his brows together. He came over to the table and placed a hand on her shoulder, a gesture that was obviously meant to be reassuring but instead made her jumpier.

"I'm fine," she replied, standing so his hand dropped from her body. "Is the food almost ready? I should go get the kids."

She headed for the stairs without waiting for his response.

10

———

After lunch and another hour of Lego building, this time with Fletcher joining in on the fun, they painted the second coat of blue on the walls. By the time that was finished, it was late afternoon, and the sun was already beginning to set. A beautiful pink hue lit up the sky as Maeve walked Fletcher out to the porch. He'd almost offered to stay and make dinner, too—he'd spied some sealed bacon in the back of the fridge that he knew he could work with—but he figured he shouldn't push too hard.

Maeve shut the front door quietly behind them as they stepped onto the porch. "Thanks for all your help today. Andy's really thrilled with his walls."

"I'm glad," Fletcher said. "I hope you don't mind having a two-toned room."

She waved off any worry about that. "I don't care what their walls look like as long as they're happy within them."

Fletcher appreciated the way she cared for her kids' happiness. Not all women would be willing to let their children do something offbeat like paint a bedroom two opposite colors. He imagined how Christa would have responded to a request like that…probably with disgust and immediate refusal. She would have said it looked cheap or hideous.

The differences between her and Maeve couldn't be starker, and Fletcher wondered why he hadn't seen Christa's negative traits for so long. But deep down, he knew he hadn't *allowed* himself to see them because he was so preoccupied with the potential life Christa could have given him. He'd been so distracted by visions of babies and white picket fences that he spent ten years in a relationship that probably shouldn't have even lasted ten months.

It was no use focusing on the past, though. He knew he was where he was meant to be now.

"And hey," he said to Maeve, "if you ever decide you want to paint over them, I'll be there to help."

Maeve's gaze snapped to his, as if she was surprised he would make a comment about the future. Little did she know that he planned to be in her life for a long time. Or maybe she did know, and she was just choosing to pretend she could ignore their chemistry.

"Well, drive home safely," she said, her green eyes as wide as a deer's in the headlights.

"Maeve," he said, taking a step toward her. Just as his foot hit the floor, it went right through a rotted porch plank. Luckily, it gave way slowly, so his entire leg didn't shoot right down into the hole, just up to his ankle. "Shit," he grumbled as he regained his balance and looked down at the hole in the porch.

"Shit," Maeve echoed, following his gaze to the floor.

Fletcher lifted his head, offering her a wry smile. "What I was going to say was that I want to see you again, but now I know I will because I'm coming back to fix that."

"Oh, you don't have to," she started, but he cut her off by placing his hands on her shoulders.

"You're not that great at accepting help, you know that?" He stroked small circles on her shoulders with his thumbs, giving extra attention to the one he'd massaged before. She held herself stiff as a board, but he didn't miss her small sigh of relief. "There's no way I'm going to put a hole in your porch and not come back to fix it."

"It's not your fault," Maeve insisted. "This porch is old, and the wood is weathered."

"Just because it's not my fault it happened doesn't mean it's not my responsibility to fix."

Fletcher thought of his mother, June, and how she'd raised him. She'd be royally pissed if he created a problem and didn't make it right.

Maeve looked up at him, her expression dubious. "I'm not your responsibility."

He tilted his head to the side. "Maybe not, but this hole is. Will you be around again next weekend?"

She nodded.

"Good." He lifted one of his hands to her face and stroked one of those soothing circles over the base of her jaw. "I'll be back." Then, he leaned down and kissed her cheek—just a light brush of his lips—and turned to walk back to his car before she could even react.

Maeve sipped cautiously on her steaming hot coffee as she sat on the porch the next morning. She'd gotten the kids off to school a mere eleven minutes late before coming home to enjoy a few minutes of the brisk, early morning spring air. The experience was only slightly less enjoyable in light of the squawking mama and papa sparrows perched on a nearby power line. She gave them the side-eye as she blew on her drink. They were the ones who had chosen to build their nest in such close proximity to her favorite coffee-drinking spot, after all.

The dew-tipped grass of the lawn began shimmering as

sunlight poured over it. Maeve released a long exhale as she took in the dazzling sight. When she and Connie had first arrived, the lawn was overgrown to the point that it was really more of a field. She'd had a hell of a time mowing the tall grass with the secondhand push mower they'd managed to get for cheap, but it was worth it for her current view.

To her delight, daffodil shoots had begun springing up around the base of the porch. Connie hadn't known what foliage or flora may have been left at her father's house, and Maeve looked forward to finding out what other surprises awaited her. There were still defined flowerbeds, like the one she'd found Peeve in, that appeared to have some vegetation. They could be perennial plants or just weeds—they would have to wait a few weeks to find out.

The daffodils served as a first sign of spring, despite not yet boasting their brilliant yellow blooms. Like most good things, those would come with time. Along with the sparrow eggs, the sight of the daffodil shoots filled Maeve with a renewed sense of hope. New beginnings were all around her, sprouting, growing, and holding the promise of good things to come.

The door to Connie's unit clattered open, and she emerged with her own mug in hand. Just as she went to make her way to the empty seat, Maeve remembered the rotted porch plank.

"Careful!" she cried, lurching forward as if to knock her friend out of harm's way. Connie managed to sidestep the hole just in time, but Maeve did *not* manage to halt her forward motion before hot coffee flew from her mug and spilled onto her jeans.

Connie froze, her eyes growing wide as she watched the disaster unfold. Once Maeve had placed the half-empty mug back on the table and squeezed what excess coffee she could from her pants, Connie regained movement and rushed to her side.

"Are you okay?"

Maeve gave up wringing out the denim and sat back in her chair. "Yes. The coffee was already cooling down, and these jeans are thick. I'm fine."

Connie grabbed her upper arms, catching and holding her gaze. "No, I mean, are you *okay*?"

Maeve understood the intensity in her stare. Connie was always on high alert for anything that may bring back unwanted memories. "I'm okay. Really," she replied gently.

Connie gave her arms a reassuring squeeze and dropped into the seat beside her. "Well," she said, already sounding back to her usual cheeky self. "I guess that's one way coffee can wake you up."

Maeve let out a soft chuckle and returned to sipping her drink. "I'd prefer the caffeine to make it inside my body, but I guess that's true."

Connie tucked into her own coffee, enjoying the idyllic Northeast spring morning for a few minutes before speaking again. "So, Mr. McNally spent quite a bit of time here this weekend."

"You can call him Fletcher," Maeve said, avoiding the leading tone of Connie's statement.

Connie grinned. "I'm so used to hearing Mr. McNally. The kids are always talking about Mr. McNally this, Mr. McNally that. It's like he's a celebrity or something."

Maeve grinned back. "To them, he is."

"And to you?"

Her grin slipped at Connie's pointed question. "He's a friend."

Connie's brows drew up skeptically. "I'm your friend, and I don't kiss you goodbye on the cheek before I leave. And the way he looked at you…shit, woman, he is smitten as a kitten."

Maeve's jaw dropped open. "You were watching us?"

Connie put her hands up in defense. "I was getting ready

to go out to the store when I saw you two saying goodbye through my window. I can't help what I saw."

Maeve shook her head. "He was just…being nice."

"Mae," her friend said, turning to look her squarely in the eyes. "That man is more than nice. He's completely into you. You should go for it!"

Maeve sighed. "Can you please just drop it? I told you—things are too complicated for me to be dating right now. I'm still getting the house in order, getting the kids settled, and I haven't even started looking for a job yet."

Connie cocked her head to one side and began ticking things off on her fingers. "One, the house seems to be just fine to me—your bedroom and the kids' bedrooms are fully furnished and decorated. That was the biggest project that needed to be done. Two, the kids seem awfully settled—they love school and they're making friends. So, I guess it's time to get you a job so you can finally focus on something that will make you happy other than basic life logistics."

Maeve took a slow sip of her coffee before responding. "Basic life logistics are all that's keeping me afloat right now."

That sobered Connie right up. She placed her mug on the table so she could clasp one of Maeve's hands in hers. "I know, honey. But you deserve so much more. So, seriously, what do you think you want to do? It's your fresh start. The options are endless."

Maeve shrugged. "All I've done are desk jobs, and there's nothing really pulling me toward those again. I'd love to try something new, but I have no idea what."

"Well, what are some things you enjoy?"

Maeve shot Connie a dubious look because her best friend already knew the extent of her limited hobbies. She took care of her kids, took care of their home, and read when she could squeeze it in.

Connie crossed her arms and leaned back. "Humor me."

"I like playing *Scrabble*," Maeve replied.

Connie pinned her with a glare. "Let's try and think of things that involve being out in public."

Maeve let out a sigh, trying to think of hobbies or passions that could potentially be turned into paying jobs. She thought back to who she used to be. Who she *really* was.

"Well, before…" She paused to clear her throat. "Before I met Jason, I liked going to yoga. I loved going to coffee shops to sit and read and people-watch. I used to go to the movies a lot, too."

The joy she felt when thinking of all the things she used to enjoy doing was quickly eclipsed by sorrow over the memories of why she had stopped doing them. Jason hadn't like her going to yoga because he thought it gave people free access to admire her body. He hadn't wanted her reading alone in coffee shops because he was afraid she might get hit on, and he rarely wanted to accompany her to them because he wasn't a coffee drinker. If Jason didn't get anything out of it, he wasn't going to do it. And she'd stopped going to the movies after a particularly bad experience during which she'd convinced Jason to take her and he got the impression that the popcorn man was making eyes at her. A bag of hot, buttery popcorn had wound up dumped over the worker's head, and they'd been kicked out of the theater.

"Okay," Connie said with a clap of her hands. "So, we've got yoga teacher or studio manager, barista at a coffee shop, movie theater crew or manager… I'm sure all those places need marketing people, too, and I know you have some expe-rience with that on your resumé. You have options, Mae."

Maeve's shoulders dropped. "I don't know. I haven't worked since I had the kids. Any experience on my resumé will be considered outdated."

"Give yourself some credit," Connie said. "Raising kids gives you a whole new set of skills. Time management, conflict resolution, patience… Any smart employer would see that."

"I guess," Maeve replied. "Once I get to know the area more, I'll have a better idea of what my options are. I'll need to be close by in case the kids get sick or something and need to be picked up from school."

"You know I'm always available, too," Connie reminded her. "We're in this together, honey."

Maeve smiled, all traces of worry or uncertainty fading with that reminder. "Thank God for that."

11

I t was the day of the big bake sale to raise money for field day, and Maeve had baked brownies as promised. When she arrived at the school early that morning to drop them off along with the kids, she saw the school moms setting up a long table by the school's entrance and headed over to give them her contribution.

"Hi!" Tiffany called out, waving two arms above her head as if Maeve would miss her. How could she ever miss that blinding blonde hair? Her head was like one of those reflectors they used in professional photoshoots.

"Hey," Maeve said, placing her pan of double-chocolate brownies on the table.

Rebecca, one of the brunettes, glanced at it. "Oh, you made…plain brownies."

Maeve glanced around at the other treats already laid out. Ornate cupcakes, intricately decorated sugar cookies, and all sorts of other fancy desserts littered the table. She frowned down at her brownies, which now looked downright shabby in comparison to the rest of the offerings. "I guess I didn't realize how all-out you guys went for these bake sales."

Stephanie, the redhead, patted her on the shoulder. "It's okay. Everyone likes brownies, right?"

Maeve thanked her with a small smile. Though Stephanie's red hair wasn't authentic like Maeve's was, she still saw her as somewhat of a kindred spirit.

"Well, I hope you guys are successful today," Maeve said, itching to retreat to her car and go home to Connie so they could laugh about the over-the-top school moms again.

"Oh, you're not staying to help us run the bake sale?" Jennifer, the other brunette, asked.

"Oh, er…I didn't realize you needed any help." *And I didn't sign up for that,* Maeve thought to herself.

"I'm sure we can handle it on our own," Tiffany said, "but we'd really love for you to stay and help so we can get to know you better as well!"

Maeve considered turning them down. It would be so much easier to just go home and not have to deal with these pretentious women anymore. She had done everything she'd committed to when she placed those brownies on the table. She could wipe her hands clean and walk away now if she wanted to. But she also didn't want to get on anyone's bad side, especially if their kids might wind up being friends with hers.

"Okay, I guess I can stay and help."

Tiffany clapped her hands as if Maeve had just agreed to donate a million dollars. Stephanie grinned kindly at her, and Jennifer and Rebecca both shot her tight smiles.

Parents began arriving to drop students off, and business at the bake sale picked up rapidly. Each time a bus pulled up, kids got off in droves, many of them armed with dollar bills that they used to purchase early morning treats. The glass jar the women had left out was already stuffed with cash, and half the school hadn't even shown up yet.

During a lull in business, Fletcher appeared, sauntering toward their table and looking better than he had any right to in his work attire of chinos and a blue pin-stripe button-up. "Hey, everyone," he said. "Wow, everything looks fantastic."

"Thanks, Mr. McNally," Jennifer piped up. "We all worked *so* hard to put this together."

Maeve could have sworn the woman shot her a sidelong glance when she said the part about working hard, but it was over so quickly she couldn't be sure it had ever really happened.

"I can tell." Fletcher took in the array of food, his eyes scanning the over-the-top selection.

"What would you like, Mr. McNally?" Tiffany asked. "I made these chocolate-ganache cupcakes. They're infused with raspberry filling." She pointed at the cupcakes, then to a neighboring plate of cookies. "These frosted chai cookies that Rebecca made have also been super popular. If you want one, you'd better snag it now because they're going fast!"

Maeve briefly wondered if Tiffany had been a saleswoman in a past life, before becoming the peppy PTA president.

Fletcher considered his options before pointing at the tray of brownies in front of Maeve. She'd managed to sell a few of them to kids who didn't know better, but most people hadn't even noticed them amidst all the fancier options.

"These look delicious," he said, licking his lips. Maeve tried not to recall what that tongue felt like between *her* lips.

"Oh, are you sure you don't want something a little more…unique?" Jennifer asked. "We've got so many great options. How about one of these seven-layer bars? They're made with authentic Swiss chocolate!"

Fletcher's eyes didn't leave their target. "No. I'm in the mood for a brownie. I want this one, please." He pointed to a particularly plump brownie in the corner of the pan.

Maeve's lips ticked up. "You're a corner guy, huh? I prefer corners to middle pieces, too."

Fletcher grinned at her, his brown eyes lighting up along

with his smile. "Well, it seems we have something in common, then."

She vaguely registered the other ladies scowling in their direction, but with Fletcher's eyes locked on hers, it was as if they were in their own little world. He was wearing his genuine smile, not the polite one he put on for the other women, and his eyes held a playfulness, as if they had their own little secret.

Maeve reluctantly broke eye contact to scoop the brownie out of the pan and lay it on a napkin. Fletcher stuffed a five-dollar bill into the donation jar and held his hand out to receive the brownie. Her fingers just brushed his palm as she passed it to him, but the light contact felt almost scandalous in the presence of all these other women.

Fletcher's eyes locked onto hers as he brought the brownie up to his mouth, and he let out a low, masculine moan as he bit into it. Maeve bit her lip to hold back laughter. The other women were openly gawking now, and Jennifer wore a particularly jealous sneer. Fletcher seemed to know exactly what he was doing. He was putting on a show just for her. To make her smile.

Maeve raised one eyebrow as he chewed. "Good?"

Fletcher's eyes burned into hers as he answered, "Delicious."

A shiver stole down her spine at the hunger in his voice. She didn't think it was hunger for more brownie. "I'm glad you're enjoying it," she replied, working hard to keep a straight face. She was caught between wanting to crack up at Fletcher's antics and wanting to lean over the table and lick the brownie smudge off his lips.

He finished the treat in a couple of large bites, then began licking the pads of his fingers to clean them. Maeve squirmed as she watched him, unable to tear her gaze away even to gauge the other ladies' reactions, which were sure to be hysterical.

"Well, that was a great way to start my morning," Fletcher said with a wink.

One of the other ladies audibly gasped, and Maeve bit back a smile. "I hope the rest of your day is just as sweet," she said, playing into his hijinks by saying something totally unlike her. In fact, it sounded exactly like something Tiffany would say.

Fletcher seemed to suppress his own grin, pursing his lips slightly and clearing his throat. His eyes lingered on her for a moment more before sweeping over the other women. "I hope you all have great days. Thanks again for your hard work."

Maeve allowed herself to appreciate Fletcher's glorious backside as he walked away only because the rest of the women were doing the same. Once he was gone, she went on serving the next customer as if nothing had happened. Somehow, she just knew that would rankle the others.

After another twenty minutes of passing out treats and collecting donations, the bake sale finally ended. They'd managed to sell every single item—even her boring brownies. Sure, they were one of the last things to go, but they sold in the end. And Fletcher had obviously enjoyed them, which was really all that mattered to Maeve.

She helped them break down the table before grabbing her empty tin and heading for her car. She'd only made it a few steps in that direction when Fletcher was suddenly at her side, matching her pace.

"Here, let me carry this for you." He grabbed the tin from her hand.

"I really could have handled that myself," Maeve said, stuffing her now-empty hands in her jacket pockets.

"I know," Fletcher murmured as they walked along. "But I needed an excuse to come talk to you again."

Her heart fluttered, and she focused on her footsteps for a moment so she wouldn't stumble. "Thank you for defending my brownies earlier."

They reached her car and turned to face each other as they leaned against it.

"They didn't need defending. They were delicious."

"Well, I'm not sure the other ladies cared too much about the taste. They didn't look anywhere near as impressive as anything else on the table." Maeve grimaced, thinking of her faux pas. She should have known women like the school moms would expect more than a tin of plain brownies cut into haphazard squares.

Fletcher's smile was thoughtful as he responded. "That's the thing. Some people only care about looks. They try to make it seem like everything's perfect, that they have everything together. But none of that's real, and frankly, I don't have time for that type of bullshit anymore."

Maeve's eyes widened at the curse, especially since they were still in the parking lot of the elementary school.

Fletcher brought a hand up to cup her cheek, and she was too distracted by how good the contact felt to care about the fact that they might be seen. "You're not like that, Maeve," he said. "You're real. In fact, you're the realest person I've met in a long time."

She snorted, burrowing her hands deeper into her pockets. "If, by real, you mean a real mess."

"You're not a mess," he said. "You're a single mom of two beautiful and very energetic children. I think you're doing a great job."

She gazed up into his sincere eyes, relishing the feeling of his thumb stroking her cheek. "Thank you."

He stroked her skin once more before dropping his hand, his eyes remaining glued to hers. "And you can always ask for help. Even though I know you're not great at accepting it."

"Hey, I accepted your help carrying this brownie tin," she said as she snatched it back from him.

He chuckled. "That you did. And you're going to accept it again this weekend when I come to fix the porch, right?"

She wanted to say no. That she would just slap a piece of wood over the hole so no one fell in and call it a day. But with two kids constantly tromping around, that probably wasn't the safest idea. And once again, it was a fantastic excuse to see Fletcher without leading him on to think that she was open to more than the idea of being friends.

So, she found herself saying, "Yes."

Hello again, Mae.

I know you're reading these texts.

It wasn't very nice of you to block me, but don't worry, I got a new number.

With shaky fingers, Maeve blocked the number as fast as she could, which wasn't very fast with the way she fumbled with the phone. Maybe *she* should be the one getting a new phone number. One more text sailed in before she was able to delete it.

Where are you? Tell me or I'll come find you.

The ominous words sent a shiver down her spine, and she placed the phone on the countertop so hard it was a wonder the screen didn't shatter. Even if he did come looking, Jason wouldn't be able to find her. Connie had made sure of that. Nonetheless, the thought of him getting anywhere near her or her children again made Maeve's stomach twist. A sudden wave of nausea had her doubled over. Her knuckles turned white as she gripped the edge of the counter for support.

"Are you okay, Mommy?" Andy asked as he entered the kitchen. It was a school morning, and the kids had been finishing up getting dressed.

Maeve forced herself to take a deep inhale and exhale, which helped relieve the nausea a bit, but her stomach still churned and roiled. "I'm fine, baby," she said a little breathlessly. "Why don't you grab your backpack and wait by the door?"

Andy did as he was told, though he shot her a worried glance as he headed for the door. She hated seeing anything but a smile on that cherubic little face, so she gathered every ounce of strength in her body and stood up straight, taking deep, even breaths through her nose.

She really needed to get her stress under control. Sure, the constant worries about Jason ate away at her, and receiving texts from him was understandably concerning, but this physical manifestation was just a little too much. How was he still able to ruin her well-being when he wasn't even in her life anymore?

"Let's go!" Allie shouted as she came barreling down the stairs to grab her own backpack. Maeve's eyes snapped shut at the volume with which her daughter spoke. She felt almost hungover, but she hadn't had even a sip of alcohol since that first night with Fletcher.

She dropped the kids off at school in a haze, vaguely wondering if she should even be driving. Amidst the brain fog, she noticed a black SUV pull up behind her at a red light on the way home. It inched forward until they were practically bumper to bumper. Whatever stick was up the driver's ass, he was going to have to deal with it. It wasn't the day to mess with Maeve.

As soon as the light turned green, she zoomed forward,

eager to put space between his car and hers. He followed at a steady pace, driving just a little too close for comfort. Maeve took the left turn that led to the last main road before her journey branched off onto back roads all the way home. To her chagrin, the SUV took the same one. After a moment of separation resulting from the wide turn radius, he went back to tailgating her.

Maeve grunted her displeasure as she tried to make out the driver in her rearview mirror. His hat and sunglasses obscured any recognizable features. She couldn't imagine it was anyone she knew intentionally annoying her. She didn't have any enemies. She hadn't even lived in Boston long enough to make any enemies yet.

Then, a chilling thought hit her. Could it be Jason following her?

No. It couldn't be. She'd given him no possible way to track her, and besides, less than an hour ago, he'd sent a text about coming to find her. If he knew where she was, he would have sent something a lot more sinister.

She attempted to calm herself with a deep breath. *It isn't Jason.* She was still just shaken up by his text.

Debating whether she should continue driving home or try to lose the SUV first, Maeve decided to go with the former. She truly didn't feel well, and she was eager to get home to her couch. If he followed her onto the back roads, she would know something was really up and devise a different plan then.

Maeve breathed a sigh of relief as she took a right turn, and the SUV continued going straight down the main road. The rest of the drive home was much more peaceful, save for the lingering foggy feeling and slight nausea she couldn't seem to shake.

As soon as the front door swung shut behind her, Maeve's eyes filled with tears. She honestly wasn't sure whether it was the physical discomfort or the emotional turmoil that was getting to her, but she just plain felt like crap.

This was supposed to be her fresh start. Jason had ruined her life once already. He wasn't supposed to be able to do it again.

Maeve collapsed on the living room couch as tears flowed down her cheeks. Her gut had settled a bit, but now she felt weighed down by fatigue. Suddenly, she felt as if she'd run a marathon. And she was cold. Freezing, actually. Pulling a fuzzy blanket off the back of the couch, she wrapped herself in it like a cocoon and slipped into a horizontal position on the couch. Salty tears coated the fabric of the pillow beneath her cheek until she fell asleep.

That afternoon, Fletcher sat behind his desk after enjoying a great lunch with Beau and Emma to celebrate their engagement. Their joy had been palpable, and he was beyond happy for them but was once again left with mixed emotions. Emma hadn't been able to stop twiddling with her ring, and Beau hadn't been able to stop staring at his fiancée. It was equally sweet and dispiriting.

"Fletcher?" He looked up to find a worried Bethany in his doorway.

"What's up, Bethany?"

"Andy and Allie haven't been picked up yet. They're the last students here."

Fletcher glanced down at his watch. It was well after the end of the school day, and while Maeve was often on the later side to drop the kids off, she was rarely late to pick them up.

"Let me try to call their mom." Fletcher pulled out his cell and clicked on the *Ravishing Redhead* contact. The phone rang and rang until a robotic pre-recorded message played. *Damn.*

He didn't bother to leave a voicemail and, instead, shot her a quick text.

"Let's give her five minutes to respond," he told Bethany. "And let's find the kids something to do in the meantime."

Bethany smiled. "Already done. Come see."

Fletcher followed her out into the main office, where Andy and Allie were decorating the front desk with a colorful paper chain. Allie was, frighteningly, wielding a stapler while Andy wrapped strips of paper around each other to form the chain.

"Wow, that looks beautiful," Fletcher said.

Both children grinned widely.

"Thanks, Mr. McNally!" Allie said. "We're beautifying your office. And don't worry—I'm making sure the stapler is finger-free before I push it down."

"Glad to hear it," Fletcher said, still not fully trusting her with something that could be construed as a weapon. "Did your mom say she was going to be late picking you up today?"

"No," Andy said. "But…"

Apprehension was written on the boy's face, so Fletcher knelt beside him.

"It's okay, Andy. Whatever you're worried about, you can tell me."

Andy swallowed and looked up at Fletcher with eyes as wide as saucers. "It's just that…Mommy wasn't feeling too good this morning. She was looking at her phone, and then she was bent over, and she looked like I do before I throw up."

Fletcher frowned. Was Maeve sick? Or had something happened? Had she gotten some kind of bad news?

"Thanks for telling me, bud," he said, patting Andy on the shoulder. He checked his phone, but no new texts from Maeve had come in. He stood and walked over to Bethany. "I'm not sure what's going on, but I'm starting to get a little worried. I'm going to zip over to their house and make sure everything's okay."

Bethany sent him a questioning look but nodded her

approval. Principals didn't usually do house calls, but this was Maeve they were talking about. He wasn't legally allowed to drive the kids home, but there was nothing stopping him from driving himself there.

Fletcher took the roads just a little too fast as he headed for Maeve. What if something bad *had* happened? It was so unlike Maeve not to pick up her kids. She was so attentive to them. It wasn't as if she would have forgotten. And she hadn't found a job yet, as far as he knew, so that wasn't the reason. He could only imagine that something had held her up, and the endless list of possibilities had his head spinning.

Pulling into her driveway, he noted that her car was there. So, either she was home, or she'd gone out with someone else. But either way, why hadn't she answered her phone?

He knocked on the door. No answer. He rang the bell. No answer. He decided to knock on Connie's door in the hopes that she might be home and know where Maeve was.

A moment later, the door cracked open to reveal half of Connie's face. Her hair was all tied up in a bright-red scarf today, and her eyes were narrowed to slits until she recognized him. "Oh. Hi, Fletcher," she said, opening the door wider.

"Hey." He plowed his fingers through his hair. "Do you know where Maeve is? She never picked the kids up from school."

Connie frowned down at her watch, then peered over at Maeve's car parked in the driveway. "As far as I know, she's here."

"I tried calling and texting, but I didn't get an answer," Fletcher said, his concern growing. "I knocked and rang the bell, too. Nothing."

Connie's frown deepened. She reached for something on a small shelf, then shuffled out her front door and over to Maeve's. Fletcher noticed then that she wore fuzzy, fire-engine-red slippers that matched her headscarf.

"Let's check if she's inside." Connie inserted the spare key she'd procured into the lock, and the door creaked open. "Maeve?" she called out.

There was no answer, but then Fletcher heard a soft sound coming from somewhere inside. Was that...snoring? A second noise joined the first—a soft *thump* of paws against the hardwood floor. Peeve traipsed into the entryway, wove a figure-eight through Connie's legs and then Fletcher's, then began prancing purposefully away. It seemed as if he wanted them to follow him. They shared a puzzled glance before doing just that.

Peeve led them straight to the living room before jumping onto the armrest of the couch and curling himself into a ball. A distinctly human-shaped lump of blankets was perched on the couch, an eruption of red hair jutting out the top of it like lava from a volcano.

"Maeve?" Fletcher asked, more out of bewilderment than trying to get her attention. Had she just fallen asleep in the middle of the day?

Connie rushed over and knelt beside the couch. "Mae, what's wrong?" she asked, lightly shaking her shoulder.

Maeve's eyes slanted open slightly on a grunt. "Hmm?" she mumbled, clutching at the blankets to pull them tighter.

Fletcher came over and placed the back of his hand against her forehead. "She's burning up."

Connie rocked back on her heels. "She must have caught a virus or something."

Fletcher dropped his hand with a sigh. Maeve's eyes had closed again, and her soft snoring was already starting back up. "She looks miserable. Would you mind picking up Andy and Allie? I'll stay with Maeve."

"Of course," Connie replied as she stood. "Why don't I take them over to my place, too? All their shouting and running around will disturb Maeve's rest."

"That would be great," Fletcher said. "I can stay as long as needed."

Connie seemed to study him for a moment before her lips tilted into a grin. "Great. I'll check in with you later." She shuffled back over to her place—probably to change into real shoes and grab her keys—and Fletcher took a seat on the far end of the couch where he assumed Maeve's feet were. He couldn't tell beneath the mountain of blankets atop her sleeping body.

Poor Maeve. The virus must have come on quickly and taken her by surprise. Andy had said she looked like she was about to vomit that morning. The part of his story about her looking at her phone must have just been an irrelevant detail. Kids had a habit of adding those.

Fletcher kicked his feet up on the already-scuffed coffee table and spent a few minutes scrolling on his phone to pass the time. Maeve probably needed medicine, water, and food, but more than anything, she needed rest, so he would let her stay asleep as long as she needed.

He immediately became alert a few minutes later when a low groan escaped Maeve's mouth. The pile of blankets began to shift, and he realized she was stretching her legs out. A second later, her feet bumped into his thigh.

"Hi, Maeve," he said.

She sat up slowly, sniffed, and stared at him. "Fletcher?" Her thick red hair stuck out at odd angles, and her creased cheek held proof that it had lain against the seam of the couch cushion for some time now.

"Connie and I came to check on you when the kids never got picked up," he explained softly.

"Shit! The kids." Maeve attempted to slide out from beneath the blankets but got all tangled up and only managed to get half her body uncovered.

"It's okay." Fletcher patted her bared shoulder. "Connie's got them. You need to focus on getting yourself better."

She let out a large yawn, then pouted. "I feel like crap."

He swallowed a chuckle. Something about Maeve's

disheveled appearance and sleepy spunkiness was quite endearing. "I'll bet. When did your symptoms come on?"

"This morning. I was fine one minute, and the next, I was nauseated and exhausted." She rubbed her temples as if she had a headache, too.

"You definitely have a fever," Fletcher said, using that as an excuse to place his hand on her forehead again. Her smooth skin was hot to the touch. "Do you want me to take you to the doctor?"

Maeve shook her head as she yawned again. "It's just a virus. A couple of kids in Allie's class were out sick with it last week."

Fletcher nodded. A nasty virus had been spreading through the school. "Do you want me to expel them for getting you sick?"

That earned him a small smile despite her obvious discomfort. "No." Maeve laced her hands together and stretched her arms over her head. The movement caused her shirt to rise up just enough to show a strip of creamy skin above her waistline. The sight snagged Fletcher's gaze, and he began imagining what else was hiding under the rest of that shirt.

He was still dying to see Maeve in full. The taste he'd gotten of her a few weeks ago was nowhere near enough to satiate his hunger. His lust had only increased over the time they'd gotten to spend together as he watched her love her children, hold her own with the school moms, and continue to sass him in that feisty way of hers. He was fascinated by every facet of Maeve, and he hoped to continue to get to know the other parts of her.

Her voice brought him back to the present moment. "Thank you for checking on me and having Connie go get the kids."

Fletcher lifted a brow. "Are you trying to kick me out right now?"

She shrugged slightly, as if the weight of the world sat on her shoulders. "There's nothing else you can do."

He blinked at her. "Of course there is. I can stay and take care of you."

Maeve's eyes flashed with contempt. "I don't need anyone to take care of me."

He sighed and gestured to her blanket-clad body. "Maeve," he said. "You were fast asleep in the middle of the day, you have a fever that's probably somewhere in the hundreds, and you can't even get yourself out from under those blankets you've wrapped yourself in. Have you even eaten today? Taken any medicine? Have you been drinking water?"

Her shoulders drooped as he ticked off the list of tasks. "No," she mumbled.

"Didn't think so. So, until you're feeling better, I'm going to be here taking care of you."

"Fletcher, you don't have to—"

"Ah, ah, ah," he interrupted her objection. "No backtalk. I don't want to hear any complaints from you."

Maeve scowled and crossed her arms over her lap. "You're talking to me like I'm one of your students."

Fletcher grinned because she was absolutely right. "If you don't want me to talk to you like a child, then don't behave like one. Just let me take care of you without any whining."

She stuck her tongue out at him but didn't object further.

He stood from the couch. "I just need to know one thing from you: what's your favorite kind of soup?"

Maeve's features softened as she answered, "I love chicken with rice."

"Then, I'm going to go get stuff for chicken-and-rice soup and get you some medicine to see if we can bring that fever down. Is there anything else you need from the store?"

She thought for a moment. "Would you mind getting me some chocolate, too? Maybe a bag of M&Ms?"

Thrilled that she was finally asking him for what she wanted, Fletcher nodded eagerly. "You've got it. I should be back in about a half hour. Why don't you rest until then?"

Already halfway back under the blankets, Maeve gave him a thumbs up and closed her eyes.

13

Consciousness tugged at Maeve's brain. As she lay with her eyes still closed, the day's events began slowly trickling into her mind: the texts from Jason, feeling horrible as she drove the kids to school, collapsing on the couch when she got home, then Fletcher and Connie checking on her before leaving to take care of the kids.

Inching her eyes open, she saw that it was already getting dark outside. She decided to get up to close the shades, which meant hauling the mass of blankets off her body. Once she was finally free, she stood, her body feeling like lead—stiff and heavy—as she staggered over to the windows. She hadn't quite made it to the first one when a noise snagged her attention.

Maeve looked around until she realized the noise was the doorknob on the front door. Someone on the other side was twisting it, trying to open it to no avail. That must have meant the person didn't have a key. If it was Connie or one of the kids, they would be using a key and would be able to open the door just fine. So, that could only mean one thing.

Someone was breaking into the house.

Perhaps it was lingering fear from Jason's *I'll find you* text, or perhaps she was experiencing fever-induced delirium, but either way, Maeve decided it would be a fantastic idea to grab the bug zapper Connie had given her and attempt to fight off the intruder. Snatching the zapper off a side table, she tiptoed toward the door, wielding it like a baseball bat.

When the door finally lurched open, she let out a wild cry and stumbled forward, lashing out with the zapper to deter the intruder from coming any farther inside. She still hadn't seen his face as he held two large, brown, paper grocery bags in his arms. She felt her makeshift weapon connect with a body part just as the realization dawned that an intruder wouldn't have been bringing her groceries.

"Jesus!" cried a familiar deep voice as the bags fell from the man's grasp. Loose carrots and celery stalks rolled through the foyer, and a wrapped chicken dropped to the floor with a thud.

Maeve lowered the racket slowly and watched in horror as Fletcher knelt down and began gathering the escaping produce. "I thought you were an intruder," she whispered.

"Nope, just the guy who said he was going out for groceries and would be back soon."

"I'm sorry. I…I was a little out of it. Did I hurt you?"

Fletcher's eyes softened as he glanced at her. "No, I'm wearing a thick jacket, so I didn't feel the zaps."

"Oh, good," she replied as she fiddled with the zapper in her hands.

Fletcher stood and gently took the item from her grasp. "Why don't you go sit down before you hurt yourself."

Maeve grimaced at the command but had to admit that it wasn't a particularly bad idea. She obviously wasn't in her right mind if she'd forgotten Fletcher's plan to return with food and medicine and then thought it smart to fight off what she thought was an intruder with a bug zapper.

On shaky legs, she made her way over to a chair at the kitchen table. Fletcher followed soon after, placing his now refilled bags on the counter.

"I got you two kinds of fever medicine—one for daytime and one for nighttime," he explained as he unpacked the boxes. "I figured you could take the daytime one now, then rest while I make the soup, eat, and then you'll be ready for the nighttime one in about four hours, before you go to bed."

Maeve nodded. Chills had begun wracking her body, and her teeth were already beginning to chatter now that she was no longer under the comfort of her blanket mountain.

Fletcher must have noticed, because he grabbed a blanket off the couch and handed it to her before doling out her medication. He handed her two pills along with a glass of water, and Maeve realized he was treating her kitchen as if it was his own—locating glasses, getting her water, preparing to make soup…

"Wait, you're *making* me soup? I thought you would just buy some canned stuff at the store."

Fletcher gawked at her. "The canned stuff is full of unnecessary sodium, and it's practically tasteless. I can whip up some fresh chicken-and-rice soup in about an hour."

Her mouth watered at the thought of hot, fresh soup. "Can I do anything to help?" she asked, glancing at the unsliced vegetables and chicken.

"No. You can go sit and relax." He pulled a couple of magazines from the grocery bags. "I got you these." He passed the trashy tabloid magazines over to Maeve. "I know my sister-in-law and future sister-in-law love these, and I figured they're the best mindless thing to read when you're not feeling well."

Maeve accepted the magazines, touched by Fletcher's thoughtfulness.

"And…" he added, pulling a large bag of M&Ms out of the bottom of the bag. "I got you these."

Maeve's mouth watered anew, and she made *give me* hands until he passed her the bag. She immediately tore it open and popped a handful of the candies into her mouth. "These are all the medicine I need."

"But you will take the fever medicine, too," Fletcher said —a command, not a question. His stern tone elicited memories of commands he'd given during their one night together. *Lie back. Grab onto the headboard. Hold on tight.*

Maeve's belly tightened—not with nausea this time, but with lust. Heat that had nothing to do with her fever flooded her veins. She'd never had any kind of schoolgirl fantasies, but she wouldn't mind getting to hear more of Fletcher's principal voice in bed. Too bad that would never be happening.

She knocked back the two pills and made a show of swallowing them with a large swig of water. "Done."

Fletcher's lips drew into a half-smirk at her dramatic display. "Good girl."

The tightness in her belly grew taut at the affirming words. He'd used those in bed, too—another thing Maeve had never known she had an inclination for. But clearly, Fletcher realized it, because he was smiling to himself as he began chopping the carrots and celery into thin slices. Once again, he worked with ease and grace in the kitchen, showcasing the culinary skills he'd honed over years of helping feed his family.

"Do you want to rest on the couch while I cook?" he asked, glancing over even as he continued chopping.

Maeve pulled the blanket tighter around her. "Actually, I'd like to stay upright for a while. I think I was asleep for a few hours. Mind if I stay out here with you?"

He treated her to a warm smile. "Of course not. I love spending time with you. But if you stop feeling up to it, you can go lie down anytime."

She nodded, appreciative of how attentive he was to her needs. He always seemed to have a subtle awareness of her mood and mental state, and he was careful not to push past where she was comfortable.

"So," Fletcher said as he began carving the pre-cooked

chicken. "Last time we talked like this, I told you a lot about me, my family, and my job. What about you? What's your story, Maeve?"

She swallowed hard, realizing that while this was a totally natural question, it was also one she dreaded answering because she would either have to give him all the dirty details of her ugly past, or she'd have to lie. Despite how much she would've loved to have nothing but honesty between her and Fletcher, she chose the second option.

"Oh, there's not much of a story to tell, I guess. I'm the only child of loving parents. They still live in Indiana, where I grew up. I went to college for business, and I've worked in a few different corporate jobs. I was married for a few years and had Allie and Andy, obviously. Things were getting kind of stale, and I wanted a change, so we decided to move here and have this fresh start."

"That's really brave," Fletcher said, now shredding the carved chicken. "To leave everything you know and start over."

Maeve shrugged. Not that he realized it, but she'd had no other choice. It didn't matter how brave or not she felt—she had to get those kids out of that house and away from Jason.

"It was for the best," she said, recalling Fletcher using those same words to describe his own breakup.

He continued his food preparation for a few quiet minutes. Then, as he was combining ingredients into a pot, he continued his line of questioning. "No pressure to talk about it, because I understand how complicated and nuanced these things can be, but what happened with your marriage?"

Maeve's stomach dropped. There were a lot of reasons she didn't want to get into the whole sordid story with Fletcher, from maintaining his image of her as a strong, bold woman to maintaining her own safety. She collected herself with a deep breath before giving him a diplomatic answer.

"We just weren't the right fit long-term. It was better for everyone that we separate."

Fletcher nodded, his eyes focused on his cooking task, though Maeve knew he was listening intently. In fact, she suspected his lack of eye contact might have been a calculated move to get her to open up more by feigning nonchalance.

"Is he in the kids' lives at all?"

"No," she said quickly and probably a little too harshly. "No, they don't see him at all." Then, she thought of Fletcher's job and what he must think of that. "I know from a child-development perspective it's best to have both parents in a child's life, but in this case, it was making life worse for everyone involved."

Fletcher put his hands in the air. "Hey, I'm not judging. You have to do what works for your family. And I trust your judgment, Maeve."

She almost had to laugh at that. How ironic that he would say he trusted her judgment when she'd been struggling to trust her own ever since Jason. What kind of fool picks a man like that? And *stays* with him?

"Thank you," she replied quietly. "It wasn't a good marriage, and I'm glad I left it. I…" Images of her marriage to Jason rolled through her mind like a photo reel. There had been good times, of course, but for every good time, there were three bad ones. For every happy memory, there were traumas and scars to outweigh it. "I think I am going to lie down after all."

14

After feeding Maeve a hearty serving of chicken-and-rice soup, Fletcher forced her to leave the dirty dishes in the sink and walked her toward her bedroom.

"Do you want to shower before you get into bed?" he asked. He was holding onto her elbow to guide her, and he worried she wouldn't have the strength to stand in the shower, but he also knew how good a shower could feel when one was sick.

She nodded. "I'd like that. I feel disgusting."

They veered toward the bathroom, where Fletcher sat her down on the closed toilet lid. Pivoting toward the shower, he turned the water on and adjusted the dial until it reached the perfect, warm-but-not-too-hot temperature.

"Are you going to be okay doing this by yourself?"

She scowled up at him. "Well, I'm certainly not going to let you help me."

He resisted the urge to roll his eyes. She spoke as if it would be so horrible to have him help her wash herself, his hands sudsing and soaping her up, roaming along her soft, creamy skin… Okay, so maybe it was a bad idea.

"Maeve, you're sick," he said bluntly. "And as attracted to you as I am, this would be purely clinical. You can barely stand up, your body is shaky with your fever, and all I want is for you to feel clean so you can get into bed and have a good night's sleep."

Her jaw set hard. "No. No way. I'll take a super-quick shower, and I'll sit down if I need to."

He waited for a moment, but it didn't seem like she was going to budge. "Fine. I'll be right outside the door. Just call if you need me."

She nodded and shooed him out the door.

In the hallway, Fletcher leaned his back against the wall and sank down to the floor just outside the bathroom door. The water turned on, and he pictured Maeve stripping out of her clothes, stepping under the spray, foaming up her hands with soap before spreading it all over every inch of her body. Even sick as a dog, the woman tempted him.

As promised, she took a short shower, and the water turned off just a few minutes later. Fletcher sighed with relief. He could stop picturing her in there now. The bathroom door cracked open, and Maeve peeked around the corner.

"All set." She opened the door the rest of the way and revealed herself to be wearing an oversized fluffy towel draped over her shoulders and covering everything to mid-thigh.

"Why don't you get dressed—" Fletcher's voice cracked, so he cleared his throat and continued, "and I'll go get your nighttime medicine."

Maeve scurried off toward her bedroom, and he went to the kitchen for her medicine and another glass of water. He was just walking back down the hallway when her bedroom door opened. This time, she was fully dressed in long, flannel pajama pants and a big, loose t-shirt. The shapeless clothing hid her delectable curves, but somehow, she still looked sexy as hell.

She probably thought she was deterring his longing by

wearing such ratty clothing, but it was having quite the opposite effect. The fact that she trusted him enough to be vulnerable and look less than perfect, when he knew she held a wound about that from the way she'd spoken about the other moms at school, meant a lot to him.

"Thank you," Maeve said as Fletcher handed her the medicine and water. She dutifully swallowed the pills and handed him back the empty water glass. "Hopefully, these will keep my fever down so I can sleep tonight."

"I hope so, too," he replied. "But I'll be here if you need anything. I'm going to sleep out on the couch."

Maeve's jaw dropped. "You don't have to stay here."

"Maeve." He took a step toward her, placing his hands on her shoulders. She tipped her head back to peer up at him. "You're sick. I'm not leaving you alone. No one should have to be alone when they're sick."

"Connie's right next door with the kids," she argued.

"Exactly. Connie's taking care of the kids. I'm here to take care of *you.*"

She scrunched her nose in confusion, as if that was an unfamiliar concept.

One of his hands drifted to her face. Her skin was no longer hot to the touch, just soft and smooth beneath his fingers as he caressed her jawline. "Get some sleep. I'm not going anywhere."

She leaned into his touch for just a moment, pressing her cheek into his palm like a kitten seeking warmth. "Fletcher, you really—"

"Don't even think about kicking me out," he said, cutting her off. "Because I'll take the M&Ms with me."

She gasped dramatically, feigning horror. Then, her eyes narrowed. "You wouldn't."

He lifted a brow in challenge. "Try me, sweetheart."

Blush bloomed on her cheeks, and he cheered internally. He loved getting Maeve all riled up, breaking through those carefully constructed walls of hers. But now wasn't the time or place for seduction, so he brushed his thumb one last time over her beautifully pink cheek, then dropped his hand back to her shoulder. "Go to bed."

Her breath seemed to hitch at his commanding tone, and he filed away that information for later. After that sweet reaction, he couldn't stop himself from leaning in to press a chaste kiss to her forehead. "No more fever," he said, playing off the kiss as a temperature check.

She was still looking up at him through wide eyes as she whispered, "Goodnight."

"Goodnight, Maeve," he murmured as he steered her toward the bed. She walked a bit unsteadily, and he held onto her elbow to support her. Once she was safely atop the mattress, he helped pull the covers up over her body.

The blanket came almost up to her nose, and she peeked at him from beneath her light eyelashes. "Thanks, Fletch."

She looked so cozy and warm, and the bed looked so inviting. There was nothing he wanted more than to hop in and snuggle up with her. Instead, he took a step back. "Sleep tight."

As he exited the bedroom, he left the door open a crack so he would hear Maeve if she called for him, then headed for the living room. He was setting up the couch with a spare set of sheets he'd found in the hall closet when a soft knock came at the front door. He answered it to find Connie on the doorstep, back in her red slippers and headscarf. He opened the door wide and welcomed her in.

"How's our girl doing?" Connie asked as Fletcher shut the door softly behind her. He felt a pang of tender affection at her words. As much as he wished he could claim Maeve as *his girl*, he knew he hadn't won her over just yet. But it was only a matter of time.

"She's doing better. The medicine really helped, and I got some food and liquid into her. How are the kids?"

"Oh, they're fine. Thrilled to be having a sleepover at my place, actually. It's a novelty for them. They got to eat pizza and ice cream. And don't worry, they got their homework done," she said with a wink. "They're asleep now."

Fletcher nodded. "So is Maeve. She wasn't thrilled about the idea of me staying over, but I think I convinced her it was for the best."

Connie looked past him to the couch, now all made up as a bed for the night. "You're going to sleep here?" Twin creases appeared between her eyebrows as she frowned slightly. "Is Maeve okay with that?"

Fletcher appreciated Maeve's friend looking out for her, and, looking back, he *had* threatened to take away her M&Ms if she didn't let him stay. But knowing Maeve, if she'd had any real objections to the idea, she would have made them crystal clear.

"Yes. I think maybe she just wants me to stick around and make her breakfast," he teased. "But I'm more than happy to play night nurse. I like taking care of people."

Connie's frown eased, her lips tugging into a pleased grin. "Maeve's not great at letting people take care of her."

Fletcher grinned back. "I've noticed. But I think she's starting to get better at it."

"I hope so," Connie said. "I'm glad she met you."

"Me too," he replied, though that was an understatement. "Maeve is a really special person."

Connie gave him a pointed look. "She is. And she's been through an awful lot. I wouldn't want to see her get hurt anytime soon. This fresh start has been really good for her."

"Neither would I," Fletcher agreed. He understood Connie's concern. It was obvious Maeve had been hurt by her marriage, and now he was here, trying to woo her. Of course Connie would worry about him breaking her heart again. "I really like her, and I would do anything to make her happy," he promised.

Connie seemed appeased by his words, nodding once before turning to head back to the front door. "Well, I'll get out of your hair. If anything comes up, you know I'm right next door. The kids will have to come by in the morning to get dressed and ready for school, but I can drop them off."

"That would be great, thanks. I'll have to work tomorrow, but I can check in and see if Maeve needs me to come over again afterward."

"She'll tell you not to even if she does," Connie warned.

"I know," Fletcher said with a low chuckle. "But there's plenty of leftover soup in the fridge, so even if she insists that I stay away, at least I'll know she's eating. And she has medicine now, too."

"Thank you for taking such good care of her," Connie said as she stepped out the door.

"Thanks for checking in," Fletcher replied, waving goodbye before making a quick trip out to his car, where he kept a gym bag with extra clothes. Changing into some sweats and a t-shirt, he carefully folded his chinos and button-up in case he had to wear them again tomorrow.

As he headed back to the couch, Peeve appeared, trotting down the stairs and into the living room. The footfalls of his furry paws were practically silent against the hardwood.

With a soft *meow*, he leapt onto the couch beside Fletcher. The cat had apparently become his best friend after he'd given him some leftover chicken from the soup. The feline had also been uncharacteristically well behaved all day. He must have known Maeve wasn't feeling well.

Settling in for the night, Fletcher stretched his body out along the couch cushions, careful not to jostle the cat. As soon as he stilled, Peeve curled up right into his chest and began purring like a tractor. The soothing sound put him to sleep in minutes.

∼

Fletcher awoke to something tickling his face. Still half-asleep, he scrunched his nose a couple of times before peeling his eyes open to see what was causing the odd sensation.

He groaned when he laid eyes on the culprit. "Peeve," he muttered, batting the cat's tail away from his face. During the night, Fletcher had rolled onto his back, and now Peeve sat square on his chest, his tail flicking back and forth and hitting Fletcher's nose on each pass.

Disturbed by Fletcher's shooing, Peeve stood and stretched, sending his backside right into Fletcher's unsuspecting face.

"No!" he shouted, swatting Peeve onto the couch beside him. "Is this you making up for being so polite yesterday?" he asked as he sat up, taming his bedhead with a couple strokes of his hand.

"He can't risk ruining his reputation," Maeve said from somewhere behind him.

Fletcher whipped around to find her sitting in the kitchen. "You're up."

"And fever-free," she said with mock gusto, holding up her mug in a *cheers* motion.

"I'm glad you're feeling better." He stood and made his way into the kitchen, noticing that the inviting aroma of freshly brewed coffee permeated the space. "And you made coffee."

"Yes," she said, taking a sip from her mug. "I slept like a log, but I still feel a bit like I got hit by a truck."

Fletcher nodded. "A fever will do that to you." He had experienced many a fever during his years as an educator. After the first few years of teaching, he built up a pretty strong immune system but still got taken down at least once a year by some kind of virus.

"Help yourself to coffee." Maeve gestured toward the pot.

"Thanks." Fletcher grabbed a mug from the cabinet and poured himself a cup. "So, Connie offered to take the kids to school today. There's leftover soup in the fridge. There are plenty of M&Ms left. Can you think of anything else you need before I go to work?"

Maeve shook her head. "No. You've been so helpful, Fletcher. Thank you."

"No problem."

They sipped their coffees in silence for a few moments, during which Fletcher tried to think of anything she might need. Anything that would give him an excuse to come back after work. Extra tissues? More trashy magazines? Another type of chocolate?

Before he could come up with anything, the front door swung open, and the kids came crashing in. They both stopped suddenly when they reached the kitchen and saw Maeve and Fletcher sitting there.

"Hi, Mommy," Allie said in the loudest voice possible that could still be considered a whisper. "Connie said we have to be quiet because you're not feeling too good."

Maeve gave her daughter a tired smile. "Hi, sweetie. I'm feeling a lot better today."

"Can I hug you?" Andy asked around a yawn, his copper hair still all askew from sleep.

"Of course," Maeve said, and the little boy flew into her arms. "I think you both would've caught this bug already if you were going to."

"Connie's going to take us to school today!" Allie said, clapping her hands together as if this was the biggest treat.

"I heard," Maeve said as she rubbed Andy's back while he clung to her like a koala. "Make sure you say thank you to Connie for taking care of you."

"Oh, we did," Allie said, her eyes wide and serious. "But I'll make sure to say it again."

"What is Mr. McNally doing here?" Andy asked as he watched Fletcher from his vantage point in Maeve's arms.

Before either of them could offer an answer, Allie piped up with, "Is he your boyfriend?"

Maeve's hand stilled on Andy's back. "No, sweetheart. Why would you ask me that?"

The little girl shrugged, her strawberry-blonde curls bouncing over her shoulders. "He's here a lot, and he does lots of nice things for you—like a boyfriend would do."

Maeve replied slowly, as if choosing her words carefully. "He does do a lot of nice things for me, doesn't he? That's because we're friends."

"Oh, okay." Allie shrugged it off easily.

Maeve's shoulders visibly relaxed. "Why don't you two go get dressed? Connie doesn't tolerate being late like Mommy does."

Both kids scurried up the stairs toward their bedroom, and before Fletcher had a chance to debrief with Maeve about the boyfriend comment, Connie entered the kitchen with a cheerful, "Good morning!"

"Morning, Con," Maeve said, turning toward her friend. With that one slight movement, she seemed to block him out entirely. "I hope the little buggers haven't been too much trouble."

"No trouble at all," Connie said. "You look like you're feeling much better."

"Oh, you mean because I'm not half-dead on the couch, completely delirious and hardly able to open my eyes?"

"Well, it seems you've got your fire back, too. And did you thank Fletcher for taking care of you?" she asked, unknowingly mirroring the exact words Maeve had said to her children moments before.

Maeve scowled at her friend. "Of course I did. I'm not a complete heathen."

Connie patted her on the shoulder. "That's my girl." She turned toward the staircase. "I'll go check on the kids."

Once she was out of sight, Fletcher ran a hand through his hair. "So, Allie's pretty observant, huh?"

Maeve closed her eyes, tented her fingers beneath her chin, and leaned forward on the table. "She's too smart for her own good."

"It's not really that surprising that she would jump to the conclusion. I *have* been here a lot lately," Fletcher said. "And I *am* always really nice to you," he added in a teasing tone.

A ghost of a smile crossed Maeve's lips before she let out a long sigh. "They've never seen me with a man other than their father."

"Oh." Fletcher processed this information quietly, understanding just a little more why Maeve might be so resistant to a relationship.

Opening her eyes, she met his gaze. "It's good, though, for them to see us together as friends. And you're a really good male role model for them."

Fletcher's heart sank at the words *friends* and *male role model*, when what he really wanted was to be so much more. But he was slowly sinking his claws into her—he knew it. He was chipping away at her walls, and it might take a while, but he was going to eventually get her to admit that she liked him as more than a friend.

Once Connie wrangled the kids out the door, Fletcher offered to cook breakfast, but Maeve declined, saying she wasn't very hungry, but she promised to have some soup for lunch. Now that she was back at seemingly full health, he no longer felt the need to push his care onto her. Plus, he knew the boyfriend comment had bothered her more than she was willing to admit, and he didn't want to upset her further. So, he packed up his gym bag and left, luckily having enough time now to go home and change into fresh clothing before work.

As he drove the short way back to his apartment, Fletcher

worried that his excuses to visit Maeve's home were running low. He still had to fix that hole in her porch, but other than that, he had no good reason to go there unless she agreed to pursue some kind of relationship with him, which didn't seem to be likely to happen anytime soon.

Her getting sick had been a happy accident. Not happy for her, of course, but Fletcher was certainly thrilled to have used it to rationalize spending more time with her. He would just have to come up with some new reasons to drop by the house. He wasn't above pretending one of the kids had left something at school, or thinking up some other home project that absolutely *had* to get done.

He might have to get creative, but he would find a reason to see Maeve again.

15

———

"Mommy!" Allie's high-pitched voice called from the porch. "They're hatching!"

It was Saturday morning, and Maeve had sent the kids outside to do an egg check—a daily habit they'd adopted since she'd shown them the nest the week before. Apparently, the daily checks were finally paying off because the eggs were hatching.

Maeve rushed outside to find Allie standing on a porch chair, her face buried in the hanging plant that housed the nest.

"I can see a baby bird!"

"I wanna see!" Andy howled from where he stood on the porch, too short to get in on the action.

Maeve pulled the second chair over next to Allie's and hoisted her son up onto it. She could just see over the top of the nest while she stood on the ground, and all three of them watched in awe as a baby bird pushed its way out of its temporary home.

At first, all they could see was a small tuft of gray fuzz spouting from a hole in the egg. Then, ever so slowly, a little alien-like creature emerged. Its skin was red and almost translucent, and two large, black orbs that looked like bug eyes dominated its face. Only its petite yellow beak confirmed that it was a baby bird and not, in fact, an alien.

"It's so ugly," Andy said, nose scrunched with distaste.

"It's cute," Allie argued as she watched the baby break completely free of its egg.

"It's amazing," Maeve breathed, the moment instantly transporting her back to the births of her children. She thought back to the pride, love, and utter adoration she had felt in those magical moments post-birth when she'd held her babies on her chest, watched them breathe, and stroked their soft skin. Those two kids were the only good thing she ever got out of her marriage.

A squawk pierced her ears, and Maeve realized the mama and papa sparrow were perched on a nearby tree branch, desperately attempting to divert attention away from their young.

"Okay, guys," she said, patting Andy and Allie on their backs. "Let's put those birds out of their misery and go inside for breakfast."

A chorus of *awww*s followed her instruction, but the kids dutifully backed away and hopped off their chairs.

"We can check on them in a few hours," Maeve promised. "Maybe they'll all be born by then." She got both kids settled with bowls of cereal at the kitchen table, then sat down beside them with her coffee. "Don't forget Mr. McNally is coming by today to help fix the hole in the porch."

"Can we show him the baby birds?" Andy asked, his little green eyes wide with wonder.

"Of course," Maeve replied. "But remember, he's just here to help with one little project, not to play with you guys all day."

Allie pouted. "But what if he *wants* to stay and play all day?"

Maeve sighed, worried the kids were getting too used to

having Fletcher around the house. "Mr. McNally is just coming over to help with one quick thing," she said. "He probably has other things he has to do afterward."

"But what if he doesn't?" Allie pushed.

Maeve shook her head, silently cursing her daughter's tenacity. "Al, please just let it go."

Allie huffed but returned to eating her cereal.

Andy paused his own meal with his spoon halfway to his mouth. "We can still show him the birds, though, right?"

Maeve sighed. "Yes, we can still show him the birds."

The kids were stationed in front of a window, watching the driveway like hawks, when Fletcher's Honda Civic pulled in.

"He's here!" Andy called. Allie was already halfway out the front door. Maeve followed them out onto the porch, reminding them not to run into the driveway. Fletcher emerged from his car and shouted a greeting, then opened up the door to the backseat and pulled out a toolbox and a couple pieces of wood.

"Whoa," Andy silently mouthed as he watched Fletcher pull out the long, thin planks.

Fletcher, bless him, must have noticed the boy's fascination, because he called out, "Hey, little man. Do you think you could give me some help?"

"Yeah!" Andy cheered, then looked up at Maeve for permission. When she nodded her approval, he took off toward Fletcher, wrapping his leg in a quick hug before following his instructions of how to hold the wood to avoid splinters. Allie was preoccupied with checking on the nest and didn't seem to mind being left out of the task.

The boys gradually made their way across the driveway and up the porch steps, the wood balanced between them.

Andy beamed with pride as they set it down on the porch, and Fletcher rewarded him with a high-five.

"What, no comments about how handy I am today?" he asked Maeve as he straightened to his full height.

She smirked up at him. "I think I'll wait until the job is done to decide how I'm feeling about your abilities today."

Fletcher waggled his eyebrows. "I always get the job done."

Heat streaked across Maeve's cheeks, and she turned away so he wouldn't notice. "We have a bird's nest," she blurted. It was the first thing that came to mind when she spotted Allie on the porch chair.

"Another one hatched!" Allie gestured for Fletcher to come over. "Come see, Mr. McNally!"

"Wow," he said, walking over to her, but not before catching Maeve's gaze and sending her a wink. He peered over Allie's shoulder to see into the nest, and something about the size difference between the two of them had Maeve's breath catching.

"Look at them," Fletcher said. "So small! And such a neat science lesson about nature. You should take some pictures to show your class."

Allie gasped, clearly thinking that was a great idea. "Can I take some pictures on your phone, Mommy?"

"Of course," Maeve replied, handing her cell to her daughter. "Always thinking like a teacher, huh?" she said to Fletcher.

He grinned. "It's impossible not to. It *is* pretty cool to have such an up-close view."

Maeve nodded. "The kids have been so excited, checking on the nest every day. I swear it's better than television for them."

Fletcher took one more peek into the nest as Allie began her photoshoot, then stepped back and gestured to the hole in the porch. "Why don't we get this hole fixed so they can spend lots of time out here without risking falling through the porch.”

“Can I help you, Mr. McNally?” Andy asked.

“Well, bud, I’m going to be using a hammer, and they’re dangerous for little hands. But you can sit with me while I work, if you want.”

Andy nodded. “Cool!”

“I have a couple things to finish up inside,” Maeve said. “I’ll come check on you two in a little while, okay?”

Both boys nodded, though Fletcher’s exuberant expression fell a fraction when he realized she wasn’t staying outside with them. Truth be told, she was tempted to, but watching him interact with Andy and Allie made her heart flutter in unwelcome ways.

Heading back into the kitchen, Maeve began searching for tasks. She didn’t *actually* have anything to “finish up inside,” so she spent the next half hour puttering around the kitchen, making up jobs for herself. She dug through the fridge and got rid of anything that was spoiled, washed the counters until they sparkled, and turned all the spices so the labels were facing forward. She had her head in the cabinet beneath the sink, organizing all the cleaning products, when she heard Fletcher call out her name.

She began backing out of the cabinet only to bump her head on the frame of it. “Ow!” she muttered to herself. Rubbing at the sore spot, she still hadn’t gathered her wits to respond to Fletcher when he said her name again, sounding a little closer this time. When she didn’t answer right away, he called out a third time, this time shortening her name to “Mae?”

Her head snapped up, injury forgotten. She stood and marched out to the foyer where Fletcher was standing in the doorway.

“Don’t call me that,” she said. “That’s not my name. It’s Maeve.”

Fletcher took a step backward, surprise crossing his features. "S-sorry." He put his hands up. "I just wanted to show you the patch."

Taking in his defensive stance, Maeve shrunk back, appalled at her overreaction. Hearing him use that name had shocked her, and she'd reacted without thinking. Now, he probably thought she was bizarre for reacting so strongly to a simple nickname.

She let loose a sigh. "No, I'm sorry. I just… No one calls me that." Well, no one except Connie. She was the only one Maeve tolerated calling her that remnant of her old life.

"It's no problem," Fletcher said, his eyes assessing.

She took a step toward the doorway. "Let's see how handy you were today."

Her attempt to diffuse her dreadful behavior with humor was only partially successful, as Fletcher watched her for a beat longer before turning toward his handiwork.

"It's all patched up." He pointed to the new planks now nestled into their spots. "The wood in that spot obviously isn't weathered the same way the rest of the porch is, so it'll be a little lighter like this for a while. You could try to stain it to match the rest, but your best bet is just to let Mother Nature do the work."

"This looks good," Maeve said, crouching down to run her finger along one of the new planks. The wood looked pristine, so smooth and—"Ouch!" she yelped as her skin caught on the wood. She instinctively lifted her finger to her mouth to soothe it before realizing that wasn't going to help much with the small sliver of wood that had lodged itself in her skin.

"Let me see." Fletcher held his hand out.

"It's fine," she insisted, even as she cradled her hand to her chest.

"Let. Me. See," he repeated.

Sensing that he wouldn't take no for an answer, she tentatively placed her hand in his, palm up so the pad of her finger was visible.

"That's a nasty splinter," Fletcher said as he inspected it. "We're going to need tweezers to take this out."

"No!" Maeve said a little too loudly as she yanked her hand back. "No. It'll come out on its own, won't it?"

He arched a brow and stared at her. "No, Maeve. It won't."

"Are you sure?"

"I'm sure. Let's go inside, and I'll take it out. I promise you won't feel a thing."

"But...but..." She tried to think of another magical solution for removing the splinter, but came up with nothing.

"Come on," he urged, grabbing her other hand and tugging her inside.

"Fine," she muttered. She waved to Allie and Andy. "Come inside, guys. Why don't you go finish that castle you were building earlier?"

They chased each other to their bedroom while Fletcher led Maeve to the bathroom.

"Tweezers?" he asked, all business, as she sat down on the closed toilet.

She bounced one knee up and down. "In the medicine cabinet."

Fletcher grabbed the tweezers and sat on the edge of the tub across from her. "Settle down." He placed a hand on her jumping knee. "I'm not going to hurt you."

Maeve's leg stilled, and she looked into his warm brown eyes. Those words held so much more meaning than he would ever know, and somehow, she trusted them implicitly.

"I know," she whispered.

"Good." He took her hand and lifted it close to his face so he could see the splinter. "Just close your eyes and relax."

She let her eyes drift shut but immediately began imagining the splinter sliding out of her skin and cringed, jerking her hand in his grip. "Wait!"

He paused, still grasping her hand, and patiently waited for her to go on.

"Can you tell me a story or something to distract me?"

"A story?" Fletcher looked up at the ceiling as if there was something interesting written there. Then, his face broke into a wicked grin. "I know. Why don't I tell you the story of my tattoo?"

Maeve's eyes snapped open. "You have a tattoo?" She was shocked that this practical, straight-laced man would do something so permanent and potentially unprofessional.

He nodded silently, still wearing that impish smile.

"Can I see it?" she asked, her curiosity burning bright.

"I'll show it to you once I get this splinter out."

Her shoulders drooped, but she took the deal. "Fine."

"Close your eyes, and I'll tell you the story."

She obeyed, shutting her eyes tightly and focusing on the sound of his voice, low and steady.

"I was twenty-eight, and I'd just gotten my heart broken. I was feeling a little reckless, so I went out driving and wound up totaling my car."

Her eyes popped open again. "Oh my God. Were you okay?"

"Close your eyes," he said, watching her expectantly until she did. "I was fine," he went on. "But my car was not. I got a friend to tow it back to my house, and my youngest brother, Beau, who was sixteen at the time, found it in the garage. He threatened to tell my mom, who was already worried about me after the breakup. I begged him not to, and he blackmailed me into acting as his guardian so he could get a tattoo in exchange for not ratting on me."

Maeve grinned as she kept her eyes shut. "Smart kid."

"Foolish kid," he muttered. "But it worked. I brought him to the tattoo parlor, and he got a ridiculous snake tattoo that winds all around his upper arm. I ended up acting like a fool, too, because I was still hurting and pissed off, and I got the best revenge tattoo I could think of."

Maeve's smile widened as she imagined what it could possibly be. "And what was that?"

"A set of lips just above my ass," he answered, dead serious.

Laughter burst from her throat, and she struggled to keep her eyes closed.

"When we broke up, I told her to kiss my ass," he explained. "The tattoo felt like closure."

"I'm sorry"—Maeve choked around heaves of laughter—"but that is just too good."

Then, she felt a very real set of lips pressing against her open palm, and her laughter died quickly.

"You can open your eyes," Fletcher said softly.

She did, and she found his gaze pinned on hers as his lips lingered on her skin. Then, he held up her finger. "It's out."

"Oh," she breathed. "I didn't even feel it."

"I know," he replied. "I got it out around the time I was talking about the car accident. You didn't even flinch."

"What? It was out for almost that entire story?"

"Yep," he said with a smug grin.

She shook her head. "I can't believe you didn't tell me."

He shrugged. "I had a story to finish."

"Now show me that tattoo," she demanded, even more intrigued now that she knew of its placement.

He grinned and turned to the side. Tugging up his shirt a few inches, he told her, "Hold that there." Maeve held her breath as she took the fabric of his shirt into her hand. Fletcher lowered the waistband of his pants just until the tattoo became visible between the stretches of fabric.

Maeve shook with laughter anew as she stared at the set of plump pink lips on the left side of his lower back. "How did you choose which cheek?" she asked, tears streaming down her face now.

He sent her a grin over his shoulder. "I told the tattoo artist to make it a surprise."

For some reason, that sent her into another fit of laughter. His shoulders began shaking, too, and Maeve lost her grip on his shirt, letting it fall back over his skin and covering the tattoo.

Fletcher turned to face her, reaching up to wipe away some of the amused tears lingering beneath her eyes. "I love seeing you laugh like that."

His heartfelt words sobered her, and her laughter faded. "Thank you for getting my splinter out."

He took the affected hand in his and laced their fingers together, resting their joined hands on her knee. "No problem."

Maeve realized how close they were sitting, their knees almost knocking together between them. Fletcher had placed the tweezers on the side of the sink, and his other hand now rested on her thigh, his thumb lightly tracing circles on the inside of her knee.

"You're always taking care of me," she whispered as she leaned infinitesimally closer.

"I like taking care of you," he said in a low voice, his hand trailing from her thigh, up her side, to the back of her head, where he slid his fingers into her hair.

She stared into his brown eyes. "Why?"

"Because." He rubbed his thumb over the back of her neck. "I like you."

That simple answer charmed Maeve more than it should have, and she leaned into him, seeking. Seeking what, she wasn't entirely sure. Connection? Comfort? She didn't have time to decipher it before his lips met hers, soft and seeking in their own way.

To her dismay, her throat released a moan as she melted

into Fletcher's kiss. Each touch of his lips offered exactly what she was looking for, even though she hadn't figured out what that even was. He held onto the back of her head tightly enough to be possessive but loosely enough that she didn't feel trapped.

Fletcher managed to take away her worries by taking control while still ensuring she felt safe. How did he do that? How did he *know* to do that? At the moment, she didn't know, and honestly, she didn't care. She simply reveled in the feeling of his hands on her skin and his lips on her mouth.

The spellbinding kiss came to an abrupt halt when one of the kids came skidding by the doorway.

"What are you doing in the bathroom?" Allie asked, her hands on her hips and her head cocked to the side in a pose eerily similar to one Maeve often found herself in.

"Oh." Maeve pulled back and attempted to surreptitiously draw her hand out of Fletcher's. He held on tight. "Mr. McNally was just helping me get my splinter out."

Fletcher held up their joined hands. "All better."

Allie narrowed her eyes at their hands, and Fletcher finally let Maeve pull hers back.

"Is everything okay, honey? Did you need something?"

"No." Allie uncrossed her arms. "I just wanted to see what was so funny. I heard you laughing."

"Oh, Mr. McNally just told me a funny joke," Maeve said.

"Can I hear it?"

"You know, Allie," Fletcher cut in. "It was a joke just for grown-ups. But I can tell you a kid joke if you'd like."

Allie nodded in delight.

"Okay," Fletcher began. "Where did the sheep go to get his haircut?"

Allie thought for a moment, tapping her chin as she tried to come up with a punchline. "I don't know."

"To the baa-baa shop!" Fletcher said with enthusiasm.

Allie cracked up, proving that Fletcher knew his audience

well. "I've got to go tell that one to Andy," she said breathlessly, then ran off to entertain her brother.

Fletcher turned back toward Maeve. "Sorry about that," he said with a frown.

She sighed. "It's fine. But Allie is getting suspicious. She knows something's up with us."

Fletcher's eyebrows drew up. "*Is* something up with us?"

Maeve dropped her head into her hands. "I don't know, Fletch. All I know is I just made out with you in my bathroom because I don't seem to have any self-control these days."

She had fought so hard to keep her feelings to herself, to keep Fletcher strictly in the friend zone, but then he went and did cute things with her kids and told her embarrassing stories while he removed her splinter, and—

Fletcher leaned back a bit, an amused smile curling his lips. "We did not just make out."

"What?" she asked, distracted by her inner musings.

"If I made out with you, you would know it," he said, his gaze darkening with lust.

"Oh."

"Yeah, oh. Though, trust me, I would love to make out with you sometime."

"Fletcher…" she said. "This is just…hard for me. And confusing for the kids. You're their principal, and now you're my friend, and…"

"And now we're heading toward something more," he finished for her. "Maeve." He placed his hands on her shoulders, shaking her out of her spiral. "Stop overthinking this. Kids are really adaptable. They're going to be just fine if you get a boyfriend. This is about you and what *you* want."

"But what if we start something and things go wrong? And it hurts the kids?"

"Nothing's going to go wrong," he said. "But even if it did, like I said, kids are adaptable. I don't know how long you and your husband have been apart, but look how well they're doing now. They're thriving with you as a single parent. And not to toot my own horn, but I think Andy and Allie like me a lot. I don't think they'd mind having me around more."

His words struck Maeve right in the heart. The kids *were* thriving with her. But it wasn't just her—it was her and Fletcher. They saw him every weekday at school and, lately, every weekend at home. He helped them with big tasks like painting their room and small ones like opening a stuck container lid. And he was responsible for Maeve's perpetual good mood lately because, even though she tried to fight her feelings at every turn, every time she thought of him, her heart began beating overtime.

"Please, Maeve, let's give this a chance," he pleaded as she chewed on her lip, undecided. "We can take things as slow as you need to. If you want me to come over again under the guise of helping you with something around the house, I'm willing to do that. But either way, give me another house project to work on or let me take you on a date, because I need to see you again."

"I don't need any more help on the house," she said, too prideful to continue accepting his charity. "But I want to see you again, too," she admitted, her gaze down at her shoes.

He tipped her chin up until she met his gaze. "Maeve Walsh, will you go out with me? No kids, no cats, just you and me getting to know each other better."

At that moment, it struck her as hilarious that they were sitting in her bathroom, post splinter removal and ridiculous tattoo reveal, and this gorgeous, capable man was asking her out.

Her lips widened into a grin as she worked to hold back laughter.

Fletcher's smile mirrored hers. "Should I take that as a yes?"

16

The invitation arrived via text bright and early on Monday morning. Beau and Emma were having an intimate wedding ceremony in just a month's time. It would be small, including only Fletcher's family (his mother, June; his brother, Jack, and his wife, Natalie; and their two children, Carter and Noah) as well as a few friends of Beau and Emma's, including Beau's former police partner and his wife. The ceremony would be held at a remote beach called Madequecham in Fletcher's hometown of Nantucket. The reception afterward would take place at Danny's Place, the café Jack and Natalie owned.

The whole event sounded lovely, but as Fletcher read through the details on the invitation, all he could think about was the fact that he'd be attending alone. Beau and Emma were madly in love. Jack and Natalie couldn't keep their hands off each other. And Beau's friend Diego and his wife, Isabella, while less into PDA than the others, were constantly whispering and giggling in dark corners.

For the past few years, Fletcher had enjoyed the privilege of having a built-in date for events like these. Even if Christa hadn't exactly been the most fun person at parties, at least she was someone to walk in with. He supposed he would wind up attending this wedding with his mother, which, no matter how much he loved the woman, felt beyond pathetic.

He longed to ask Maeve, but it seemed like the type of thing that might scare her off. She had finally agreed to go on an actual date with him—they'd settled on dinner next weekend—and asking her to be his plus-one might be a step too far. Not only would bringing her to the wedding mean making their relationship public, but it would also mean meeting his family. He hadn't been lying when he'd said they could take things as slowly as she needed them to. He wouldn't risk doing something that might make her throw her walls up again.

When Friday night rolled around, Fletcher left work right after the last school bell rang and headed home to change and get ready for his date. Maeve had roped Connie into babysitting for the night, and Fletcher would be picking her up at five o'clock to take her out to dinner. If all went according to his plan, she would then be coming home with him.

He spent agonizing minutes in front of his closet, trying to decide what to wear before choosing dark jeans and a navy-blue Henley shirt. Maeve had specified that she wanted to go somewhere casual. He wasn't sure if that was because she was trying to make the evening the least date-like she possibly could, echoing the stunt she'd pulled with the macaroni and cheese and chicken nuggets she'd cooked for their first dinner together, or if she just didn't care for fancy restaurants. Either way, Fletcher would do anything to make her comfortable, so he'd chosen a family-friendly Italian restaurant and was making sure to dress down while still looking put together.

Fifteen minutes before he was set to pick Maeve up, he

hopped into his car and took off to a florist down the street where he picked out a bouquet of daisies and carnations. It had been a long time since he'd been on a first date, but bringing flowers felt like the right move. Returning to his car, his hands trembled slightly as he drove the rest of the way to her house. As he pulled his car into her driveway, he had to remind himself that he'd already spent many hours with this woman, kissed her, and slept with her. This was just a date. It was no big deal.

But it felt like one.

Maeve answered the door on the first knock. She was wearing a forest-green wrap dress that swung around her knees and accentuated her curves. The color made her eyes look even more vividly green than they usually did. Those gorgeous eyes lit up as she took in the bouquet in his hands.

"You brought me flowers?"

"Sure did." Fletcher handed them over the threshold into her awaiting arms.

She smiled up at him, genuine gratitude in her expression. "Thank you. They're beautiful."

"You're welcome. *You* look beautiful," he replied, his gaze eating up the way the dress flowed over her hips. The top was tapered into a generous V-cut that showed off the pale skin at the top of her breasts. He wanted to lick that skin.

"Let me put these in water," Maeve said, disrupting his lascivious thoughts.

Fletcher cleared his throat before responding, "Of course."

She turned and sashayed to the kitchen, her hips swaying as she rushed. She was going to kill him in that dress. He would spend the entire evening with an erection. And despite the torture that would be, he would enjoy every damn minute of it.

Connie's husky laugh emanated from the depths of the house, followed by Andy's and Allie's childish laughter.

Fletcher wondered what had caused their amusement, but he had no time to come up with an answer before Maeve came rushing back and grabbed her brown leather jacket off a hook by the door. It paired well with the brown boots she wore on her feet. Shrugging on the jacket, she hid that dress Fletcher was having trouble dragging his eyes away from and stepped out the door. "Let's go."

They drove to the restaurant Fletcher had picked, making small talk all the way. He was hoping to ease her into some more serious conversation by beginning with benign topics like the weather and what the kids were up to at school. By the time they reached the restaurant and got seated, they'd run out of meaningless chatter.

The waiter had just brought over their wine when Fletcher finally broke the ice. "So, I was hoping to get to know more about you."

Maeve took a healthy sip of her drink. "What would you like to know?"

Everything, he wanted to reply. While he felt like he'd divulged quite a few details about his family and his past—including but not limited to his embarrassing tattoo story—he really hadn't learned much about Maeve's. It was as if her mission to keep personal details out of the picture had continued after their first night together, while he had chosen to open the floodgates about himself.

Sure, she talked about Andy and Allie a lot. He could recite their favorite foods, colors, books, and more, but he was realizing he didn't know all those same things about Maeve, and that bothered him.

"Well, for starters, where did you grow up?"

She placed her glass on the table, her shoulders lowering slightly as if she was relieved by the easy question.

"Indiana," she answered. "My parents still live there."

"Any siblings?"

"Nope. It took my parents a while to get pregnant with

me, and my mom had a difficult pregnancy, so they decided to stop after one."

"How were your pregnancies?" Fletcher asked, figuring those types of difficulties could be genetic. He was suddenly worried that she had suffered through both nine-month periods. The thought of Maeve in pain was like an ice pick to his heart.

Her eyebrows shot up. "You really want to know about my pregnancies?"

He kept his gaze locked on her vivid green eyes. "I want to know everything about you."

She swallowed visibly before answering. "Well, my pregnancies were actually pretty smooth. But then, I had to have an emergency C-section with Allie, so I went for an elective C-section two years later with Andy. Those weren't too fun."

Fletcher nodded, remembering how she hadn't wanted to take her shirt off, blaming the scars and stretch marks. "That sounds rough. I'm glad everyone ended up happy and healthy."

She treated him to a coy smile. "That we are."

He smiled back, hoping he contributed to that happiness. Maeve may have only just been beginning to let him in, but there was no denying that she'd enjoyed the time they had spent together so far. If her smiles and near constant blushes were any indication, she had *really* enjoyed it.

Their food arrived—chicken parmigiana for him and gnocchi for her—and he took that as a sign that it was time to get into the really deep stuff. After a few bites of his chicken, Fletcher asked, "How long were you and your husband together?"

Maeve froze, her fork halfway to her mouth, and he could have sworn she stopped breathing for a second. Then, she cleared her throat and answered, "We were together for ten years. We met when I was twenty-six, and I had Allie two years later."

Ten years was a long time to invest in someone to then end things. He should know—he'd been with Christa for about the same amount of time. "How long ago did you two split?"

Maeve shifted in her seat. "Our marriage dissolved a few months ago, but we haven't been on the same page for a lot longer."

Fletcher made a sound of agreement. "I can relate to that."

Maeve resumed eating, probably relieved he was turning the conversation back to himself. "How about your last relationship?" she asked. "How long were you two together?"

"Almost ten years," he replied. "But, like you, we'd been drifting apart for a while."

"When did you break up?"

He pushed some pasta around his plate with a fork. "Actually, it was the day you and I met."

Maeve sucked in a breath, and his gaze immediately lifted to hers.

"Did you break up with her because of me?"

"No!" he answered a little too quickly, desperate to wipe the horrified look off her face. "I mean, no. We had officially ended things that morning."

"Oh." He could see the gears in Maeve's head turning. "So, that was why you were in the bar that night. That was the reason for your pity party."

Fletcher winced and clenched his jaw, wishing he could say anything other than, "Yes."

She wiped her lips with a cloth napkin. "I see."

"But I swear, it wasn't a rebound thing. I wasn't looking for anything but a drink when I went to the bar. Honestly, I didn't even think I *wanted* anything for a while. But then, I saw you and...you took my breath away, Maeve. You were so poised and alluring, and then we had such similar ways of thinking. I know it was weird timing that I had just gotten out of a relationship, but—"

Maeve settled her palm on his forearm, the contact instantly silencing him. "Fletcher, it's okay," she said. "We both have pasts. I'm not going to judge you for yours if you won't judge me for mine."

He reared his head back. "Of course I won't." What would he ever have to judge about a woman getting married, having kids, then getting divorced? He wasn't one of those people who insisted that parents stay together. He firmly believed that two happy parents that were apart were better than two unhappy parents that were together. Although, the kids' father wasn't present in their life, so perhaps they didn't fall into either of those categories.

"Then, we're all good," Maeve said with a reassuring smile.

Fletcher let out a breath. "Good."

The rest of the meal felt lighter. He was glad he'd gotten the chance to dig a little deeper with Maeve and that both of their pasts were now out in the open. He also finally got answers to his questions about her favorite color, food, and book: green, any type of pasta, and the *Outlander* series.

After dinner, Fletcher somehow convinced Maeve to come back to his place. Maybe it was the second glasses of wine they'd gotten, maybe she was just happy to be spending time away from her kids, or maybe—just maybe—she was finally starting to give in to the idea of a relationship with him.

"Do you want another drink?" he asked as he slid her coat off her shoulders.

She wandered into the apartment, glancing around as if looking to see if anything had changed since she'd last been there. "Sure."

Fletcher stepped over to the bar cart set up between the kitchen and living room. "I have everything for a vodka soda with lime, if you want one of those."

Maeve spun to face him. "You remember my drink order?"

He shrugged. "Of course."

Her lips curled slightly at the corners. "That would be lovely."

"I'll have one, too," he said as he began concocting the drinks. Maeve drifted around the open space for a few more moments before settling herself on the edge of the couch. Her dress shifted a bit higher on her legs, showing off more of her enticing skin. Fletcher tried not to stare at it as he placed their drinks on coasters on the coffee table.

Maeve leaned forward to squeeze the lime wedge he'd supplied into her drink. The movement brought her cleavage into full focus, and he couldn't help himself from openly staring. She either didn't notice or didn't care, because she just continued doctoring her drink as if she wasn't a goddess sitting in the middle of his living room.

She tapped the *Scrabble* box sitting on the table before leaning back against the couch. "Do you play?"

Fletcher's voice came out raspy as he answered, "Yes." He cleared his throat before going on. "I love it, but I don't have too many people to play it with. My future sister-in-law, Emma, is pretty much the only person I can convince these days."

Maeve took a sip of her drink. "Why, are you really good? Is everyone else tired of losing or something?"

He bit back a grin, knowing it would be a dead giveaway of his expertise. "Something like that."

"Huh." She shrugged. "I'm not the best, but I do enjoy the game."

"Want to play?" he asked. "Maybe I could teach you a thing or two."

Her eyes blazed as she met his gaze. "Sure."

Taking in the lustful look she was giving him, the passion in her eyes, and the way she was leaning toward him as if she was desperate to get closer but didn't quite know how, Fletcher decided to take a leap. "What do you say we make things a little more interesting?"

Maeve crossed her legs, inching her dress even farther up her thighs. "How so?"

A wide grin spread over his lips. "Have you ever played strip *Scrabble*?"

17

———

Maeve wasn't sure what possessed her to agree to strip *Scrabble*. Sure, she was almost three drinks in, and Fletcher looked sinfully sexy with his Henley rolled up to his elbows, exposing his muscular forearms. Perhaps it was the lingering effects of Jason's texts and her determination not to let him control her anymore. Being with Fletcher would certainly be a huge *screw you* to Jason—not that Maeve was using him for that. But she did feel an increased desire to move on and show him who was boss every time Jason managed to butt into her life from afar.

Plus, she was the reigning runner-up *Scrabble* champion in her online league, which she played most nights before she went to bed. Only one user managed to consistently beat her. Damn *user56824*. She was pretty confident she could get Fletcher stripped down to his skivvies, and boy, would she enjoy that sight. But still, it wasn't wise to play with fire, and playing a game that revolved around removing one's clothing when she couldn't remove her dress without revealing even more secrets was definitely risky.

She supposed she would just have to win.

"We need to set the rules first," she said.

Fletcher rubbed his thumb over his jaw as he thought for a moment. "For every twenty-five points a player gets, the other has to remove an article of clothing."

She narrowed her eyes, knowing how easy it was to reach twenty-five points. As a seasoned player, she was sure he did, too. "Make it one hundred points."

"Fifty," he countered.

"Seventy-five."

"Fine, seventy-five points."

"And you have to take your socks off before we start."

"What? Why?" he asked.

"Because," Maeve explained patiently, "I'm already starting with less clothing than you because I'm wearing a dress. You have pants *and* a shirt. We need to even the playing field a little. I get to keep my socks on to start, but you have to take yours off."

"Hold on," he said, throwing one hand up in the air. "I may have an extra outer piece of clothing, but women wear two undergarments. Men only wear one. So, technically, we have the same amount of clothing on right now."

She took a long, slow sip of her drink. "Who said I'm wearing any undergarments at all?"

Fletcher's jaw fell open, and she let out a husky laugh.

"I'm kidding," she said, worried he'd catch flies with his mouth open so wide.

"Jesus." Fletcher clutched his chest. "Warn a man before you're going to throw something like that at him. I was ready to forego the game just to see if you were serious."

She reached out and tapped the *Scrabble* box with her toe. "No way. You want to find out what's under here, you're going to have to earn it," she said, knowing very well she wouldn't be allowing him to see anything above her waist. She *had* worn some very sexy lace panties, though, that she wouldn't mind showing off.

He pulled the box toward them and began setting up the

board. "While we're discussing the nuances of socks in strip *Scrabble*, I should mention that both socks count as one item of clothing."

Maeve thought for a moment but could find no fault with that. "Deal."

He held out the velvet bag of letter tiles. "Pick seven."

She did, and she lined them up in front of her, already plotting what high-scoring words she could make with them. The game began with her earning a whopping twenty-seven points, hitting a double-word score with both the *z* and *a* in *zebra*.

"It's a good thing we didn't go with twenty-five points as our stripping interval," she said, sitting back in her seat.

Fletcher raised an eyebrow. "Or maybe it's not."

She cast a glance over his bare forearms, dusted in golden hair just as she knew his chest was beneath his shirt. She could recall the outline of each muscle in his chest, shoulders, and abdomen, and she longed to trace them all with her fingers again. Maybe he was right, and they should have just gotten to the steamy stuff, but she was having far too much fun to rush things.

Fletcher put up a good fight, getting a respectable eighteen points with *aback*, the *k* hitting a double-word score, but Maeve hit seventy-five points first, and he dutifully tugged his socks off. He soon caught up in score, and Maeve removed her socks as well.

A few minutes later, she placed down four tiles that made Fletcher bang his head against the back of the couch. She had reached one hundred fifty points thanks to a triple-word score on the word *queen*.

"I thought you said you weren't very good at this game," he said.

She shrugged. "Or maybe you're just not as good as you thought."

He scowled playfully at her before standing. Reaching

back with one hand, he deftly pulled the Henley over his head in that sexy, one-swoop way men somehow pulled off. The move revealed that contoured chest and flat stomach Maeve couldn't stop thinking about.

Fletcher slung his shirt over the back of the couch and took his seat again, cracking his knuckles in front of him as he prepared to take his turn. He was still almost fifty points away from catching up to her but clearly eager to reach the one-fifty mark as well. The few minutes he spent in concentration, staring at his tiles as he chose his next word, allowed Maeve a perfect opportunity to admire his bare torso without him noticing her gawking.

"It's hard to think with you staring at me like that," he said a moment later without looking up from his tiles.

Okay, so maybe he *had* noticed.

"Sorry." She turned her gaze to the board.

"I wouldn't mind," he replied, "except I'm trying really hard to focus over here so I'm not the only half-naked one in the room."

She couldn't hold back the retort crawling up her throat. "I like you being half-naked."

His brows flew up. "Is that so?"

Maeve reached for her drink and took a large sip before responding, "Yep."

Fletcher's lips curled into a sly smile. "That's good to know." He returned his gaze to his tiles. The smile remained on his mouth as he began setting down his tiles. She watched in shock as he covered one of the other coveted triple-word score squares with the word *joker*.

"If I'm correct, that brings my score up to…" He feigned counting on his fingers. "One hundred fifty-one." He sat back into the couch as if settling in for a show.

All the blood drained from Maeve's face as she realized what she had to do. Not wanting Fletcher to see her squirm, she flattened her expression, stood up straight, and reached beneath her dress. Fletcher watched with eagle eyes, so she decided to give him the show he was looking for.

Maintaining eye contact with him, she hooked her thumbs into the elastic band of her panties and gently tugged them down her legs. Once she'd removed the lacy black scrap of fabric, she folded it neatly before laying it over Fletcher's shirt. Then, she sat primly on the couch, crossing her legs and waiting for his reaction.

He stared at their respective pieces of clothing layered on top of one another for a long moment before turning his gaze to her. "Very creative, Maeve," he said in a low voice as he gave her still mostly clothed body a once-over, clearly having expected her to remove her dress first.

"Thank you, Fletcher," she replied, her voice coming out just as husky as his.

"Your move," he said, his gaze pinned on her lap.

Her hands were a little shaky as she laid down her next word, but that didn't stop her from earning a double-digit score. They continued on, sneaking looks at each other in between turns, racking up points, and building tension until Maeve felt like a bow string ready to snap.

Their tiles were beginning to dwindle, and she knew the end was near. She grinned triumphantly as she used up the last of her high-scoring letters to spell out *wavy*, earning her enough points to pass the two hundred twenty-five mark.

Fletcher looked down at the board in dismay. "I think I've been hustled."

She smirked. "I told you I wasn't the best. I never said I wasn't good."

He sent her an accusatory glare. "You minced your words."

She shrugged. "Don't hate the player. Hate the game."

His glower turned into a predatory grin as he stood, deftly removing his belt and laying it over their growing pile of clothing. Maeve gulped as she watched his long fingers unbutton his jeans and pull down the zipper.

"Maeve, sweetheart," he murmured. "You've got to stop looking at me like that."

Her gaze remained glued to his now-open fly and the sliver of skin and golden hair now visible to her. "I don't want to stop," she whispered, her tongue unconsciously darting out to wet her lips.

Fletcher growled, actually growled, from somewhere deep in his throat. In one fluid movement, he shucked off his jeans and tossed them over the couch, no longer worried about folding or laying them out gently.

Now in only a pair of black boxer briefs, he stalked over to where Maeve sat and knelt in front of her, putting them at eye level. Taking on a significantly gentler tone, he stroked a hand over her hair and said, "Tell me you want this."

She nodded, unable to speak for fear of her voice shaking. The mere fact that he'd thought to stop and make sure she was with him, that he'd had the self-control to mellow himself before he did so, sealed the deal for her. Fletcher was tender care and tantalizing temptation all rolled into one.

"Tell me," he insisted.

"I do."

Placing his hands on the couch on either side of her hips, he hoisted himself up just enough to capture her lips with his. Her hands found their way into his hair, linking behind his head. As his lips guided hers, teasing and taunting and driving her wild, she hardly noticed that he'd slowly pushed her dress up until it was bunched around her waist. His lips wandered to her neck, sucking and licking as he kneaded her thighs with his hands.

"So fucking soft," he muttered between swipes of his tongue over the delicate skin of her neck. She moaned as his fingers drifted over her inner thighs, stroking closer and closer to that sweet spot that was just begging to be touched.

With her eyes closed and head thrown back as she enjoyed his hands and mouth on her, it took Maeve a moment to realize Fletcher had sat back on his heels on the floor. He was gazing between her thighs as if completely enthralled by what he saw there.

Suddenly feeling shy beneath his scrutiny, she began to shut her legs, but he caught her thighs, keeping her bared to him.

"I need to taste you," he said.

"Y-you don't have to."

He tore his gaze away to meet hers. "I want to."

"Are you sure?" she asked, unable to stop the nervous babbling that burst from her mouth. "Because my ex…he never wanted to. It'll take me a long time to…you know. So… it's okay if you don't want to."

"Maeve," Fletcher rasped. "I want to taste you more than I want my next breath. But only if you want me to."

"Yes," she breathed. A split second later, his head dipped low, his lips scorching as they met her heat. Startled by how good the sensation felt, she squirmed beneath his mouth. He held her steady, inching her legs wider as he feasted on her.

After long moments, Fletcher pulled back slightly, nipping at her inner thigh. Apparently unable to get the angle he wanted, he swiftly stood and dragged her legs over the end of the couch, balancing her bottom on the armrest. He grunted as he shifted her entire body without any help from her, as she was halfway to incoherent, blown away by the feeling of his mouth on her. It had been a very long time since anyone had touched her that way, and Fletcher did it with such care and fervor that she was left with no qualms that he wasn't enjoying himself.

In this new position, her hips were elevated in a way that felt sexy and scandalous and gave him access to every intimate part of her. As if he couldn't get enough, Fletcher lowered himself again and began licking at her with renewed passion.

Her hips bucked up, trying to arch even closer to his face. Moans of pleasure rang from her throat as he worked her over with his mouth, then added his fingers into the mix.

Minutes passed, but Maeve didn't have time to worry about how long it was taking her to reach her peak, because she was too focused on soaking in every ounce of pleasure Fletcher was giving her. But eventually, he pulled his mouth away and wiped his lips with the back of his hand, coating his skin in glistening moisture.

There it is, she thought. She was taking too long, and he was over it. She was too high maintenance. Too hard to please. Now he would never want to do it again, just like Jason.

Fletcher shocked her by grabbing her hips and lowering them back onto the couch. "Fuck, Maeve, I can't get close enough to you. Will you please sit on my face?"

"W-what?" she stammered as he propped her body upright to make space for himself to lie down on the couch. He motioned for her to come closer, but she hesitated, gaping at him.

He motioned for her with two fingers. "Maeve, please. Come."

Normally she would have tried for a sassy response like, *I'm trying to*, but Fletcher seemed so serious about his request that she just silently scooted atop him. She'd only made it as far as to straddle his hips when he grabbed the backs of her thighs and pulled her forward, practically knocking her over. She grabbed the armrest of the couch to catch her balance and positioned her hips over his mouth.

Fletcher craned his neck to reach her, his hands attempting in vain to pull her closer. He let out a frustrated grunt when she remained steadfastly an inch above his mouth.

"I didn't say hover, Maeve. I said sit," he said sharply, all traces of gentleness forgotten.

On a groan, she released every bit of tension from her

body and relaxed atop him. Fletcher made a noise so feral she would have sworn Peeve was in the room, yowling, if she hadn't had very clear evidence that the noise was coming from the man below her as his mouth vibrated against her most intimate parts.

The combination of Fletcher's lips and tongue worshipping her, his hands gripping her and holding her open, and the sheer eroticism of what he was doing had Maeve climbing higher and higher. Yearning to appease the ache growing inside her, to satisfy that primal need clawing at her, she began riding his face, her hips moving faster and faster with increasing need.

When Fletcher released another one of those rumbling growls, she rode right into her release, crying out as the onslaught of sensations tore through her. He gripped her even tighter, treating her to a few more sensual kisses as she rode the wave of her orgasm. When he finally released her from his grasp, she scrambled off him, but he immediately sat up and gathered her into his chest.

"Maeve," he whispered as he nuzzled into her hair. "You are spectacular."

She grinned like a fool as she cuddled into him. "Maybe you should have used a big word like that in *Scrabble*. Then, you might have won."

She felt his smile against her forehead.

"Contrary to popular belief, I think I just did."

18

Lying on his couch with Maeve in his arms, limp and sated, was as close to heaven as Fletcher had ever gotten. She lay against him, so open and trusting with no walls in sight. His chest warmed with male satisfaction at having achieved what she seemed to have thought would be impossible. It had hardly been a chore. Her taste, the feel of her, the sounds she made... Maeve was exquisite in every sense of the word.

Taking one of her hands in his, Fletcher noticed the ring she wore. For the slightest moment, he worried that Maeve still wore her wedding ring, but relief swept over him as he realized the gold band was on her right ring finger, not her left. There was a heart at the center of the band, held in a pair of little golden hands and wearing a gold crown. The unique design struck his curiosity, and he ran his finger over the symbols.

"What's the story of this ring?" he asked.

"It's a Claddagh ring," she said, her fingers absentmindedly stroking up and down his arm. "It's an Irish tradition. My parents gave it to me when I turned eighteen. If the heart is turned inward, it means your heart is taken. If it's turned outward, it means your heart is open to love."

Fletcher smiled into her hair, pleased by the idea that her heart was open to love. "Have you always worn it?"

Her stroking fingers paused momentarily before picking back up again. "No. I took it off when my ex and I got engaged. I didn't wear it for years, but when I left, I decided it was time to put it on again."

"It's beautiful," he said as he laced his fingers through hers. "Just like you." She turned her face up to his, and he leaned down to catch her lips in a kiss. "Will you stay here tonight?"

Maeve chewed her bottom lip, indecision clearly gnawing at her. "I really shouldn't."

He rubbed his thumb along hers. "Why not?"

"Because…the kids…" she trailed off.

Fletcher glanced at his watch. It was ten thirty-six p.m. "I'm sure Connie has already put the kids to bed by now."

"But what about in the morning?" she asked. "Or what if one of them wakes up with a nightmare and needs me?"

"I'm sure Connie can cover all that," Fletcher said, trying to carefully tread the line between cajoling Maeve into giving in to her desires and convincing her to do something she didn't want to do. He desperately hoped he was succeeding at the former.

"I don't know…" she said. "I haven't spent a night away from them in a long, long time."

He nudged her nose with his. "Maybe it's time, then."

She leaned into his chest, resting her cheek right over his heart. "I want to, Fletch. Don't get me wrong. It's just… I need to make sure I'm always doing what's right for my kids."

"I know," he replied. "I respect that a lot. It's one of the things I like most about you. But you staying over tonight won't lead to any suffering for your kids. They love staying with Connie, and you deserve a night off."

She sighed, her breath tickling his chest. "You're probably right."

"I am right." He pressed a kiss to her forehead. "Plus, a happy mother makes happy children. And you'll go home tomorrow happier than ever. I'll make sure of that."

She smiled against his chest.

"Please stay," he whispered.

"Okay."

Fletcher didn't give her a chance to change her mind as he stood and swept her into his arms. "Good. Because I want to find out what else makes you scream like that."

Maeve didn't respond as he carried her to his bedroom, but one glance down at her face showed that her cheeks had turned the loveliest shade of pink. In his bedroom, Fletcher placed her gently down on the bed.

"I know I didn't earn this fair and square, but will you please take this thing off now?" he asked, fingering the bottom hem of her dress.

Maeve stilled, turning her emerald gaze away from him. "Fletcher, I…"

He waited for her to finish her sentence, but after a few moments of silence, he realized she wasn't going to.

"You're not going to be comfortable sleeping in that." He motioned to her dress.

"I'll be fine," she said, showing that hint of sassy defiance that he knew and loved.

He let out a sigh. As much as he wanted to pull the dress right over her head and worship her entire body, she was clearly uncomfortable, and she'd already come such a long way tonight. He gestured toward his dresser. "If I give you one of my t-shirts, will you change into that?"

Maeve nodded eagerly, clearly amenable to his solution, so he grabbed one of his favorite t-shirts—a faded Boston Red Sox one from their 2018 World Series win—and handed it to her. He turned away without being asked, wanting to show that he supported her even if he didn't quite understand her wishes.

"Okay," she said quietly after a few moments. Fletcher turned and found Maeve on the edge of the bed, his t-shirt draped loosely over her body. The sight brought a smile to his face, and he walked over to loom above her sitting figure.

"Lie back," he instructed, pleased when she enthusiastically obeyed. Her scooting backward dragged his shirt higher up her thighs, and he inched it up the rest of the way until it rested just above her hips. A glance at the apex of her thighs revealed that she remained wet and ready, so he made quick work of shedding his boxers. Now fully naked, Fletcher slid up the mattress until his body hovered over Maeve's.

Her bright eyes met his, and she treated him to a cheeky grin. "Hi."

"Hi," he said back before leaning down and kissing her slowly, his tongue stroking into her mouth in long, languid pulls. He gently lowered his body over hers, relishing the feel of her silky legs tangled with his.

Maeve moaned and gripped his hair, tugging at it almost to the point of pain. He let out a low grunt of pleasure and moved his mouth from hers to trail kisses over her jawline and neck. Her busy hands made their way over his chest and down his abdomen, stroking and rubbing and generally turning him into a sensitized mess.

"Fuck," he said as she slipped her hand around his erection, using just the right amount of pressure to totally unhinge him. Her soft sounds of encouragement had him bucking into her hand, but after a few strokes of his hips, Fletcher came to his senses and realized that it wasn't her fist he longed to be inside of.

"Maeve," he whispered, pulling back so he could see her face. Her cheeks were flushed, her green eyes hazy.

"Hmm?" she mumbled, still stroking him in her tight fist.

He shuddered at the sensation. "Sweetheart, I need you."

A lazy smile touched her lips before she craned her neck up to reach his mouth. Her kiss was unhurried, long and slow and full of longing. It briefly crossed Fletcher's mind how different this time was from their first encounter, because while he had been equally determined not to rush that one, the nature of their relationship and the expectations for that night had made it far less meaningful than this one.

This time around, Fletcher knew just how much it meant to have her.

"I need you, too," Maeve whispered as she reached down to guide Fletcher into herself. They both groaned as he entered her, and he slid in easily on his first thrust, filling her to the hilt. His eyes almost rolled back in his head at how unbelievably perfect she felt. Tight and hot and wet, yielding to his hard length.

"You feel so fucking good," Fletcher said as he pulled almost all the way out before thrusting back in. Maeve cried out and arched her back, taking every inch of him. Her eyes had screwed shut, her fingers fisting in the sheets. The erotic sight turned him on almost as much as the feeling of her squeezing him, tighter than her fist had been and slicker, too.

He was almost lost in the sensation when a dreadful realization dawned on him.

"Shit," he muttered, forcing himself to stay still. "I didn't put a condom on yet."

"It's okay." Maeve nipped at his collarbone. "I'm on birth control."

A spike of adrenaline coursed through Fletcher's veins at the thought of coming inside her with no barriers, literal or metaphorical, between them.

"Are you sure?" he asked.

"As long as you don't have any STDs, then we're golden. I was checked out after I left my ex."

Fletcher breathed a sigh of relief. "Same." He began moving again, his pace slower but rapidly building. Maeve wrapped her arms around him, her nails clawing at his back. She was

surely scoring his skin, but the carnal undertone of her actions made him supremely grateful he hadn't made her grab onto the headboard this time.

He was up on his hands, his palms supporting him on the mattress, when Maeve wrapped her legs around him and urged him in closer. "Don't hover, Fletcher," she demanded, throwing his earlier words back at him.

Floored by her cheeky comment, he lowered himself until his body covered hers. She clung to him like Velcro as he drilled into her, bringing them both higher until he knew he was about to blow. Wanting to get her there again first, he changed the angle of his body a bit so he rubbed against her clit with each stroke of his hips. Maeve gasped and shifted, her own hips quickly catching onto the movement.

"Shit, sweetheart," Fletcher breathed as she rocked beneath him, getting herself off on his body. She felt so good —too good—and as soon as she clenched around him, her orgasm pulsing and vibrating, he exploded, too. He came long and hard, filling her as he panted and quivered above her.

After a long moment that felt like a little slice of forever, Maeve's grip on him loosened. Her arms and legs remained around him, one hand trailing sluggishly up and down his bare back.

"Wow," she said with a sigh. Fletcher grinned triumphantly and pressed a kiss to the crook of her neck before carefully pulling out of her.

"Wow is right," he replied as he gently disentangled himself from her limbs.

"Where are you going?" she asked, a slight frown on her mouth as he scooted toward the edge of the bed.

"Just going to clean up," he said. "Don't worry, sweetheart —I won't be far, or long."

True to his word, he raced to the bathroom and wiped

himself off, wetting a cloth with warm water to do the same for Maeve. When he returned to the bedroom, she had propped herself up on his pillows and pulled the t-shirt down to cover all the luscious skin he'd been enjoying just moments before.

"Uh-uh," he chided playfully as he sauntered back over to the bed. "Got to clean up first." Getting up on all fours on the bed, he crawled before Maeve and lifted the shirt up again. She sat stock still as he began tenderly wiping away all traces of his pleasure from her intimate skin. She squirmed slightly as he parted her lips, gently dabbing between them. Just for good measure, he traveled a bit higher and brushed over her sensitized clit, making her squeal.

"I'm clean, okay?" she shrieked. "I'm clean."

Removing the cloth, Fletcher leaned in for a quick kiss. "On the contrary, I think you're very, very dirty."

Her cheeks blushed bright red, and he chuckled as he tossed the cloth on top of his hamper. Settling back into the bed, he brought the covers up over their bodies. Maeve immediately cuddled into him, resting her head on his chest and slinging her arm around his waist.

Fletcher nuzzled his face against her hair and released a content sigh. "You're not going to leave this time, are you?" he asked, his lips resting against her temple.

She shook her head. "No. I won't leave this time."

He pressed a kiss to her forehead. "Good."

19

When Maeve awoke in Fletcher's arms, she felt safer and more secure than ever before. She'd promised him she wouldn't leave during the night, but even if she had wanted to, she would have missed her chance since she slept so soundly. His embrace was a balm she hadn't even realized she needed.

Morning light streamed in through the slats in the bedroom's shades. It was likely another chilly spring morning that would blossom into a pleasantly warm afternoon. She snuggled into Fletcher's warm skin as if that would protect her from the impending chill she would feel when she had to leave.

"Hmm, good morning," he mumbled against her shoulder.

"Morning," she replied, stretching her legs and bumping her knee into something hard.

"Oomf," Fletcher grunted, and she realized what the hard object had been.

"Oh. Good morning," she repeated playfully, reaching down to cup him in her palm.

He nipped at the shell of her ear, pushing his hips into her touch. "It *is* a good morning."

After another round of sweet, sensual, mind-boggling sex, Fletcher offered to take her out to breakfast.

"I don't know," Maeve said, worrying her bottom lip with her teeth. "The kids will probably expect me to be home for breakfast."

He attempted to tame her unruly bedhead for a moment before giving up and dropping his hand down to her hip. "They won't mind. In fact, they'll be thrilled. Connie will probably make them a breakfast full of sugar. They'll love it."

Maeve grinned at the truth in his words. Connie spoiled those kids rotten. She'd probably return to two sugar-high children, but it would be worth it to spend a bit more time with Fletcher.

"Okay."

After a quick clean-up on both of their parts, during which Maeve threw her now-hopeless hair up in a bun, Fletcher took her to a diner down the street from his apartment. Its red leather booths were cracked and had stuffing popping out from the holes, and the surfaces of each table were scratched and covered in rings from coffee cups, but he assured her they made the best breakfast in town.

Maeve perused the menu, feeling as giddy as her kids probably did at the prospect of a breakfast with Connie. She couldn't remember the last time she'd been out to breakfast, let alone been taken out to breakfast by a handsome man. In fact, she wasn't sure that had *ever* happened.

"What are you going to get?" Fletcher asked as he took a sip from his mug. Maeve had to admit, the coffee they'd brought them already was quite good, despite being served in chipped, off-white mugs that made her wonder if they'd always been that color, or if they'd become discolored over years of use.

"I'm thinking of going for the western omelet," she said as she continued to scan the menu. "Oh, or the eggs Benedict."

"You can't go wrong either way," Fletcher said, and she realized he had never even opened his menu.

She looked from the closed menu to his face. "What are you going to get?"

"I always get the *big boy breakfast*," he answered, supplying the silly name of a meal that came with two eggs, two sausages, two pieces of toast, home fries and a side of fruit.

She smirked, thinking of their late-night and early-morning activities. Of how much he stretched her and how incredible it felt. "Well, that name suits you."

Fletcher's eyes danced with humor. "I like to think so."

Maeve shook her head, glancing back at the menu for one more perusal. A flash of dark hair caught her attention at the corner of her vision. Her gaze whipped toward it, the color so familiar that her breath caught in her throat. That was *Jason's* hair. Same color, cut, and everything. It had to be him. He was facing away from her, seemingly gathering up his things to leave.

Her gut flip-flopped. Suddenly, nothing on the menu seemed appetizing.

"Hey." Fletcher reached across the table for her hand. "Everything okay?"

Maeve turned toward his worried gaze. "Y-yeah," she said, craning her neck for another glimpse of the man who was halfway out the door. She blinked a few times. "I just thought I saw someone I know."

She gripped Fletcher's hand as her nerves settled. It couldn't have been Jason. If it had been, he surely would have confronted her. It wouldn't be like him to go silently or without a fight. There was just no way. *It wasn't Jason.*

With that thought settled in her mind, Maeve's appetite returned with a vengeance. Thankfully, their meals arrived quickly after they ordered them. She was grateful she'd decided on the western omelet because it came with home fries while the eggs Benedict had not. After seeing how delicious and crispy Fletcher's looked, she would have been jealous if she hadn't gotten her own.

She moaned as she bit into one of the larger pieces of potato. It was soft on the inside and crispy on the outside, perfectly seasoned and bursting with flavor. She unintentionally let out another sound of pleasure, and Fletcher shifted in his seat.

"Maeve," he growled. "Stop with the orgasm noises, or I'm going to strip you naked and give you one right here, and I don't care who's watching."

"Sorry," she said quickly, her cheeks heating even as she bit back a giggle. "Let's change the subject."

He speared a home fry with his fork and dragged it across the small dollop of ketchup he'd put on his plate. Popping it into his mouth, he chewed silently, then took a deep breath, as if working up the courage to say something.

She stayed quiet, giving him the space to say whatever it was he needed to say.

The look on Fletcher's face was vulnerable, almost uncertain, when he eventually spoke. "So, I told you that my brother Beau is getting married," he began.

Maeve nodded, encouraging him to go on.

"It turns out they're going to be having a small, intimate wedding in a few weeks. It'll be on Nantucket with an outdoor ceremony on the beach and an indoor reception at my brother Jack's café. I was wondering…" He paused, placing his fork on his plate and reaching for one of her hands across the table. "I was wondering if maybe you would go with me?"

Maeve squeezed his hand, a bit surprised by his timidity. He was usually so self-assured, so in control of any situation he found himself in. Though, of course, he probably expected her to turn him down. She'd done it enough in the past few weeks. But after how blissful the past twelve hours had been, she had no choice but to say, "I would love to go with you, Fletcher."

A relieved grin lit up his face, and she was glad to have been the one to put it there. After a moment, though, her mind flooded with thoughts.

"So, I'll be meeting your family?" she asked. "And we'll have to travel… How many days will we be gone? I'll have to make sure Connie will be able to watch the kids. And I have to make sure—"

"Maeve," Fletcher interrupted, squeezing her hand in reassurance as she had just done to him moments ago. "Stop worrying. We'll make sure the kids will be all set. And yes, you'll meet my family, and they'll all love you. I swear it's not a huge deal. The wedding will be small and casual. Just consider it a weekend trip."

"A weekend trip with you feels like a big deal," she argued, already imagining the kids' reactions when she told them she and Fletcher were going away together. She may have to recant her statement about Fletcher not being her boyfriend, and that would bring up its own host of questions from their hyper-curious minds.

He nodded, stroking his thumb over the inside of her wrist. "I know. It *is* a big deal. You're right. We're both recently out of long-term relationships, and this is a significant step."

She nodded, grateful he acknowledged the seriousness of going away together. Hell, they had only just slept together for the second—okay, and third, and fourth, and fifth—time, and now he wanted her to meet the family.

"You can tell the kids whatever you want about it," he said, as if reading her mind or, at the very least, anticipating the direction of her worries. "And I'll introduce you however you want to my family. I can say you're a friend, or even just a parent of some of my students, though I think they'll be able to tell from the way I look and act around you that you're a whole lot more."

Maeve couldn't help but grin at the accuracy of that statement. If the school moms had been able to tell he was smitten with her, there was no doubt that Fletcher's own family would be able to read his feelings about her loud and clear.

"I'll think about what I want to tell people," she said. "But I really would love to go with you, Fletch. It would be great to get to see where you grew up and meet the brothers you helped raise. And your mother, of course."

Fletcher beamed at her. "My mom is going to adore you."

"Did they like your last girlfriend?" Maeve asked, unable to help herself from worrying about what she may have to measure up to. She didn't know much about Fletcher's ex, but any woman who scored him had to be pretty fantastic.

Fletcher's smile fell into a small frown. "They said they did —well, except for Beau, who outright disparaged her behind her back—but I think they mostly just put up with her because I liked her. To be honest, she never really fit in with my family. She was too pretentious, and we were too small-town and homey, I think."

Amused by his description of his family, Maeve replied, "I think I'm pretty small-town and homey."

He smiled happily at her again. "I know. That's why they'll love you."

Maeve arrived home around noon. After breakfast, Fletcher had made one more stop before dropping her off: a bookstore, where he cheekily invested in a *Scrabble* dictionary and insisted she pick out a book for him to purchase for her. She'd gone with a new fantasy she hadn't stopped hearing about. The thick, almost eight-hundred-page tome was a hardcover and on the more expensive side. She had hemmed and hawed in the aisle until Fletcher came up, grabbed it from her, and brought it to the register without a word.

At Maeve's request, he dropped her off just beyond the house so the kids wouldn't see his car and come running out to greet him. She wanted to tell the kids about them—how they were together as something more than friends—but she wanted to do it alone so they felt comfortable asking her any questions that were on their minds. If Fletcher was around, they might not fully open up.

She didn't want to use words like *boyfriend* or *relationship* for fear that the kids would slip up and accidentally spread the word around school that she and Fletcher were together. If things moved forward with him, they would obviously have to discuss how to handle other parents and staff finding out. For now, saying that she and Fletcher were becoming *good friends* seemed like an accurate and age-appropriate explanation for the kids.

She felt like a teenager coming home from a forbidden tryst as he dropped her off just down the road. After a scorching parting kiss, Maeve doubled back and walked up her driveway. She climbed the porch steps and stopped to glance into the bird's nest. Oftentimes, when she peered in, the babies were sleeping, but today, they were up and at 'em, reaching their necks up long and opening their beaks wide as they searched for food. She smiled at the sight and let them be, knowing one of the parents would be back soon with nourishment for them.

She had nourishment for her own babies in the form of a box of donuts from the diner. As soon as she opened the front door, they came running, their little eyes bugging out when they noticed the pastry box in her hands.

"What did you bring?" Allie got up on her tiptoes to get a better glimpse.

Maeve laughed. "Come to the kitchen and find out."

Connie awaited her in the kitchen, wearing a sly grin that said *someone had a fun night.* Maeve gave her a surreptitious thumbs-up and received a wink in return.

Placing the box on the kitchen table, she opened it to show the kids. "I got three chocolate, two vanilla, and one strawberry."

"I call strawberry!" Allie said immediately.

"You don't even like strawberry," Andy complained, crossing his arms. "You only want that one because it's special."

"He's right, Al," Maeve said. "Last time you tried a strawberry donut, you said it tasted like grass. You can choose chocolate or vanilla."

Allie huffed and grabbed one of the chocolate donuts. "Fine."

Andy grinned like the Cheshire cat as Maeve handed him the single strawberry donut. She grabbed the vanilla ones for herself and Connie.

"So, guys," she said as they all began munching on their treats. "You know I've been spending more time with Mr. McNally lately and that we're becoming good friends. In fact, in a couple of weeks, we're going to be going away together. His brother is getting married on Nantucket—that's an island off of Cape Cod—and he asked me to go with him. I'll have to ask Connie to watch you guys for a couple of days."

"Yay!" Andy shouted, unperturbed by her announcement and more focused on the fact that he would get to spend time with Connie.

Allie didn't look quite so easily accepting. Her face was scrunched into a wary expression, and she narrowed her eyes as she processed Maeve's words. "So, is he your boyfriend *now?*" she asked.

Maeve chose her words carefully. "We're good friends. We might become better friends, but that's all it is for now."

"Well, *will* he be your boyfriend?"

Maeve rolled her neck out so her daughter's questions wouldn't give her a headache. "I don't know," she answered. "Maybe. But right now, we're just getting to know each other better."

Allie shrugged, returning to her donut. "Okay."

Maeve reared her head back, shocked that there weren't a million more questions on Allie's mind. "Okay?"

"Yeah." Allie wiped some crumbs from her upper lip. "I like Mr. McNally. I'm glad he's your friend."

Maeve couldn't help the smile that stretched across her lips. "So am I."

The kids finished their donuts, and she helped clean off their faces before remembering one more thing she'd meant to add.

"I want you both to remember that just because Mr. McNally is Mommy's friend, doesn't mean you can get away with anything at school," she said. "He's still your principal, and you have to treat him with respect."

They both nodded, taking her decree seriously.

"We will, Mommy," Andy said, his eyes wide and sincere. Maeve stroked his hair, knowing that, realistically, her kids were probably some of the most well-behaved ones at the school, despite the sass and mischief they sometimes presented with at home. She just felt the need to get it out in the open that, no matter what changed with her and Fletcher, his role as their principal wouldn't change.

"I know," she replied.

20

After dropping the kids at school, Maeve returned home, eager to begin a serious job hunt. She had thought over the options Connie had presented but decided none really appealed to her. Working at a yoga studio, coffee shop, or movie theater might be fun for a while because those were places she enjoyed, but none of those jobs would be overly fulfilling. She wanted to find something that would make a difference in the world. Something that would make this fresh start even more worth it.

As she exited her car, the hair on Maeve's arms pricked up, anxiety immediately washing over her. She had been so on edge lately, any little thing out of place caught her attention. She quickly realized the source—a strange noise coming from the front of the house. Suddenly, her mind was spinning a mile a minute. Was someone breaking in? Casing the place and scrambling to hide in the bushes so she didn't see? Had Jason finally found her?

Frozen halfway up the driveway, she scanned the front of the house. Peeve was in the window, jumping impossibly high, as if trying to open the damn thing. The noise she heard was him batting at the glass, his furry paws hitting it over and over.

His mouth kept opening wide then closing as if he was howling.

Despite locating the source of the noise and determining it was harmless, Peeve's agitation stoked Maeve's unease. Animals were intuitive, so if he was upset, something might really be wrong. Why couldn't she have found an abandoned guard dog in her gutter, who would protect her, instead of a small, silly cat who wouldn't even kill a fly?

Noticing that Peeve's attention was directed toward the porch, Maeve took a few cautious steps in that direction. She couldn't see anything overtly out of place until she got a bit closer and noticed a tiny creature plopped on the porch floor. It sat almost directly below the hanging plant that housed the birds' nest. Glancing in horror from the nest to the floor about five feet below, Maeve realized that one of the babies had taken a big tumble.

She puffed out a gasp as she rushed over and knelt beside the baby bird. It was a pathetic little thing, its eyes barely open and its feathers nowhere full enough to protect its delicate skin. "Oh no," she breathed as she watched the bird open its mouth, either searching for food or crying out in pain. No matter which it was, the creature clearly needed her help.

Okay, think, Maeve. She'd watched enough viral videos of people saving abandoned baby animals, though they were usually of the mammal variety, and the people were doing cute things like feeding them with syringes or swaddling them like infants. What were you supposed to do with a bird? Grind up worms and spoon-feed them? Because that was so not happening.

She surveyed the bird for a moment, his anguish nearly tearing her heart in two. *You're a mother*, she reminded herself. *You can handle this.* Setting her shoulders back in determination, Maeve stood and marched into the house to find a pair of gloves. Though she was pretty sure it was a myth that the parents would abandon the baby if it smelled like a human, she wasn't willing to take any chances.

Before slipping on a pair of food gloves, she took a moment to try and soothe Peeve. The cat was going absolutely bonkers, alternating between hissing and yowling as he attempted to launch himself through the window. Unable to calm him down, Maeve just shook her head and left him there. He would tire himself out eventually.

"Here we go," she murmured as she knelt down and scooped the bird up in her gloved palm. She figured the best bet was to just place it back in the nest where it would be safe and hope the parents didn't reject it. The second she picked it up, however, she noticed that its leg was bent at an odd angle. A stifled sob caught in her throat, tears springing to her eyes as she inspected the bird's leg. It was clearly broken, a fact that placing him back in the nest wouldn't solve.

Shit. She considered calling Connie, but her friend was at work, and Maeve knew how important her work was. She really shouldn't bother her unless it was an emergency—a human emergency, that is. Keeping the creature cradled in her palm, she pulled out her cell phone and called the only other person she knew would be willing to help.

Fletcher answered after the first ring, almost as if he'd been awaiting her call.

"Hello?"

Relief swept through her at the sound of his voice. Deep and strong, nothing could reassure her more than knowing this man was on the other end of the line. He would know what to do.

A tear trailed down Maeve's cheek. "Fletcher," she whispered, unable to keep the emotion from tainting her voice.

"Maeve?" he asked, a scraping sound rattling out in the background as if he'd pushed his chair back quickly. "What's wrong, sweetheart?"

The affectionate pet name sent more tears sliding down

her cheeks. She glanced down at the poor critter in her hands. "I...I just got home and found that one of the baby birds fell out of the nest. His leg...I think its broken. I don't know what to do, Fletch. He was all alone."

Indignation suddenly tugged at her. Where had the bird's parents been? Had they even noticed it had fallen out? They hadn't been doing their usual squawking as she rescued it. Did they even care that it had gotten hurt?

"Okay," Fletcher said, his tone soothing. "Okay, so one of the birds fell out and broke its leg. We can fix that."

"How?" she wailed.

"We'll look up local wildlife rescues and see who takes cases like this. I'm sure there's someone out there who rehabilitates wildlife like that."

"B-but what do I do with it in the meantime? It's so small, Fletcher. What if it's cold or hungry?"

Fletcher let out a sound almost like a sigh but from deeper in his throat. "I'm coming over." There was some background noise, as if he was already moving through the office. "Why don't you look for a box and something warm to line it with? Put the bird in that, and I'll be there soon."

Clutching the phone between her shoulder and her ear, Maeve used her free hand to wipe away some of the tears. "Don't you have to work?"

"I have vacation days," he replied over the sound of a car door slamming shut. "What I *have* to do is take care of you and that bird."

Maeve sniffled. "Thanks, Fletch," she whispered into the phone before hanging up and searching for the items he'd recommended. Luckily, there was still a shoe box laying around from some new shoes she'd bought the kids. She cracked it open and lined it with paper towels, the process painfully slow as she could only use one hand. She did her best not to jostle the bird in her other, desperate not to make its hurt leg any worse.

"There," she said as she gently placed the bird into the box. Her momentary satisfaction was soon chased by despair as the bird settled into the bed of paper towels, its leg splayed out to the side in an almost grotesque manner. Tears welled in her eyes again, and she willed them away, hoping to look at least somewhat composed when Fletcher arrived.

A knock on her door had her eyes filling all over again, so she gave up all pretenses of composure and answered the door. A worried frown creased Fletcher's brow as she opened it.

"Hey," he said, immediately stepping into the door frame and wrapping her in his strong arms. She released a pent-up sob into his chest, likely ruining his shirt with her snot and saliva, but he didn't seem to care. "I'm here now," he whispered, soothing her with long strokes up and down her back.

Maeve was tempted just to stand there in the safety of his embrace, soaking up his strength, but she didn't want to waste time wallowing in her own pity when the bird was suffering just a few feet away. After a moment, she pulled back and led Fletcher to the kitchen.

"Here's the little guy." She gestured to it, only sparing it a quick glance. The sight made her too sad.

Fletcher visually inspected the bird and nodded. "Yep, it's definitely broken. Poor little thing." He indicated for Maeve to sit down in one of the kitchen chairs, then sat beside her and pulled out his phone. "I'll see who's around that might take him in."

As he scrolled on his phone, one of his hands absentmindedly made its way to Maeve's thigh. She silently relished the comfort in his touch, wondering if he knew how much it meant to her that he'd come.

"This place looks promising." Fletcher held out his phone to show her a photo of two women in front of a wildlife rescue sign. One was feeding a tiny rabbit from a bottle, and the other held a plump squirrel in her arms. They looked just like the people in the videos she'd seen, and the image of the two healthy animals planted a little seed of hope for the baby bird in her mind.

"That looks great."

"I'll call them."

As Fletcher spoke with the people at the wildlife rescue, he linked his fingers with hers, again offering that silent support. "Good news," he said after hanging up. "They take birds, and they're open now. I'll drive you over."

"Are you sure?" Maeve asked, still worried about him taking time off work to help her with something that seemed a little silly now that she'd calmed down a bit.

Fletcher placed a kiss on the crown of her head. "I'm sure."

Once she was settled into the passenger side of his car, Maeve began her own internet research. She hoped to get some insight into how the baby bird had wound up on the floor. Was it common for birds to try and fly prematurely and end up hurt on the ground? Or was there a chance it had been kicked out of the nest for some reason?

She let out a sound of discontent that had Fletcher's head turning toward her.

"What is it?"

"According to this article, sometimes as birds get bigger, there's not enough space for them all in the nest, so one just gets jostled out."

He turned his gaze back to the road and shrugged. "That sucks. It sounds very *circle of life*."

Maeve pocketed her phone with a sigh. "I just don't understand where its parents were. Where was the mother? Why didn't she protect her baby better?"

"I don't know, sweetheart," Fletcher said.

Maeve sighed, deflated, and drummed her fingers on the top of the shoebox in her lap. "Do you think it'll be okay?"

"I do," he answered, reaching for her restless hand and

wrapping it in his own over the center console. "Because even if its mother wasn't able to save it, you were."

~

Once the bird was safely in the care of the wildlife rescue, Fletcher drove them to a nearby coffee shop to decompress. Maeve already felt a thousand times lighter, knowing the bird was in good hands, but the whole situation had shaken her up more than she cared to admit. Something about seeing the baby bird so helpless, with no parents in sight, had pulled at a thread of shame embedded deep within her.

"Do you want decaf?" Fletcher asked, glancing at his watch. It was a little after one o'clock. The process of saving the bird then the trip to the wildlife rescue had taken up a good chunk of time. It hadn't exactly helped that Maeve insisted on taking a tour of the place. It was just so amazing! This particular rescue accepted both birds and small mammals like squirrels, rabbits, foxes, and more. The workers had brought her through their treatment rooms, where they provided any necessary medical care, as well as their rehab rooms, where animals who didn't need urgent care but weren't ready to go into the main space yet resided.

Then, they had walked through a maze of large indoor and outdoor cages separated by species, pointing out some of the animals and giving brief glimpses of their stories. Each and every one was heartbreaking—a wolf runt abandoned by its pack, a brood of ducklings whose mother had been killed trying to cross the road, a rabbit that had suffered a dog attack. The stories were emotionally taxing to listen to, yet seeing the animals thriving in this supportive environment had hope blooming in her chest.

"Nah," Maeve replied. "Get me the real stuff." Caffeine

would be necessary to get her through an afternoon with Allie and Andy after the exhausting morning she'd had.

Fletcher brought two coffees over to the table where he had insisted she sit while he paid.

"Here you go." He handed her one of the drinks. "One cup of the real stuff."

"Thanks, Fletch," Maeve said, taking the drink and blowing lightly on it before putting it to her lips for a tentative sip.

Fletcher watched the whole action before sitting down and surreptitiously adjusting himself.

Maeve's lips kicked up in a smirk. "Getting a little too excited there?"

He sent her a glare that held no malice. "It's been too long since I've had you," he confessed.

She bit back a laugh. "It's been less than a week."

He took a long slug of his coffee. "It's been four days. That's too long."

She toyed with the cup in her hands. "Unfortunately, that's what you get when you date a single mom. I can't just run out for a quickie or sleep over on a whim. Trust me, I'd like to be able to do those things. I'd like to be able to see you every day without having to worry about scheduling sex around my kids' calendar. But that's not an option for me."

Fletcher placed his coffee on the table and reached for her hand. "I know it's not. I didn't mean to make you feel like I was expecting anything or like I was upset that it's somewhat complicated to find time to be together. I just enjoy being with you so much. But I don't mind waiting. You're more than worth waiting for."

Maeve squeezed his hand, savoring those sweet words. "I'm sorry I got defensive. I think I just sometimes wish I *could* be wild and carefree for a while. I never got that opportunity, and I feel like I missed out."

Fletcher nodded. "I know what you mean. After my dad

died, I was never able to be a normal teenager. I went straight into caretaker mode for my brothers. Then, I chose a career that didn't allow much room for acting out. But maybe we both can still have our wild and carefree days, even if they look a little different."

Maeve arched a brow. "What do they look like?"

"Just think," he said, sitting back in his chair. "In a couple of weeks, we'll be away on Nantucket together, in a private hotel room, with no one else around. No one asking for our help, or needing anything from us, or threatening to walk in on us."

A grin took over Maeve's face. "I like the sound of that."

21

"Have you seen my lipstick?" Maeve asked as she rustled through her make-up bag. She could have sworn she'd just seen it in there, but then she had walked away from the bathroom to pack some clothes in the bedroom, and now the lipstick was missing.

"Uh," Allie sputtered as she rounded the corner into the bathroom. She had red lipstick smudged over her petite mouth in an eerily clown-like fashion. Her eyes grew wide and apologetic as she took in Maeve's scowl. "I just wanted to try it out."

Maeve heaved a sigh as she took in the dulled lipstick in Allie's grasp. So much for going for a bold lip at the wedding.

"Next time, you can ask me, and I'll help you put it on, okay?"

Allie nodded and carefully put the cap back on the now-ruined tube of lipstick.

It was the day before Beau's wedding, and Maeve had been packing all morning, rushing to get things together before Fletcher picked her up at noon. They would drive to Hyannis to catch a two o'clock ferry, and they were slated to arrive on the island around three. There would be a rehearsal dinner that night, though there was barely a need for a rehearsal due to the intimate nature of the wedding. Fletcher and his brother Jack would stand up for Beau, and Jack's wife, Natalie, and Emma's good friend Isabella would stand up for her.

Maeve was somewhat relieved by the small number of people she would have to meet, but the fact that they were also the people closest to Fletcher was daunting. Their approval would be paramount if she was going to pursue a relationship with him, and it had been a long time since she'd had to impress someone's family. In fact, she'd never really felt the need to make a perfect impression on a significant other's family before. Jason hadn't been close to his parents, which perhaps should have been yet another red flag. At the time, it had seemed like one less step to worry about.

Despite her nerves, Maeve was still beyond excited to see Fletcher's hometown and the iconic island of Nantucket. Being early June, he assured her it wouldn't be overly crowded yet, and he had promised to show her all his favorite spots. And, of course, there was the hotel room they'd booked for the next two nights, where they'd get that uninterrupted time together.

Maeve had felt nothing but peace since deciding to give things with Fletcher a chance. He made her feel safe and comfortable while still eliciting butterflies in her belly—a combination she'd never felt with any man before. There was still a niggling sense of worry about something going wrong and the kids getting hurt in the mix, but everything was going so smoothly that she felt safe letting her guard down a bit.

"When are you coming back again, Mommy?" Allie asked.

"I'll be back on Sunday," Maeve replied, zipping up her overstuffed suitcase. The prompt given for wedding attire had been vague, leaving her unsure what to wear. It wasn't like she had a huge wardrobe, but she wanted to ensure that she wouldn't stick out like a sore thumb from the other guests at the wedding. It was enough that she would be a new face. She didn't need a fashion faux pas making her stand out more. In the end, she'd packed a sundress, a flowy skirt and blouse, and a cocktail dress she'd found on a sale rack the day before on an emergency shopping trip with Connie.

"I'm going to miss you," Allie said, sticking her lower lip out in a pout.

"Oh, baby, I'm going to miss you, too." Maeve pulled her daughter in for a hug. "But you'll have so much fun with Connie and Andy and Peeve. And I'll make sure to call you both nights before bedtime."

Allie seemed satisfied by that as she pulled out of the hug and skipped over to the doorway. "And maybe you'll bring us souvenirs?"

Maeve grinned at her daughter's lack of subtlety. "Sure, if Connie reports good behavior, then I'll bring you both some souvenirs."

Allie's lips pulled into a mischievous smile. "How about if we're good, we get *two* souvenirs each, but if we're not so good, then we only get one?"

Maeve resisted the urge to roll her eyes. She was hoping to avoid Allie picking up on that particular mannerism, knowing it would frustrate her to no end if she did.

"Why would I give you a reward for being not so good?" she asked, honestly curious what creative reasoning her daughter would come up with. The ringing of the doorbell interrupted their negotiation, and Allie clapped her hands.

"He's here!"

She took off down the stairs while Maeve followed at a slower pace, lugging her heavy suitcase behind her. Allie and Andy had already let Fletcher in the front door by the time she made it to the bottom of the staircase.

"Hey," he said, lunging forward to grab the suitcase.

"Hey," Maeve replied, flexing her hands to work out

the fatigued muscles. After a quick glance at the kids to gauge their reaction, she stepped forward and enveloped Fletcher in a hug. His arms immediately came around her, holding her to his chest, and she breathed in his scent—crisp and clean, like freshly washed towels mixed with a hint of something spicy. After a moment, she pulled away and stepped back, but not before catching Connie watching them from the kitchen with a shrewd smile.

"Well, we have to get going," Maeve announced to their onlookers. "We don't want to miss our boat."

Connie came forward to give her a hug goodbye, whispering in her ear to have fun and enjoy herself. Allie smacked a kiss on Maeve's cheek as she knelt down to say goodbye, likely marking her with evidence of her mischief with the red lipstick. Lastly, Maeve turned toward her son and found his eyes filling with tears. The sight threatened to break her heart in half, but Allie, her brave, beautiful little girl, took his hand and squeezed it.

"It's okay, Andy," she said. "Mommy's going to call us before bed every night she's gone."

Maeve nodded. "That's right. And I'm going to bring you souvenirs, too."

"But only if we're good," Allie clarified.

Maeve reached forward and pinched her cheek. "I think we both know I'll bring something either way."

Allie beamed as Andy wiped away his tears with the back of his hand. "I love you, Mommy," he said, and Maeve's heart stitched itself right back up.

She was a good mom. She knew that. She gave her kids her all, protected them fiercely, and cared for them to the absolute best of her ability. Going away for one weekend with Fletcher didn't make her a bad mother. It didn't make her selfish or greedy—none of those things she'd once been accused of incessantly. At least, that was what she was trying to convince herself as she stood up and waved a final goodbye to her children.

They got on the road, making good time and hitting Hyannis well before their boat was set to leave. They chose seats on the outer deck so they could watch the ocean pass them by. It was chilly with the ocean breeze, and Maeve pulled her jacket a little tighter over her chest.

"Cold?" Fletcher asked, reaching over to intertwine their fingers and resting their hands atop his thigh.

"A little, but it's worth it for this view," Maeve said, settling into his side to soak in his warmth. The cerulean waves splashed up against the side of the boat, their rhythmic sound relaxing her to her core. Or maybe it was the feeling of being tucked into Fletcher's embrace that was doing that. Either way, she wasn't going to let a slight chill keep her from this utter euphoria.

"It *is* a great view," he said, but when Maeve went to look up at him, he was staring down at her. Warmth bloomed in her belly, and she looked back out over the ocean, unable to formulate a response to the sweetness of his comment.

Thankfully, she was saved from having to come up with an equally meaningful remark when her cell phone rang. She fished it from her pocket as she remained anchored to Fletcher's side.

"Hello?" she said into the phone.

"Hi, Maeve," said a woman's voice. "This is Rosa from the wildlife rescue. I'm just calling to give you an update on the baby bird you brought in. He's doing very well—eating and gaining weight. His feathers are even starting to come in!"

"Oh, that's great news!" Maeve replied, relief pouring into her veins. As silly as it seemed, she had thought of that little bird a lot since they'd dropped it off. Was it scared? Lonely? In pain? Did it miss its mother? She had spent countless hours over the last handful of years entrenched in those worries over her own children.

"Thank you so much for calling," Maeve added. "I really appreciate the update." She hadn't always been able to protect her kids the way she had wanted to, and that guilt still plagued her. Knowing the bird was safe and healthy, and her kids were as well, would grant her a greater capacity to relax and enjoy her weekend.

"Of course," Rosa said. "I can call again with another update before we release him back into the wild if you want."

"That would be great," Maeve replied, thinking of the tiny creature she had found on her porch floor being strong enough to live on its own. "Do you think... Would it be possible for me to be there for that?"

"For the release?" Rosa asked. "Sure, I don't see why not. I'll let you know when we plan to do it."

"Thank you so much." Maeve was already excited at the prospect of seeing the baby bird fly off on its own. After hanging up, she snuggled into Fletcher's chest.

"Who was that?" he asked, resting his chin on her head.

"A woman from the wildlife rescue. She says the baby bird is doing really well, and they're going to let me be there when they release it back into the wild."

Fletcher gave her a squeeze. "That's excellent. I imagine it will be very gratifying for you to watch that."

She grinned at the way Fletcher understood her so easily. "I was thinking I might like working at a place like that," she said. "A place that rehabilitates wildlife, or maybe a shelter where stray cats like Peeve end up. I think it would be really satisfying to watch animals get better and get a second chance at life."

He placed a kiss on the crown of her head. "I think that's a fantastic idea. You could help give animals a fresh start, just like you did for yourself."

Maeve's heart swelled. Without even knowing the extent of her fresh start, Fletcher realized just how important it was to her. He understood her drive to help others do the same, whether human or animal, and he encouraged her idea without questioning the logistics or practicality of it. That level of support was so foreign but oh-so welcome.

She squeezed his hand. "I think I would really love that."

～

Once docked, Fletcher hauled his and Maeve's suitcases off the ferry toward the sidewalk. The hotel room he'd booked was right in town, so they set off toward it on foot. He hadn't wanted to pay to take his car over just for the weekend, so if they needed to go anywhere farther than walking distance, they would just take a cab or get one of his family members to drive them.

"These streets are so bumpy," Maeve commented as she inspected the cobblestone streets of downtown. "You must have to drive so slowly over them."

Fletcher smirked. "Well, you're supposed to. But trust me, we tested that limit quite a bit as teenagers."

She grinned up at him. "What other limits did you test?"

He bumped her hip playfully as they walked down the sidewalk. "Wouldn't you like to know."

"I really would."

He ran his fingers down his jaw. "Well, I was obviously the most well behaved of the bunch. I had to try and set a good example for Jack and Beau. But they were young enough when I was in my late teens not to pick up on most of the stuff I was doing, like driving too fast down Main Street or drinking at beach bonfire parties—that sort of thing. Not that those even happened very often."

Maeve shook her head. "Why am I so surprised every time you admit to doing something reckless?"

He shrugged. "Well, I suppose because I come off pretty..." It took him a moment to choose an adjective. "Straightlaced."

"You do," she said. "You've got the nice clothes, and the clean apartment, and the respectable job. But then you do things like suggest strip *Scrabble*, or show me a tattoo on your ass, and I realize that you're so much more than that, too. You're fun and a little bit daring. And yes, you may have made a mistake or two in your life, but you're just human, Fletcher. I like when you let me see that side of yourself."

He wished he could reach out and grab her hand, give it a squeeze to thank her for reminding him that it was okay for him to be human, but the bags in his hands kept him from doing that.

"It's not always…easy…for me to just let loose and enjoy life. My position in my family, my job…they don't leave a lot of room for hedonism. I've spent a long time trying to fill my father's shoes and be an upstanding citizen and an overall good role model. But it wasn't always what was best for me. I think that's what led me to stay too long with Christa. I had the job, and the partner, and all the things people expected me to have at my age, and I never wanted to rock the boat.

"To be honest, I think that's part of what drew me to you at first. Taking you home that night at the bar felt so…carefree. For once in my life, I wasn't doing the thing everyone expected me to. I don't know. I guess I'm sowing my wild oats."

Maeve was silent for a few moments, and the longer it lasted, the more worried he became. Peering down, he tried to gauge her reaction.

Her brows were drawn together in bewilderment. "Are you saying I'm an oat?"

There was humor in her words, but they were also laced with vulnerability, and Fletcher sensed that her question was an important one.

"Not at all," he said. "You're more like the whole container of oats. Everything I've ever needed and everything

I didn't even realize I wanted. I don't need any other oats because I've already found a lifetime's supply of them in you."

It took him a few seconds to register that Maeve was no longer beside him. She'd stopped in her tracks a couple of paces back on the sidewalk. Fletcher backed up until they were side by side again.

"Is something wrong?"

She stared at him, slack jawed. "No, it's just...how do you always know the sweetest things to say to me?"

He shrugged. "I'm not really trying to be sweet. Just honest."

She shook her head, wearing a look of disbelief mixed with a dash of wonder. "I can tell. The things you say...the things you do...they're not calculated. Not manipulative. Just straightforward."

He narrowed his eyes at the incredulity in her tone. "Is that not what you're used to?"

As if only then realizing what she'd revealed, Maeve shrugged and began walking again. "I guess not."

Fletcher allowed her to brush off the subject, understanding that it would be a big step for her to tell him more about her past relationship, but filed away that information. Maeve didn't talk much about her ex-husband. Then again, he supposed he didn't talk much about Christa.

But Maeve's ex had been a spouse. The father of her children. One didn't just end a relationship like that and leave unscathed. That type of breakup left a mark.

Fletcher had already seen evidence of that mark in her reluctance to let him in. In the way she'd run off in the middle of the night that first time they slept together. In the insistence that he didn't have to use his mouth to pleasure her because her ex hadn't been patient enough to do so. And now, in her surprise that his words and actions were always so genuine.

He wondered if the fact that she never wanted to remove her top during sex was a residual effect of that marriage as well. He had to assume so. There were other oddities, too, like when she had insisted he not call her Mae. Was that because her husband had called her that? There were so many things he still didn't know.

One day, Fletcher would ask about that bastard and every single thing he'd ever done to make Maeve insecure or uncomfortable, and then he would do all the opposite things. But it wasn't quite time to dive into that conversation. Slowly —so slowly—she was letting down her defenses, but getting to know Maeve was a bit like coaxing a cornered animal. It required time and tenderness, patience and persistence.

Hopefully, this weekend and meeting his family would deepen their relationship to a point where she trusted him with her full story. Little by little, bit by bit, Maeve was becoming an important fixture in his life. It didn't bother him that she was taking time to open up, but it sure would be great to know all of her.

22

After checking in to the hotel and dropping off their bags, Fletcher took Maeve on a tour of all his favorite spots in town. They walked the perimeter of downtown while he pointed out the movie theater where he'd gone on his first date, the candy shop where he'd spent all his allowance as a kid, and the library where he'd learned to love books and reading.

In the end, they wound up dangling their legs over the edge of the dock at Easy Street harbor. At low tide, the water was far below their feet, but the breeze off the ocean kept them refreshed. A family of ducklings swam laps around the boats anchored there as they bobbed up and down over the gentle waves.

"This is so beautiful," Maeve said as she rested her head against his shoulder.

Fletcher glanced down at her and kissed the top of her head. "I agree."

He could hear the smile in her voice when she said, "Stop doing that."

"Stop doing what?"

"Stop taking my comments about the beautiful views and turning them back on me. It's cheesy."

"I think it's romantic."

She squeezed his thigh. "It is. But it's also cheesy."

He kissed her hair again. They lounged there for a few more minutes, enjoying the view and being in each other's arms, before Fletcher glanced down at his watch.

"The rehearsal dinner starts in about an hour and a half. We'd better get back to the hotel so we can get ready."

Maeve let loose a hefty sigh, snuggling further into his chest for a moment before retreating.

He cocked a brow. "Nervous?"

"Yes," she replied in a tone that said *duh*.

"It'll be fine," he said, standing and reaching a hand down to help her up. "In fact, it'll be great."

"Great for you, maybe," Maeve said as she got herself up off the ground, and they began the walk back to the hotel. "I'll spend the whole time hoping I don't have pit stains on my dress from the nervous sweating I'll be doing."

"Do you want to borrow my deodorant?" he asked. "It's extra strength."

Maeve punched him gently in the arm. "I'm serious."

"So am I."

"No," she said, reaching for his hand and interlacing their fingers. "I just need your hand to hold."

Donning her favorite forest-green wrap dress like armor, Maeve slipped into a pair of wedges and applied some fresh makeup to her face. Fletcher was out in the main part of the hotel room, getting dressed, while she used the bathroom mirror to beautify. He was just pulling on his shoes when she entered the room.

"Damn," he said, his gaze blazing a trail from her head to her toes, lagging when it reached her chest. Maeve knew her breasts looked fantastic in the dress—that was why she'd worn it both on her first date with Fletcher and to this rehearsal dinner—but from his reaction, one would think she'd come out wearing an evening gown.

"You've already seen me in this dress," she pointed out.

"It doesn't matter," he said. "Every time I see you, I'm blown away."

A blush that had nothing to do with the makeup she'd just applied seeped into her cheeks. There he went again with the sweet comments.

"You look...dashing," she replied, taking in his crisp button-up shirt, dress pants, and sharp loafers. She took a few steps closer until they were side by side.

"Dashing, huh?" he teased, lifting an eyebrow.

"Sounds like one of our *Scrabble* words, doesn't it?"

Fletcher ran his fingers over her exposed décolletage, eliciting a full-body shiver. "We may just have to play again one of these days," he said in a low voice.

Maeve subtly halted his hand before it could slip beneath the shoulder of her dress by twining their fingers together. "Are you sure you're not afraid of losing again?"

He grinned and leaned in to whisper in her ear. "If I recall, losing turned out pretty well for me last time."

When his lips came back into view, Maeve dropped a kiss on them, her wedges putting her at an ideal height to reach him. Fletcher wrapped his arms around her and pulled her close, stroking his hands up and down her back and just holding her. Any nerves she'd been feeling about meeting his family melted away as she relaxed in his arms.

"Ready to go?" he asked.

She pulled back, grateful Fletcher kept her hand tucked safely in his.

"Ready as I'll ever be."

They walked, hand in hand, a short distance down the street to Danny's Place, where the rehearsal dinner was being held. Maeve was a little unsteady on her feet as she attempted to cross the crushed-seashell driveway in her wedges, so Fletcher tugged his hand away and, instead, wrapped an arm around her waist to keep her steady.

They entered the establishment that way, with her clinging to his side, and they instantly garnered curious stares from almost everyone in the place. There was a momentary pause as every single person there inspected them before Maeve managed to distance herself by a couple of inches.

"Hi!" called a young woman with gorgeous, beachy, blonde waves—the first to break the silence.

"Bro!" exclaimed the man beside her, his messy brown curls flopping over his forehead.

"Hey, Jack, Natalie," Fletcher said. "This is Maeve."

Fletcher's brother and his wife shook her hand, and she donned her brave face—the one no one would ever question. The one she'd perfected long ago.

"Nice to meet you both."

"It's so great to meet you," Natalie said. "We're all so excited that Fletcher brought you."

Jack nodded his agreement. "And welcome to Nantucket. Have you ever been to the island before?"

"No," Maeve answered. "I'm from California, and this is my first time on the East Coast, actually."

"Oh," Jack said. "Well, welcome. What brought you here?"

"Uh…" Maeve floundered for a moment. She really should have anticipated the question, given that most people didn't just decide to up and leave their home to move clear across the country without a good reason. "I just felt like we needed a fresh start."

"Fletcher mentioned that you have kids," Natalie said. "We have two of our own, Carter and Noah." She pointed to a little blond boy and a chunky brunet baby, who were both currently in the lap of an older woman that Maeve guessed was Fletcher's mother.

"They're adorable," she replied, smiling as the older boy gently ran his hands over the baby's hair. She remembered when Andy and Allie were those ages. These boys probably had a similar age difference as her own children, so she trusted that they would grow up to be good friends just like hers were.

"Thanks," Natalie said as she watched the interaction herself.

Another couple began making their way over, and Jack and Natalie stepped to the side as the other man pulled Fletcher into a bear hug. It caused him to let go of Maeve, but only for a moment. Once he was released, his arm found its way back around her, draping over her shoulders this time.

"Hey, Fletch," the man said as he, too, reached out for his woman.

"Hey, Beau, Emma. Meet Maeve," Fletcher replied.

Emma, a petite, fairy-like woman with a halo of light-blonde hair gave him a swift half hug, then did the same with Maeve.

"Nice to meet you," she said.

"You're the bride and groom, right?" Maeve asked. "Congratulations!"

"That's right," Beau answered as he pressed a kiss to the top of his fiancée's head. "At least, we will be in twenty-four hours."

"That's so exciting," Maeve gushed. "It's an honor to be here. Thank you for having me."

Beau clapped his brother on the shoulder. "Thank *you* for coming. I haven't seen my brother as happy as he is with you in a long time."

Maeve glanced at Fletcher in surprise, but he had no reaction other than a slight narrowing of his eyes.

"I'm going to go introduce Maeve to Mom," he said, steering her in the direction of the older woman. The blond boy had already hopped off her lap, leaving only the baby bouncing on her knee. She treated them to a wide smile as they approached.

"Hey, Mom. I want you to meet Maeve," Fletcher said.

The woman stood up, bringing the baby to her hip and reaching out her hand to shake Maeve's. "Hi, Maeve."

"It's so nice to meet you, Mrs. McNally," Maeve said, and for some unknown reason, the thought struck her that Mrs. Maeve McNally had a nice ring to it.

"Please, call me June," the woman said. "And this here is Noah."

June waved exaggeratedly, and the baby imitated her, flailing his little hand in greeting.

"Hi, Noah," Maeve said, totally charmed by the little guy. Fletcher obviously was, too.

"Mind if I steal him?" he asked, even as he was already plucking the baby from his mother's arms.

June shook her head and turned toward Maeve. "You can't keep him away from the kids at these types of things. He'll probably even be sitting at the kids' table at dinner."

Maeve grinned at the thought. "Well, luckily, I'm used to that, having two of my own."

"Fletcher said that you have a couple of kids in his school. They sound really wonderful. I hope I'll get to meet them someday," June said, a knowing twinkle in her eye.

The sentiment surprised Maeve but left her feeling remarkably warm inside. "I'd like that."

"And there's the other little rascal," Fletcher said as the blond boy ran into his leg and began attempting to tickle him. Fletcher leaned down and tickled his fingers under the boy's armpit until he squealed for mercy, quickly winning the tickle fight. "Carter, this is Maeve," he said when their simultaneous laughter died down.

Carter looked up at her with big blue eyes. "Are you his girlfriend?"

What was it with kids and asking that question?

"We're good friends," Maeve replied. "Nice to meet you, Carter."

The boy seemed to accept that, easily running off and finding someone else to tickle. Fletcher led Maeve over to the one remaining couple in the room and introduced her to Beau's best friend, Diego, and his wife, Isabella. Once she'd met everyone in attendance, they continued roaming around and chatting with Fletcher's loved ones.

About a half hour later, Maeve realized that Fletcher hadn't put down or passed off the baby once since they had arrived. It was equally surprising to her that he was so interested in spending time with the baby and that she had hardly noticed because he was so natural with him. Each time the baby gurgled or made a noise, Fletcher would glance down to check on him and soothe him by bouncing or rocking him if needed.

When it came time for dinner, Fletcher opted to sit at the adult's table next to Maeve, but right beside where the kids were sitting, in case they needed help with anything. He claimed it was to relieve Jack and Natalie so they could enjoy the dinner without worrying too much about their kids, but Maeve suspected that he just really liked being with them.

At the start of dinner, June stood up to make a toast. She captured everyone's attention by tapping her knife gently against the side of her champagne flute.

"That's not nice. You might break the cup," Carter said in the matter-of-fact way that children do.

June placed the knife back down on the table. "You're right. Thank you for reminding me, Carter." Then, she looked around the table, smiling at each of their faces before beginning her speech. "Thank you all so much for gathering here as we prepare to celebrate Beau and Emma's marriage tomorrow. To be honest, I thought this day was a long way off. My youngest son has never been the most, shall we say, mature, and I certainly didn't expect him to be ready for marriage so soon."

Everyone chuckled at that except Fletcher, who tensed almost imperceptibly. The reaction was so slight that Maeve was sure no one else had noticed it, but she certainly had. She wondered what had caused it but didn't have the chance to ask.

"But somehow, the right woman came into his life, and together, they became a strong couple and even stronger people. I couldn't imagine a better partner for my son or addition to our family than Emma. Emma, sweetheart, we are so excited to welcome you into our family. I wish you both a long, happy marriage." She lifted her glass higher in the air, signaling for everyone else to do the same. "To Beau and Emma."

"To Beau and Emma." Everyone lifted their glasses of champagne or sparkling juice and toasted to the couple before digging into their meals.

As she ate dinner and continued to converse with everyone at the table, Maeve realized that she no longer felt even an ounce of anxiety around Fletcher's family. Everyone was so nice and welcoming that she had no room to worry. Though she didn't quite feel entrenched in the close-knit group yet, she no longer felt like an outsider, as she had before meeting them.

She wasn't used to big, happy family gatherings like this. Though she got along well with her parents and loved them very much, Maeve hadn't lived close to them since she'd gotten together with Jason and moved to California. In hindsight, she also realized that he had largely kept her from her family by insisting they celebrate holidays just as a family of four. He'd always convinced her not to spend her money on airline flights to Indiana when that money could be better spent on vacations. The list of red flags seemed never-ending at this point.

The fact that Fletcher made an effort to see his family and so obviously loved them was exceedingly attractive to Maeve. The thought that she could one day be part of a family like this was even more so.

23

The rehearsal dinner lasted into the night, long after Carter and Noah had gone to bed. June retired fairly early as well, and Diego and Isabella decided to leave to give the McNally men some time to hang out with just each other and their significant others. The six of them had spilled onto the beach behind Danny's to have a bonfire, an activity that had apparently become a favorite pastime when Beau and Fletcher visited. Maeve learned that the tradition had started out rocky, with a bonfire at which Jack and Natalie had broken up. After that, though, their bonfires had gone much more smoothly.

Sitting around the blazing fire, they told funny childhood stories, toasted marshmallows for s'mores, and polished off the last bottle of champagne. Close to eleven, Emma announced that she needed to get her rest before the big day, and Beau refused to stay at the fire without her, so they headed to their room for the night. Jack and Natalie lamented that they would have to be up early with the kids, so they took off as well.

After ensuring that the flames were thoroughly extinguished, Fletcher began walking Maeve back to their hotel, holding onto her extra tightly because the champagne plus the wedges equaled lots of stumbling.

"Thanks for coming tonight," he said. "Was it as scary as you thought it was going to be?"

Maeve shook her head. "I had a lot of fun. Your family is fantastic."

Fletcher's chest warmed. "I agree. I think they really liked you, too."

In fact, he knew that his family liked Maeve, because they had all pulled him aside at some point or other to tell him so. His mother had been sweet about it, saying that Maeve seemed like a wonderful woman and a good fit for him. Jack had basically said, "She's hot. Good for you." And Beau had predictably bashed Christa before saying how much better he liked Maeve. Despite their unique ways of giving their approval, Fletcher appreciated that all three of them had expressed a liking for Maeve.

"You really loved being with Noah, huh?" Maeve asked.

Fletcher grinned as he pictured the chubby baby. "Yeah. Jack and Natalie's kids are awesome. I can't wait to have some of my own one day." He was dreaming about babies and fatherhood and starting a family when he realized that Maeve had remained silent.

"Everything okay?" He glanced down at her but could only see the top of her head.

"Yeah, fine," she answered. "What about you? Something your mom said during her toast seemed to upset you."

Fletcher's steps stuttered momentarily. "You noticed that?"

He thought he'd done such a great job at hiding his feelings. When his mother mentioned that Beau was the least-mature sibling and she couldn't believe he was getting married so soon, all Fletcher heard was *I can't believe Fletcher hasn't gotten married yet.* He knew it was silly. Logically, he understood that. But the tug of jealousy still pulled at him.

Leave it to Maeve to be more perceptive of his emotions than his own family.

She shrugged. "You didn't laugh when everyone else did. I just felt like something she said bothered you."

He let loose a sigh. "It wasn't a huge deal, but something innocuous my mother said had me feeling bad about being the oldest brother and the last to get married."

"That seems like something that really bothers you."

"It is. As much as I don't want it to. But dammit, I'm the oldest. I'm the most mature. I'm the most natural caretaker. I'm the one who's always wanted a family. Why am I the last to get one?"

Maeve was quiet and thoughtful for a moment before squeezing his hand. "One day, you will. It just takes meeting the right person at the right time."

He accepted her reassurance and rubbed his thumb over her hand, desperately wishing she would accept that she was that person. Instead, she shattered the seriousness of their conversation by saying, "Innocuous. There's another *Scrabble* word for you."

Back at the hotel, Fletcher left Maeve in the bedroom to change into her pajamas while he used the bathroom, washed his face, and slipped into his own nightwear—a t-shirt and boxers that he hoped he wouldn't be wearing for long.

Seeing Maeve get along so well with his family, seeing her fit into his world so naturally, only cemented his attraction to her. She was so sweet, indulging his nephews with attention the same way he did. She was intuitive, reading him so clearly when he thought he could hide his emotions from the world. And that green dress she had worn...well, he had some memories of the last time she'd worn that dress. Memories tinged with the taste of her, the feel of her heat, the sound of her moans…

God, he was going to be hard before he even got back to the bedroom.

He'd never had two nights in a row with Maeve before, so this weekend was a rare treat. The chance to worship her body all night, then wake up beside her sleepy figure not one but *two* mornings in a row was an opportunity he wasn't going to take for granted.

After brushing his teeth to ensure his breath was minty fresh and shaving off the day's stubble so he wouldn't scratch Maeve's beautiful, petal-soft skin as he ravished it, Fletcher opened the door adjoining the bathroom to the bedroom… and found her fast asleep on the hotel bed.

He couldn't help but smile as he took in her slumbering form, her red hair splashed across a pillow. To his delight, he realized she'd pilfered one of his large t-shirts from his suitcase and was wearing that as her sleepwear. One of his goals for this weekend was to coax her to bare herself fully to him by assuring her that he thought she was beautiful no matter what, but the sight of her in his clothes almost beat the theoretical sight of her fully naked.

Quietly shutting out the light, he tiptoed toward the bed. Despite his high hopes for their nights at the hotel, it would be a treat just to hold Maeve as she slept. She made a small noise as the mattress dipped and Fletcher slid in beside her.

"Shh," he whispered, draping one arm around her middle and gently tugging her closer to him until they were spooning. "Sleep, Maeve."

She didn't fight him, her breaths evening out until they were as steady as they had been before he'd disturbed her. Fletcher settled into the mattress, enjoying the weight of her body pressed against him. He inhaled the floral scent of her hair, finding it relaxing and refreshing, though that could also just have been from her closeness. When Maeve was in his arms, nothing could disturb him.

Maeve was awakened by bright sunlight filtering in through the hotel window. They must have forgotten to shut the curtains all the way the night before, which was understandable given how late they'd gotten back and how exhausted she had been. The rehearsal dinner and bonfire afterward had been so much fun, but champagne and socialization after a long day of travel had left her weary.

She began to stretch out, then froze when she registered Fletcher's arm around her waist. *Shit.* She'd fallen asleep on him. They'd had a bit of an unspoken agreement that this time away would be an opportunity to continue exploring each other, and that included in the bedroom. Now they'd lost one of their two nights. She'd blown it. The guilt of falling asleep ate at her. Fletcher had insisted on paying for this room for them, and she hadn't even fulfilled her part of the implied bargain.

Would he be mad? All signs pointed to no, but old wounds still left her feeling uneasy about his potential reaction. Yet, he hadn't woken her up to have sex. He'd let her continue to sleep. And now, he had his arm wrapped protectively around her, as if needing to be close to her.

The moment she shifted to attempt to leave the bed, Fletcher stirred. His arm left her body as he stretched it up above his head, showing off the masculine tufts of hair beneath his armpits. Why that intimate little detail turned Maeve on, she wasn't sure, but one of the many things she'd learned about herself since meeting Fletcher was that body hair got her hot and bothered.

"Hey," he said, the corners of his lips turning up in a sleepy smile. "You fell asleep on me last night."

"I know," she said quickly. "I'm so sorry, Fletch. I was just exhausted after the long day, and this bed is really comfortable." She looked down at the damn soft, cozy comforter that had lulled her to sleep prematurely. "I promise I'll make it up to you."

"Hey," he said, his lips dipping into a frown. "You don't have to apologize. And you don't need to make anything up to me." He cupped her face in his palm. "Maeve, I came into this weekend with no expectations other than to spend time with you and to see my baby brother get married. If you'd wanted to get separate hotel rooms, I would have been fine with that. Though, I have to say, I'm really glad we didn't. I love sleeping beside you."

Disbelief and delight warred for the top spot in her mind. "I love sleeping beside you, too. I just thought… I thought you wanted more than that."

"Of course I do." Fletcher stroked her cheek. "I want everything with you. But you were tired, and I wanted you to get the rest you needed more than I wanted to make love to you."

Maeve's eyes burned with unshed tears. The way he'd put her needs first felt so unfamiliar that she would have had a hard time believing he was serious if the sincerity on his face hadn't been so convincing.

"Thank you. I really do want to make it up to you tonight, though. Make it up to both of us."

He leaned in to place a kiss on the tip of her nose. "No pressure."

"Trust me, I know there's not pressure from you, but my body is putting the pressure on me."

He chuckled as he pulled away. "I know the feeling. I wish we could spend all morning in bed, but I promised Jack and

Natalie we'd come over for breakfast and help watch the kids while they get ready."

Maeve mourned the loss of his touch but looked forward to spending more time with his family. "That sounds lovely."

"If you want, we can pack up everything we'll need for the wedding and bring it all to Jack and Natalie's apartment, then get ready there. The reception will be downstairs in the café, so it'll be super convenient."

"That sounds great."

24

———

The morning passed in a rush of fancy clothes, fragrant flowers, and other wedding preparations. Maeve brought all three potential dresses she had packed for the wedding and chose the one closest to the style of Natalie's, which was a knee-length, sage-green cocktail dress. Emma's other bridesmaid, Isabella, would wear the same dress as Natalie, and Beau and Fletcher would wear gray slacks and sage-green dress shirts with light-gray ties.

Maeve's cocktail-style dress was a deep-purple number with ruffle sleeves and a skirt that hit just above the knee. She had long ago discovered that jewel tones complemented her hair and skin tone best, so she tended to stick to a color palette of emerald, amethyst, sapphire, and ruby. Though unable to do her bold lip as desired, she'd brought a plum-colored eyeshadow that complemented her dress well.

By one-thirty, they were all ready for the two o'clock wedding and were just hanging out in Jack and Natalie's apartment. Carter looked dapper in his own miniature-sized groomsman outfit. He was slated to be the ring bearer, and he was taking his job very seriously. He'd been practicing his walk down the aisle all morning. Noah had on a onesie that looked like a little tuxedo, which didn't match the vibe of the wedding at all, but he looked so precious that no one seemed to care.

At one forty-five, June came to gather everyone and shepherded them into the three Jeeps they would take to the beach where the ceremony would be held. Once there, the wedding party got into place, all lined up to walk down the aisle. Since Maeve wasn't part of that group, she was led to the small row of chairs where she sat beside Isabella's husband. Maeve had the pleasure of holding Noah in her lap for the ceremony while Diego had been tasked with snapping photos of it on his phone.

The baby gurgled and pulled at Maeve's hair, which she'd put half up and half down.

"Hi, Noah," she said, giving his chunky thighs a squeeze.

The baby giggled, and drool began dribbling down his face.

"Oh!" she said, not wanting him to ruin his adorable outfit with drool. "Here." She grabbed a burping cloth from the diaper bag Natalie had given her before spit could dampen Noah's clothing.

"You're a natural," Diego said as he lined up his cell phone camera to face the aisle.

"Raising two kids gives you lightning-fast reflexes," Maeve replied.

He chuckled. "I'll bet. Do you think you'll ever have more?"

It was a valid question, given that Maeve was still young enough to have more kids. Sure, she was at the older end of the typical child-bearing years at thirty-six, but women were having kids later and later in life thanks to scientific advancements. However, her reasons for not having more kids were a little more complicated than age.

"No," she answered. "Two is plenty for me."

Diego nodded. "I'm sure two is a handful. Actually, two handfuls! I think—"

He was cut off when music started up from the lone guitarist and singer that had been hired to play the wedding ceremony.

"Let's talk later," he said before giving his full attention to his picture-taking duties.

Maeve took another peek down at Noah. Despite knowing she never could or would have more children, interacting with him made her just a little more wistful than usual about it. She didn't have long to dwell on that sorrow because, moments later, the wedding party began their stroll down the aisle. Carter came first, bearing a box that (hopefully) contained both rings. Then came Jack and Natalie, who made a stunning couple. Natalie's long, dark-blonde hair had been woven into intricate braids, then secured into a low bun at her neck. Jack grinned proudly as he held her arm in the crook of his, and they made their way up to the wedding arch.

Fletcher and Isabella walked behind them, and even knowing that they weren't a couple and that Isabella was happily married to the man beside her, Maeve still felt a pang of jealousy in her gut, seeing them walk up the aisle together. Isabella's inky black hair wasn't long enough to be fashioned the way Natalie's had been. Instead, she'd kept it down and simply braided sections on either side to create a crown of sorts atop her head.

Fletcher looked beyond handsome in his gray and green outfit. The way his slacks hugged his ass should have been illegal. Maeve was disappointed when he got to the front of the aisle and turned around to stand and face the crowd—if Maeve, Diego, and June could be considered a crowd, that is.

The ceremony moved quickly after that, with the officiant saying a few words before June did a reading. Maeve cuddled baby Noah in her lap as June read a passage about love, commitment, and forever. The older woman teared up somewhere in the middle, no doubt overwhelmed with feelings about her youngest son getting married, and perhaps remembering her own marriage as well. Maeve gave Noah, whose namesake was June's late husband, an extra squeeze.

After that came the vows. Emma and Beau had written their own sets of promises to each other, each of which had Maeve tearing up herself. It was so clear that the two adored each other, and it was also clear they were entering into a healthy, equitable marriage.

Finally, the officiant announced that Beau could kiss his bride, and he did so eagerly, sealing his mouth over Emma's and dipping her with a dramatic flourish. When he eventually pulled away, Emma's cheeks were bright pink with embarrassment, but the wide grin she wore beneath proved that she was just as ecstatic as her new husband was.

As the brief ceremony came to a close, everyone piled back into the Jeeps and headed to Danny's Place, where all the bistro tables had been pushed together to create the illusion of one long table. Centerpieces of fragrant eucalyptus, fat white roses, and delicate baby's breath were placed at intervals all along the table. Each seat had a little place card with names inscribed in gold calligraphy.

Little white fairy lights had been strung across the large windows, and mason jars filled with the same style of lights adorned surfaces throughout the café. The jars reminded Maeve of catching fireflies as a child, when she would frolic around her yard, capturing the little creatures, only to release them minutes later for fear of forcing them to remain too long somewhere they weren't comfortable. The irony of that thought juxtaposed with how her early adult life had played out wasn't lost on her.

The diner-esque bar at the front of the room had been draped with white tablecloths and was home to many of the magical little jars. It also housed two large, glass drink dispensers filled with colorful liquids. Little chalkboard signs explained that one was a red wine sangria with notes of apple, orange, and strawberry, and the other was a mocktail of a similar fashion made with the same fruit flavors.

The atmosphere was completely transformed from the previous night, when Danny's had still felt like a café. Tonight, it felt more like a romantic villa somewhere in Europe, a place where love could thrive and even one's wildest dreams could come true. The pure magic in the air and the elegance of the reception area fleetingly reminded Maeve of how she'd never gotten her dream wedding. She'd never gotten the poofy white dress, or the acoustic wedding march, or the exquisite reception with a three-tiered cake covered in fluffy white frosting.

No, Jason had insisted on a courthouse ceremony to save money, and he'd rushed the process so much that she hadn't even had the chance to invite her parents. They had used a city employee as their witness. Regret at going along with Jason's decision, and the dozens of decisions that had come after that, swam in Maeve's gut.

There was no time to dwell on her sorrow because Fletcher soon walked into the space, marching right up to her and planting a kiss square on her lips. The wedding party must have already taken a stab at the sangria because he tasted like apples, and oranges, and happily ever afters.

"Hi," he said when he pulled away.

"Hi," Maeve replied, giving him what was surely a goofy grin, but she couldn't help the pure joy she felt in that moment. "You looked good up there."

Fletcher smirked and straightened his tie. "I'm glad you think so, because I was trying my best to impress you."

"Well, you certainly accomplished that," she said, patting his chest. "You looked great walking up that aisle. Though, I have to say, you looked even better walking away." She surreptitiously wound her arm around his waist, tucked her hand into his back pocket, and squeezed.

To her delight, Fletcher's mouth fell open in shock, and Maeve left him with his mouth agape as she took off to get herself a glass of sangria. Jack and Natalie were getting the kids settled at the table, June was fiddling with the decorations as if they didn't already look perfect, and Diego was outside taking photos of Emma and Beau as Isabella directed the photo shoot, which left Maeve and Fletcher with a touch of privacy.

As she was dispensing the sweet drink into her glass, she felt his hands clutch at her waist and his breath ghost over the shell of her ear.

"If you're going to tease me like that, we're not going to make it through this whole reception."

Maeve calmly removed her fingers from the spigot and brought the glass to her lips to take a leisurely sip. "We are going to make it through this reception, and we're going to celebrate your brother's marriage, and spend more time with your family, and then we're going to go back to our hotel room and make up for everything we missed out on last night."

Fletcher's hands tightened on her waist. "Is that a promise?"

She nodded, feeling his breath trailing along her neck as she did. "Oh yes."

He placed a kiss on the sensitive spot behind her ear. "Good. But you know it's okay if you fall asleep again."

Maeve placed her free hand over one of his on her waist. "I know it is. But I'm determined not to let that happen. We have one more night here without any kids or life responsibilities to worry about, and I'm going to take advantage of it."

Fletcher's lips found another sensitive spot on her jawline. "That's what I like to hear."

"Hey, I think they're coming!" Natalie cried.

Seeming reluctant, Fletcher slowly released his grip on Maeve's waist and turned her around so they could both watch Emma and Beau make their way inside. Everyone clapped as the bride and groom entered, and Beau twirled

Emma in the doorway before dipping her low for another impressive kiss. At this, Jack hooted and hollered, and Fletcher dog-whistled, much to the delight of the two kids who were eager to get in on the action themselves. Noah clapped his chubby hands while Carter scrambled off the chair that Natalie had finally gotten him situated in to do an enthusiastic little dance in the center of the room.

"They look so happy," Maeve murmured as she watched the couple revel in the attentions of their loved ones.

Fletcher pulled her closer into his side. "They are. Let's go celebrate them so that we can get back to the hotel and celebrate us."

25

———————

Despite enjoying the company of his family, Fletcher was dying to get out of the reception. They had eaten, drank, talked, and laughed. They had thoroughly celebrated, and he was about ready to burst with need if he didn't get Maeve out of there soon.

Every sway of her hips beneath that purple dress had him growing harder. Her cheeks were painted pink from the alcohol she'd been sipping on, and tendrils of her hair had come loose from her updo and were now draped around her face like a frame outlining the most beautiful sight he'd ever seen.

She was currently across the room, chatting with Natalie, and Fletcher was watching her like a lonely puppy. Just as he was considering grabbing Maeve and whisking her back to their hotel room, Beau stood and gathered everyone's attention by clearing his throat in the loudest, most obnoxious way possible. Once he had everyone's eyes on him, he pulled Emma into his side and made his announcement.

"My beautiful bride isn't one to enjoy being in the spotlight, so we'd like to invite everyone to join us for one dance that will be our first dance together as husband and wife."

A moment later, the opening beats of "Can't Help Falling in Love" came on over a wireless speaker, and Elvis Presley's voice began crooning about wise men and fools. Suddenly, Fletcher's burning need to leave with Maeve was replaced by a need to gather her in his arms and dance with her.

He barely noticed Jack and Natalie exchanging heated looks, or Diego and Isabella sharing a grin, or June beginning to sway side to side with baby Noah in her arms, because he was so preoccupied with winding his way across the room to get his woman. He did, however, note Carter breakdancing on the floor as if he was hearing an entirely different song. That little dude's antics were hard to miss, but that didn't stop Fletcher from catching Maeve in his embrace just as words about a river flowing to the sea rang out.

Beaming up at him, she placed one hand on his shoulder as he wound his around her waist. Their free hands came together, hers fitting into his like a complementary puzzle piece.

Each line of the song seemed more and more fitting. From their serendipitous first meeting, to realizing Fletcher was her children's principal, to every excuse he'd found to return to her home, it felt as if the universe kept pushing them together. Their relationship felt meant to be.

Maeve leaned forward so her cheek rested on his chest, and they swayed and rocked to the chorus. Fletcher couldn't help falling in love with this woman. They hadn't used the words yet, but with her face buried in his chest and her hand securely in his, he was pretty sure Maeve loved him, too. They finished out the song that way, pressed up against each other and moving slowly to the music, only breaking apart when it finally stopped.

Maeve looked up at him with hazy eyes, as if she was in a daze. He felt the same way—drugged with lust and ready to lay his world at her feet.

Luckily, Fletcher had been previously informed that there

would only be one dance, and that it would be occurring at the end of the reception, so he had no qualms about grabbing Maeve's hand and pulling her toward the door.

"Let's get going."

"Wait." She tugged him back. "We have to say goodbye to your family first."

Suppressing a groan, Fletcher hung his head. "Fine."

At Maeve's insistence, he hurried around the room, saying his goodbyes and passing out hugs and kisses on cheeks. On the other hand, she took her time, gushing to everyone about how great it had been to meet them, and how happy she was for the newly married couple, and how much she hoped she would be back on the island in the future.

Fletcher's chest ached with satisfaction at the thought of bringing Maeve back to his hometown again and again—and Allie and Andy, too. He hoped they would be taking lots of trips here and maybe, one day, even having their own wedding right out there on that beach. It was a huge jump from where they were at the moment, but nonetheless, Fletcher longed for the day that wish may come true.

"Now can we go?" he asked after Maeve had said goodbye to the last of the crowd.

"Usually you're the one talking to children, but right now you sound like one," she said with a smirk.

He took a step closer so she was forced to tilt her head back to keep his gaze. "Why don't we go back to the hotel, and I can show you just how much I'm *not* a child," he suggested.

Maeve blinked, losing a smidge of her bravado before pasting that smirk back on her face. "Trust me, I know just how much of a man you are," she said, her gaze flicking down to where his erection was beginning to become visible behind his fly. He knew it was only a matter of minutes and a few more snarky comments before he would be pinning her up against the wall and kissing her without regard for who might have been watching.

"I'm about to embarrass myself in front of my entire family if we don't leave right now," he warned.

A satisfied grin played on her lips as she uncrossed her arms. "I guess we'd better get going, then."

~

Maeve felt as if she was walking on air as Fletcher led her back to the hotel, clutching her hand in his as if she might otherwise float away like an untethered balloon. Weddings always put her in a romantic mood, and the sight of Fletcher looking so handsome in his groomsman's outfit had only fed her desire. And that slow dance… Well, it was a good thing the hotel wasn't far.

It took Fletcher three tries to successfully scan the key to unlock the door to their room, and once it finally opened, it was a race to the bed. They tumbled onto the mattress in a tangle of limbs and fancy clothing. His mouth was hot on Maeve's neck as her hands explored his back, tugging his shirt from his pants so she could press her palms against his bare skin.

A noise escaped Fletcher's throat as she ran her fingernails lightly up his spine. His lips broke free from her neck only to capture her mouth a split second later. The urgency of his kiss revealed that he'd been holding in his desire for far too long. Luckily, Maeve didn't mind being the recipient of all that pent-up lust.

"Take this off," she said in a rush of breath as she tugged at his shirt.

Fletcher's lips remained on hers for one more long, delicious moment before he slid himself backward off the bed and hastily unbuttoned his shirt. She watched from beneath hooded eyelids as he shucked off the shirt and moved his hands lower. The metal on his watch clinked against the metal belt buckle as he undid it, then tore the belt off, tossing it onto a nearby chair. His swift efficiency both made her want to laugh and had heat swirling in her low belly.

"Come here," he said as he stood before the bed, fly undone but pants still on.

Maeve scooted herself forward to the edge of the bed, and Fletcher took her hands to help her stand. Delicately placing two fingers beneath her chin, he tipped her face up for a slower, sweeter kiss. This one was far more languid and leisurely than their previous one, almost as though he had tamed his lust with their encounter on the bed, though she knew it lingered just below the surface of his calm control.

"Sweetheart." Fletcher stroked his thumb along her jaw. "You look absolutely stunning in this dress, but I'm dying to see you out of it. Can we please take it off tonight?"

"Oh, uh…" Maeve floundered, her brain only working at half speed as it used up most of its energy on craving and pure want. When she didn't finish her thought, Fletcher ran a hand over her hair, tucking it behind her shoulders.

"I promise you, whatever is under there won't change how beautiful I think you are."

Dipping her gaze to the floor, Maeve chewed on her bottom lip. It was easy for him to say that her physical flaws wouldn't change his view of her, but how could she be positive that was true? She also knew that once he saw her fully naked, he'd have questions, and then she would be stuck with the options of either getting into an uncomfortable conversation that would derail their entire night…or lying. Neither of those options pleased her, but she would rather choose the one that would allow them to have this sought-after night together.

Fletcher gently guided her gaze back to his, where she found nothing but sincerity and what looked a whole lot like love. "Trust me," he whispered.

The gentle command paired with the hunger in his eyes

gave her the courage to nod. If he wanted to see beneath her dress so badly, she might as well let him. If he didn't like what he saw, then it wasn't worth pursuing something with him anyway.

"Okay," Maeve whispered. Taking a step back, she crossed her arms over her torso and grabbed a fistful of her dress in each hand. After a single deep breath, during which she bounced between feeling fearless and feeling as if she might vomit, she ripped the dress over her head. The thick material was such that she hadn't needed to wear a bra, so when the dress was gone, she was left in nothing but her panties.

Fletcher sucked in a breath. Maeve expected the worst from his reaction, but when she dared to glance at him, his gaze was pinned to her breasts. His brown eyes were molten as they studied her well-endowed chest. Her nipples hardened beneath his scrutiny, and a pleased grin stretched over Fletcher's mouth.

After an extended moment, his gaze traveled lower to her belly, with its faded stretch marks and C-section scar at the bottom, just above the line of her panties. To Maeve's relief, the heat in his eyes didn't diminish one bit. She held her breath as his gaze wandered back upward and came to rest on the large patch of puckered skin covering her left shoulder and upper arm.

The heat in his eyes dimmed to gentle warmth and understanding, but there were no traces of the pity she had so feared she would find. He stepped toward her and lifted a hand to hover over her scarred skin, waiting for permission to touch it. With much more courage than she felt, Maeve laid her hand over his, pressing it to her skin.

"Does it hurt?" he murmured.

"Not really," she replied. The burn scar was fully healed, and pressure against it didn't hurt. The skin was quite tight, which led to discomfort at times with certain movements, but overall, she was very lucky to have healed well.

Fletcher's fingers traced the scars, a grimace overtaking his features, as if he felt the pain of receiving them. "How did this happen?"

She pulled his hand into hers and squeezed. "It was silly. I had just made a piping hot cup of coffee, and I put it up on a shelf. I was distracted, probably helping the kids with something, and I bumped into it. The whole thing spilled down onto me."

The lie slid from her tongue so easily it was disgraceful. But thankfully, Fletcher seemed to buy it hook, line, and sinker.

"You got burned." He moved their joined hands back to her shoulder so he could run a fingertip over the ugly, uneven skin.

"Yes," she said. "When you're burned by liquid, they call it a scald burn. Mine was second-degree."

Doubt slid over his expression for the first time. "A second-degree burn from a hot coffee?"

"Well," she added quickly, "because it spilled onto the shirt I was wearing, and it took some time before I could get it off, my exposure to the heat was prolonged."

"Oh," he said, seeming distracted by the sight of his fingers against her scar. "It must have hurt so badly. How long was your recovery?"

She sighed as she felt the heat they'd built up slipping away. Maybe she should have just left her dress on.

"A few months until it was totally healed. I had to wrap it, and they put me on antibiotics in case of infection. I was lucky I didn't need a skin graft."

In a slow, calculated movement, Fletcher leaned in and placed a kiss on one of the nastier notches of her burn scar. "Thank you for telling me," he murmured. And then, as if it truly did not matter to him that one entire section of her body was burnt and scarred, he began pressing open-mouthed kisses to her neck and upper chest.

Maeve stood frozen, in disbelief that he was already ready to move on from her confession. She would have expected more questions, or more hesitancy to continue with their plan for the night, or more *something*. All he seemed to care about was whether or not he could hurt her by touching her there.

"Back on the bed," Fletcher said, already guiding her there with his hands clamped on her waist.

"O-okay," Maeve said as she lay back on the bed, the soft cotton of the sheets sliding against her bare back. Fletcher sidled up next to her, resting his cheek in his palm in a pose of ultimate leisure.

"Now that I have access to these," he said, bringing his other palm to cup one of her breasts. "I plan to spend some time enjoying them."

Maeve's breath hitched when his thumb brushed over her hardened nipple.

"And once I get my fill, I'll enjoy the rest of you as well," he said as he squeezed and released, lightly kneading her breast. "How does that sound?"

"That sounds g-good," she said, stumbling over her words when his fingers found her nipple again.

"Good," he said. In the next moment, he was leaning in and finding that sensitive nipple with his mouth. Her back arched off the bed as he suckled her between his lips. A moan rang out into the otherwise silent hotel room, and Maeve was stunned to realize it had come from her.

"That's it," Fletcher cooed as he dragged his tongue along the underside of one breast all the way to the other. "So fucking soft," he muttered before nuzzling his face in the center of her chest. She relished the feeling of his lips against those inches of skin she'd kept hidden away. She'd been so worried about eliciting pity or turning him off. Yet, here he was, worshipping her as he always had.

"Fletcher," she moaned as he sucked one nipple while his

fingers toyed with the other. As good as his mouth felt on this part of her body, she wanted more. *Needed* more.

"Hmm?" he mumbled, the sound vibrating against her areola. She glanced down to find his eyes closed and his brow furrowed in concentration as he remained singularly focused on exploring this new region of her. He was like a man on a mission, determined to see it through.

"Fletcher, I need you." She shifted her hips in an attempt to find friction.

"Mmm," he hummed, undeterred from his task. Rather than change course, he simply slid a hand down her body, cupping her with the lightest pressure as he continued his exploration of her breasts.

Maeve ground against his palm, eager and greedy and uncaring how needy she may seem. Fletcher released a low chuckle, his hot breath tickling her skin.

"Sweetheart," he said, his fingers beginning to trace slow circles over her opening as his tongue lavished her nipples. "I'm nowhere near done with this yet. Why don't you just lie back and relax? We have all night."

She groaned, frustrated. "Can't we just get on with it? You'll have plenty of opportunities to get to know my breasts, I swear."

The words left her mouth before she had a chance to think about their implications. She had essentially just sworn that they would be having sex plenty more times. Of course, she hoped that was the case, but tomorrow, they would be back to real life. Back to Boston, and the kids, and school. Back to difficulty carving out time to be alone together. Back to learning how to survive on her own and hoping she got no new texts from Jason.

Fletcher's head popped up for the very first time since his mouth had met her skin. His gaze burned into hers. "Promise?"

She stared into his eyes for a moment, soaking in the passion and intensity there. "I promise."

A slow, devilish grin bloomed on his face. He removed his hands from her body, leaving her bereft and wanting until she realized he was finally getting fully undressed.

"Okay." Fletcher tugged his pants down. "We'll do this your way." His boxers soon followed, and then he was back on the bed, crawling over her and sliding her panties down her legs. Once she was fully naked, he sat back and simply looked at her, his gaze roaming over every inch of her body.

Suddenly feeling self-conscious and very exposed, Maeve began to curl her limbs inward to hide all her good bits.

"Stop," Fletcher commanded, gently tugging her arms back to her sides. "You look so fucking gorgeous right now."

Still slightly shy but bolstered by his comment and the heat in his gaze, Maeve relaxed her body, allowing her legs to fall open a bit wider. His gaze snapped to the apex of her thighs.

"Goddamn," he breathed as he mounted her once again. Grabbing a handful of each of her breasts, he gave them a squeeze. "I'm dying to take you from behind, but I just can't bear to let these out of my sight."

She pushed her chest into his touch, her usual confidence restored. "Who says we can't do both? We have all night, remember?"

His answering grin was wicked. "Atta girl."

Quickly dismounting her, he grabbed a condom from his bag and stood at the foot of the bed. Tall, naked, and hard, he looked supremely powerful and *hot*.

"Let's try this," he said. Grabbing her ankles, he slid her to the bottom of the bed in one smooth movement. Maeve gasped in surprise.

"*Perfect*," he muttered as he lined himself up. The bed put them at just the right height for him to enter her while he stood. Taking her by the knees, he adjusted her to just the angle he wanted her at, with her legs bent toward her chest and spread open wide.

"Hold your legs," he instructed, patting the backs of her thighs. She obediently grabbed onto the spots he indicated, totally entranced by him when he got into this state. In the bedroom, he became commanding and dominant, shedding the Mr. Nice Guy persona he wore so much of the time. Yet, Maeve still felt fully certain that everything he did was to bring her maximal pleasure.

"That's it," he said as he slid his length through her wet slit, teasing her.

"Please," she begged breathlessly, beyond turned on by his commands and the vulnerable position he had her in.

"Is this what you want?" he asked, inserting just the tip of himself inside of her.

"*Yes*," she hissed through clenched teeth as she concentrated on holding her legs where he wanted them.

"That's what I thought." He slammed into her, and she was more than ready for him. Rocking in and out of her, he set a steady pace before reaching forward to grab her breasts.

"Perfect," he murmured again as he kneaded and squeezed and rocked and thrusted and generally drove her wild.

Maeve whimpered and lost her grip on one of her legs.

"Hold on," Fletcher said, guiding her hand back to its original spot. "I want to make you come like this, then I'll flip you onto your hands and knees, and we'll do it again."

His filthy words pushed her ten steps closer to coming, and Maeve longed to move and grind against him. To wrap her legs around him as tightly as possible or push her heels into the bed and meet him thrust for thrust. But at his instruction, she was held immobile and totally open to the immense pleasure he was bestowing upon her.

Leaning forward, Fletcher dipped his head to press a hard kiss on her lips, then moved down to her breasts, drawing a nipple into his mouth. He tugged it between his teeth, and that was her downfall. Maeve screamed his name as she came, helpless but to release her legs and ride the waves of pleasure.

Fletcher pressed his face into her neck as she came, pulsing around his still-hard length and panting like she'd run a marathon.

"Fuck, that was so sexy," he said when they had both caught their breath.

She wove her hands into his hair, tugging his head back until he met her eyes. "*You* are so sexy."

He pressed a shockingly chaste kiss to her forehead, considering he was still inside of her and hard as a rock. Maeve squirmed and clenched her inner muscles so they contracted around him. Fletcher's eyes flew to hers.

"Your turn," she said, scrambling out from beneath him and getting into position on all fours.

26

I f Fletcher had ever questioned whether he was a breast man or an ass man, seeing Maeve's perfect, pink-tipped mounds would have cemented that he was, in fact, a breast man. However, the position she was in now, ass up in the air and bared to him, had him questioning everything.

On a growl, he went on his knees on the bed behind Maeve, admiring the smooth skin of her back and heart-shaped bottom. He ran a single fingertip up her spine, and she shivered beneath his touch. Her hair was in disarray, her updo from the wedding long since destroyed. Chunks of her silky red hair fell around her neck and shoulders, but there was still a hair elastic somewhere in there and a bunch of bobby pins adhered to different sections of her head.

Gingerly, Fletcher began removing all the pins he could see and dropping them beside the bed. Meanwhile, his erection strained toward Maeve as if it had a mind of its own, and that mind was telling it to get inside of her *now*. He willed it to cooperate while he took care of her.

"What are you doing?" Maeve asked, straining her neck to try and catch a glimpse of him.

"Relax." He patted her twice on the ass, noting her soft

intake of breath when he did. "I'm getting this shit out of your hair."

She wiggled, her hips swaying side to side and testing his self-control. "But…why?"

"Because," he explained patiently, "after I fuck you, you're going to fall sound asleep, and I don't want you to hurt yourself sleeping on these bobby pins."

She stilled, tilting her head slightly to the side. "Okay."

"And besides," Fletcher said as he uncovered the hair elastic and began disentangling it from her red locks, "I'm really enjoying the view from this position."

Though he couldn't see it from this angle, he just knew a red blush had crept up her neck and into her cheeks. Once he'd removed all the hair baubles he could find, he patted her ass again, a little harder this time.

"You're all good now."

"Thank God," Maeve groaned as she pushed herself back against his body. He sucked in a breath as his erection pressed against the soft skin of her ass. Taking himself in his hand, he guided his length into her channel, slick with her earlier release. She moaned and ground back on him as he entered her.

His hands started out on her ass, massaging the two globes as he rocked into her. Then, he reached around to find her breasts, discovering that his wingspan was the exact perfect length to hold onto them as he took her. Maeve thrust back onto him, helping keep their rhythm. But that position didn't offer the stability Fletcher would need to move the way he really wanted to, so he eventually came back to a standing position behind her.

Weaving the fingers of one hand into the roots of her hair, he twisted the bulk of her long locks into his fist. Maeve's movements stuttered, as did her breath.

"Do you trust me?" he asked softly.

She didn't answer right away, and he gave her hair a gentle tug.

"Yes," she breathed out, instantly softening. Her knees splayed wider, and she collapsed onto her forearms, pressing her cheek against the mattress. The movement lifted her ass even higher, eliciting a low moan from Fletcher.

He began moving again, one hand fisted in Maeve's hair and the other grabbing onto one of her generous hips for purchase. Her confidence returned, and soon, her hips were rocking in time with his.

"Maeve, honey, I'm going to try something, and if you don't like it, just tell me, okay?" he asked, his voice strained.

"Okay," she said, still thrusting forward and back, tempting him with that glorious behind each time it reared toward him. Keeping hold of her hair with one hand, Fletcher brought the palm of his other into the air before bringing it down on her ass, almost instantaneously turning one cheek a lovely, light shade of pink.

Maeve cried out what sounded like a mix of surprise and pleasure as her entire body clenched around him. He rubbed the spot, soothing it as he assessed her reaction. She'd clearly enjoyed it, but was it something she would want to continue to explore, or was once enough?

Fletcher was just about to ask when she whispered, "Again."

His breath caught, and he squeezed her pinkened cheek. "You liked that, sweetheart?"

"*Yes*," she replied in a breathy voice.

He leaned forward, draping his body over hers until his mouth reached her ear. "Do you want it like that again, or harder?"

Maeve released a whimper. "Harder."

"*Fuck*," Fletcher muttered under his breath, returning to his position behind her. "That's my girl."

He continued thrusting, not immediately giving her what

she'd asked for, instead keeping his timing a surprise. She kept pushing her ass back toward him, seeking, and eventually, he rained down a harder blow than before. Maeve jerked forward beneath the force of his hand, a moan spilling from her throat. Fletcher couldn't help the groan that ripped from his as he gazed at the mark of his passion.

"You look so gorgeous with my handprint on your ass."

Maeve whimpered again, squeezing his cock so hard he saw stars.

"Do you want more?" he asked, not sure how much longer he could hold out.

"That's enough," she whispered, grinding down on him and clearly seeking her own release.

He grunted and leaned forward to kiss the top of her spine. "So fucking perfect." Moving his hand between her legs, his finger landed on her clit. Maeve shuddered, clearly as close as he was. He rubbed slow circles, drawing out this pre-release bliss for a bit before speeding up his finger.

"I'm...Fletcher, I'm...." She let out a strangled noise in lieu of finishing her sentence.

"I know, sweetheart," he said, continuing his ministrations while pulling her hair a little tighter in his other hand. "I know it feels so good. It does for me, too. You're so good for me."

That set her off like a rocket. She clenched so hard around him that he could have sworn he blacked out for a second. His orgasm burst from his body, spilling into her and filling her as she milked him.

"*Sweetheart*," he said, as long and drawn out as his orgasm was. Amidst the haze of release, he forced his fist to loosen from her hair. Neither one of them moved for several moments as they soaked in the pleasure of each other's bodies.

After long moments, Fletcher looked down to find Maeve on her forearms with her knees splayed out wide, looking sexy as hell but not overly comfortable. He gently coaxed her onto her side, brushing her hair away from her face until her green eyes opened and found his.

"Hi," she said softly, her tone as serene as everything else about her was at the moment.

"Hi," he returned as he stretched out beside her.

"That was…" she trailed off, leaving Fletcher with a burning need to know the ending to that sentence.

He reached for her face, cupping her cheek in his palm. "That was what?"

She nuzzled her face into his hand as she searched for her words. Unsure how to describe it, her response came out like a question. "Earth shattering?"

A grin tugged at Fletcher's lips. "Are you asking me or telling me?"

"Telling you," she said, then paused a moment before adding, "and asking you?"

He chuckled and leaned in to drop a kiss on her lips. "Sweetheart, you rocked my world."

It felt like the final walls had come down. Maeve had finally let him see her in full, and she had proven how completely she trusted him. Fletcher couldn't ask for anything more.

A blush seeped into Maeve's cheeks that reminded him far too much of the shade of pink he'd created elsewhere, so he tucked her into his chest before he started getting stiff again. He'd just come so hard he wasn't sure there was anything left in the tank.

Maeve pressed a quick kiss to his chest. "Is this the part where I fall sound asleep?"

Fletcher grinned and ran a hand over her unruly red hair before pulling her in tighter. "Yes."

Maeve slid out of Fletcher's arms and off the bed as carefully and quietly as possible. It was early—the sun was only just beginning to rise—and she had to use the bathroom.

"Shit!" she hissed as her foot met something sharp on the ground. The sensation was almost as unpleasant as stepping on a Lego, though nothing could truly top that.

"Huh?" came Fletcher's raspy morning voice.

"Sorry," she whispered, reaching down to pick up the object. "I stepped on a bobby pin."

"Careful," he warned before letting out a yawn. "There are a bunch all over the floor."

Oh, right. She instantly remembered him taking the pins out of her hair to free her mane…and then doing other things with it. Tugging and pulling things that she never would have guessed would appeal to her. And the spanking… In no way, shape, or form would she ever have anticipated enjoying that, but *damn*. Somehow, Fletcher had known just what she needed.

"I'm going to use the bathroom," she said as she tiptoed through the room, carefully avoiding any more sharp objects. When she emerged again, a thought struck her.

"Shit!"

"Another bobby pin?" Fletcher asked sleepily.

"No. I just realized I forgot to call the kids last night."

Dammit, she thought. She had promised them she would call both nights she was gone, but then she and Fletcher had just gotten so carried away…

Add another tally to the shitty mom column.

Fletcher sat up in the bed, letting loose another yawn. "I'm sure Connie took good care of them."

"I'm sure of that, too," Maeve said as she rooted through the pile of clothing they'd discarded so hastily the night before. "But I still broke my promise."

She discovered the clutch she'd been carrying at the wedding toward the bottom of the pile. *Crap, crap, crap.* There were five missed calls and even more text messages. The kids must have been really freaking out that she hadn't called. Or...oh, God. What if something had happened? What if Jason had found them?

Maeve hurried to sit on the side of the bed to read the messages. She scrolled back to the top of the text chain before beginning to read.

CONNIE

Hope you're having a fabulous time! Wanted to let you know the kids conked out early on the couch. No need to call tonight.

Relief settled over Maeve for one blissful moment until she read the next message, which came in a few hours after the first one.

CONNIE

Hey, Mae. Andy woke up and is feeling sick. If you're still awake and want to call now, I'm sure he'd love to hear your voice.

An hour later, there were more. The time stamps showed they were sent at the same time Connie began trying in vain to call Maeve.

CONNIE

Something's wrong.

I think Andy is really sick.

I'm taking him to the hospital with Allie. Call me.

At hospital now. Please call me.

There was one last text from the wee hours of the morning that had Maeve's heart leaping into her throat.

CONNIE

Didn't want to tell you this over text, but they're bringing Andy into surgery now. Boston Children's. Call me.

The phone dropped from Maeve's shaky hand, landing on the carpeted hotel floor with a soft thud.

"Maeve?" Fletcher asked. His voice sounded far away.

"I…" Her head spun, and she suddenly felt woozy. She was going to pass out. That was what this feeling was. Her beginning to pass out. The same thing had happened after getting that first text from Jason. What had she done last time? She'd doubled over, and the gravity had helped.

Maeve dropped her forearms to her thighs and stuck her head between her knees.

"Whoa," Fletcher said, suddenly at her side and rubbing a hand over her back. "What's wrong?"

She pulled in a shallow breath before responding. "Connie texted. Andy in hospital. Surgery."

Fletcher's hand clamped onto her shoulder. "Shit."

"Yes," she agreed, the initial waves of dizziness beginning to recede.

"Sit right there," he said as he leapt from the bed, strode over to the mini fridge, and tossed a water bottle onto the bed beside her.

"Drink that," he ordered as he heaved their suitcases onto the bed and began shoving their discarded clothing and belongings into them.

"What are you doing?" she asked.

"I'm packing us up so we can get back to Boston."

"But don't you want to stay here with your family? Isn't there that post-wedding brunch today?" Of course she had to leave, but Fletcher had commitments to his family. She didn't want him to miss out on things because of her drama.

Fletcher caught her gaze and held it. "I'm not letting you deal with this alone."

Tears swam in her eyes, a combination of fear for her son and gratitude for the man in front of her. "Thank you," she choked out.

He paused his speedy packing to press a quick but passionate kiss to her lips. "No need to thank me," he said. "Just get yourself ready to go, and I'll take care of everything else."

27

———————

Fletcher drummed his fingers against the wheel as they sat in the brutal Boston traffic. They were only a couple of miles from Children's, but that could take a good fifteen minutes to travel at this rate.

Maeve had finally gotten a hold of Connie just as they boarded the ferry to come home. She'd spent most of the ride on the other side of the boat from him, talking on the phone in hushed tones and intermittently crying. While Fletcher wished she would use him for some comfort, he understood that Connie, who was more apprised of the situation and whom she'd known for much longer, was her go-to source of reassurance.

Maeve had finally hung up the phone when they reached the mainland. In the car, she'd explained to Fletcher that Andy had been diagnosed with appendicitis. At first, Connie had thought it was just a stomachache. But then, he started vomiting, and she realized he'd developed a fever, so she took him to the emergency room.

It seemed like the prognosis was good—the appendix hadn't burst or caused any complications outside of needing to be removed laparoscopically—but Maeve was understandably upset. Her child had gotten sick, and seriously so, without her present.

"How much longer?" she asked as she bounced one knee up and down.

Fletcher glanced at the GPS. "It has us arriving in five minutes, but I'm not so sure with this traffic."

"Ughh," Maeve groaned. "Connie says he's out of surgery and in recovery now. I want to be there when he wakes up."

Fletcher reached over to place his hand on her thigh. Maeve froze and made no move to cover his hand with her own as she usually would. He gave her an awkward pat before retracting his hand.

"When we get closer, I can let you out, and you can walk. You might get there faster that way."

Maeve's gaze remained out the window, where it had been since they'd gotten into the car. "Okay."

Her dejected tone troubled Fletcher, but he saw nothing to do other than drive her to her son. Nothing he could say, that he hadn't already said, would alleviate the fear and guilt she was probably feeling. All he could do was offer his silent support and chauffeur services. A couple of blocks from the hospital, he let Maeve hop out and walk the rest of the way. He would find parking, then go up to the room and meet her.

As he looped through floor after floor of the packed parking garage, Fletcher tried to come up with a plan to help support Maeve and her family in the coming days. She would definitely need meals to be made, and he could easily take care of that. She might need help watching Allie on days when Andy had any follow-up appointments. He was sure Connie would be more than willing to help with those things, too, but he desperately wanted to feel useful.

Finally locating a spot on the fourth floor, Fletcher parked and set off to find Andy's room. The hospital was well marked, and he easily found a nurse's desk. The kind, young nurse behind it was chewing gum and looking over a set of clipboards stacked in front of her. Her gaze darted to Fletcher as he rushed through the lobby.

"I'm looking for Anderson Walsh," he barked, unable to slow his racing mind enough for niceties.

Clearly picking up on his urgency, the nurse immediately turned to her computer screen and began clicking buttons on her keyboard. A small frown formed on her lips, and Fletcher's heart nearly stopped. What did that look mean?

"I don't see—" she began.

"Fletcher," came Connie's voice from somewhere to the side. He turned to find her striding toward him. "Andy's room is this way." She pointed to a corridor.

"Thanks," Fletcher said, sending a cursory wave to the nurse and following Connie down the long hallway. He barely noticed the bright, colorful murals and decals that littered the walls, turning the hallway from the stark, sterile type you'd typically see in a hospital to an almost whimsical experience.

"Is he doing okay?" Fletcher asked as he stormed over the tile floors with Connie on his tail.

"He's doing well," Connie replied a bit breathlessly. Realizing that she was trying to keep up with his brisk pace, Fletcher consciously slowed his stride. "They removed his appendix early this morning, and he just came out from the anesthesia a few minutes ago. Maeve made it just in time to be the first face he saw."

Fletcher breathed a sigh of relief. "Thank God."

Connie slowed as they approached the end of the hallway. "Room 405," she said, pointing to the room with the corresponding number. Fletcher halted outside the closed door, suddenly unsure whether or not he should go in. He'd spent all morning singularly focused on getting Maeve to her son and simultaneously attempting to keep her calm. Now, he suddenly wondered if he would be welcome. Whether it was the closed door or the distance Maeve had kept on their entire journey to the hospital, Fletcher's chest ached with unexpected unease.

But that was silly. After the weekend they had just shared, with her baring herself to him and finally dropping the last of her reservations, of course she would want him there. He gave a light knock on the door before entering to find Maeve perched on an uncomfortable-looking, straight-backed hospital chair, her eyes red and puffy. She held a finger to her lips in a *shush* gesture as he entered the room.

"He fell back asleep," she whispered.

Fletcher glanced over to the bed where Andy lay, looking so small and helpless. An IV protruded from his inner elbow, and an oxygen monitor was clipped to one of his tiny fingers. Fletcher sucked in a breath and felt sudden tears burning his own eyes. *Shit.* He had to be strong for Maeve.

Silently collecting himself, he shoved his hands into his pockets and moved farther into the room. "Connie said he's doing well," he whispered back.

Maeve rolled her head to the side, as if the weight of it was just too much to bear on her shoulders. "That's what the doctors say."

"How are *you* doing?" he asked.

She released an unamused laugh. "How am *I* doing? How does it look, Fletch? My son is lying in a hospital bed, post-surgery, and I wasn't even here for it."

"Connie said yours was the first face he saw when he woke up," Fletcher replied, trying to grasp onto any possible glimmer of positivity.

"My face should've been the last one he saw before going under, too," she retorted. "But I was out traipsing around Nantucket with you."

The accusation in her tone smacked Fletcher right in the chest, but he mentally reminded himself that she was just scared and feeling guilty for taking time for herself.

"Maeve," he said, longing to reach out and touch her, hold

her, but held back by her standoffish body language. Her arms were crossed firmly over her chest, save for the periodic moments when she swiped one hand over her eyes to catch her tears. "You can't blame yourself for not being here. You're always here. You just so happened to choose the wrong weekend to take off, and no one could have predicted this would happen. I'm sure Andy doesn't blame you for not being here."

"But *I* blame *myself*," Maeve said, releasing her tightly wound arms and pushing her hands through her hair. "It was selfish of me to leave them. I'm supposed to be here for them, to protect them and keep them safe. I'm not supposed to let things like this happen."

"Maeve," Fletcher said again, wishing he could just telepathically convince her that it wasn't selfish to do one thing for herself when she spent the rest of her life making her children's lives better. "You protected Andy and Allie and kept them safe by placing them in the care of the most capable person possible. There was nothing you should have done differently."

"I shouldn't have gone!" she argued, her voice still a whisper, but a vehement one. The hushed conversation should have been almost comical, but instead, it was just infuriating. Maybe Maeve would feel better if she could just yell and scream at him. "And I definitely should have called the kids before they went to bed, but I was in bed with *you* instead. I should have had the foresight to keep my phone near me so I wouldn't miss any calls from Connie, but I was too wrapped up to think of that. Too wrapped up in *you*."

For a woman who said that she blamed herself, she sure seemed to be placing a lot of the blame on *him*.

Fletcher took his hands from his pockets to cross his own arms. Keeping his voice gentle and even, he said, "I get that you're upset right now, sweetheart, but please don't blame me for you not being here. I didn't force you to come to

Nantucket with me. You chose to, and I'm so glad you did. Like I said, you shouldn't have done anything differently. But neither should I."

Fresh tears fell from Maeve's eyes, and her shoulders sagged. "I know," she said, her voice cracking beneath her anguish. She sniffled. "Maybe this wasn't a good idea."

"What?"

"Us." She gestured back and forth between them. "Maybe it was too soon. Maybe I wasn't ready."

"What are you talking about?" Fletcher asked, jolted by the sudden turn in the conversation. Maeve had gone from angry and accusatory to dejected and deflated in the space of a millisecond.

She sighed and sank back into the chair like a balloon letting out air in a slow leak. "I should have just stayed focused on my kids and getting our new life together. I think it was too much, moving and getting settled and trying to do things with you, too. I wasn't ready."

Fletcher grazed his knuckles over his jaw. "Stop saying you should have done one thing or another differently. You haven't done anything wrong, Maeve. I think you're backtracking and trying to come up with excuses as to why we shouldn't be together because the thought scares you. It's always scared you. But Andy would be lying in this bed whether or not we were together."

Maeve's eyes narrowed as she stared him down. "You don't have kids. You wouldn't understand," she snapped.

Whether she knew it or not, that one hit him where it really hurt.

Knowing that any further argument would just get ugly, Fletcher prepared to calmly extricate himself by offering to grab them some food. That would give them both some time to cool down and get back into their rational minds. He was just about to make the suggestion when a nurse interrupted them, poking her head in the door to check on Andy. Her gaze caught on Fletcher.

"Is this Dad?" she asked brightly, a hopeful smile tilting her lips.

"No," Maeve and Fletcher said in unison, though their inflections were lightyears apart. His tone was gently correcting, while hers was disgusted, as if the thought of Fletcher being the father of her children was the most horrifying thought she could conjure up.

"I'm going to go get us something to eat," he muttered.

"Don't bother," she said. "You can just leave. I don't want you here."

The words stung, even as he tried to tell himself she didn't really mean them. The nurse poked her head back out the door like a turtle retreating into its shell. Fletcher stood silently for a few moments, just breathing and working to keep himself from yelling or crying. Or both.

"I'll leave, then," he finally said, his voice low. "Will you please let me know how Andy is? And tell me when you get home? I have to drop off your suitcase."

"I'll pick it up," Maeve said, all hints of anger drained from her voice. Now she was just monotone, robotic.

"Okay." Fletcher cast one final glance at Andy, wishing he could have gotten to see him awake with his own eyes. "Take care of yourself, and him."

Maeve sniffed and kept her eyes on her sleeping son, not even offering a goodbye wave.

Out in the hallway, Fletcher ran into Connie, who was sitting on a bench with Allie. Apparently, the girl had been on a vending machine run when he'd arrived. She and Connie had a feast of potato chips, packaged cookies, and canned juices laid out in their laps.

"Hi, Mr. McNally!" Allie exclaimed.

"Hi, cutie," he said, unable to help the small grin that

tugged on his lips at the sight of her with her bounty of treats. "Can I talk to Connie for a minute?"

"Sure." Allie nodded and dove into a fresh bag of cool ranch chips.

Connie rose and led him a few feet down the hallway and just around a corner where they would be out of earshot of the young girl. "What happened?" she asked, eyes narrowed with concern.

Fletcher slid his glasses up onto his head and pressed the heels of his palms to his eyes. "She's sad, and scared, and feeling guilty. She blames herself for not being here when Andy got sick, and she took it out on me by blaming me for taking her away." He dragged his glasses back into place just in time to see Connie shaking her head in disappointment.

"Maeve is… She's got a lot of…stuff to work through. Please don't give up on her."

"I'm not," Fletcher assured her. "But I felt like trying to force her to talk things through right now would only make things worse. I'm going to give her some space and time to calm down."

"Good idea," Connie said. "I'll talk to her, too. She's just spooked by this whole thing."

"I get that," he said. "I thought we had really gotten through some of her guardedness, but I think she just snapped her walls right back up."

"It'll take her some time," Connie warned. "But she's worth it."

"Yeah, she is," he agreed. Then, despite every instinct telling him to go back into that room and comfort his woman, Fletcher headed back to the parking garage.

28

When Andy awoke for the second time, Maeve was right there beside him, his tiny hand clasped in hers.

"Mommy?" he asked groggily, his eyes flickering open as if in slow motion.

"Hi, baby." She dropped a kiss on his palm.

Andy blinked a few times and swallowed, coming back into his body after the anesthesia-induced slumber. "When can we go home?" he asked, his voice a bit raspy from the intubation. Nothing a few popsicles wouldn't fix.

"Probably later today," Maeve answered. Since Andy hadn't had any complications, he wouldn't need to spend any extra time in the hospital.

"Good," he said. "Because Connie was going to make me pancakes with M&Ms in them in the morning, and I never got to have them."

Maeve let out a soft chuckle. "Well, it's going to be just liquids for you for a bit, buddy, but I promise we'll get you some M&M pancakes as soon as we can."

Andy gave her a puppy-dog pout, at which she rolled her eyes and grinned.

"I'm glad you're feeling well enough to try and manipulate me with your cuteness."

He smiled widely. "Allie taught me how to make that face. She said it's the key to getting whatever you want."

Maeve shook her head. "Of course she did."

Allie came bursting into the room then with Connie at her heels, begging her to slow down so she wouldn't wake her brother. The woman released a heavy sigh as Allie skidded to a halt at the foot of Andy's hospital bed.

"He's awake!" she said, turning to Connie with a told-you-so expression. "See, Aunt Connie? I didn't need to be quiet after all!"

Connie *tsk*ed. "Hospitals are quiet places for resting and healing."

Andy looked over at them, then up at the television mounted on the wall. "Can I heal with a show, maybe?"

Allie's eyes widened. "Oh, yeah, I heard TV makes appen-mixes all better."

"Appendixes," Maeve corrected. "Yes, we can turn on a show for a bit." There was almost nothing she wouldn't do for her kids, and if they wanted to vegetate in front of the TV for a while after the rough night they'd had, she had no problem with that.

Collecting the remote, she flipped through the channels until she found one playing children's shows. Both kids' eyes were soon glued to the screen, and Connie tugged at Maeve's elbow, pulling her toward the hallway.

"Can we talk for a few?" she asked quietly.

Maeve glanced over at the kids, both entranced by the CGI monkeys currently dancing across the screen, and sighed. "Sure."

"We'll be right back, kiddos," Connie said, receiving nothing but a quick nod of understanding from Allie in response.

Connie ushered Maeve out into the hallway and toward a

bench. Its thin, blue cushion looked far from comfortable, but Maeve plunked down into it nonetheless, weary and exhausted despite her great night's sleep. Turned out, having the most mind-blowing sex of your life makes you sleep like a log.

Connie sat down beside her, placing a supportive hand on her knee. "Fletcher didn't stay very long," she said, her objective statement obviously a ploy to dig for more information.

Maeve shrugged and slumped back on the bench. "He had other things to do."

Connie squeezed her knee in a reassuring gesture, though her fingers pinched her skin just a little bit toward the end. "That's not what he said."

"What did he say?" Maeve demanded, suddenly self-conscious about what Fletcher may have disclosed to Connie. The woman was kind to a fault, but she never hesitated to call Maeve on her bullshit.

Connie arched a brow and removed her hand to cross her arms in her lap. "He said you kicked him out."

"I did not!" Maeve said a little too loudly. Connie's eyebrow drew higher. She lowered her voice. "I did not kick him out. I told him… I told him that I didn't want him here."

Connie's lips pulled into an ironic smile. "And you don't consider that kicking him out?"

"No. I didn't tell him to leave. I told him that he *could* leave because I didn't want him here."

Connie sliced one hand through the air. "Semantics." Leaning toward Maeve, she took on her heart-to-heart expression, the one with the wide-open, inviting eyes and the soft smile that said *you can tell me anything and I won't judge you.* That look always preceded serious conversations.

Sensing what was coming, Maeve moved to stand, but Connie caught her arm and tugged her back down.

"Listen, Mae," Connie began. "I know what happened with Andy was scary—trust me, I've been terrified for the past twelve hours—but you shouldn't be taking that fear out on Fletcher. He seems like a really good man."

Maeve leaned forward until her elbows were resting on her knees, her palms supporting her head as if it would otherwise topple right off her neck. "He is," she said. "But I've been selfish by being with him. I've let him consume too much of my time, my thoughts, my energy... All of that should be going to the kids, but instead, I keep letting them down. I can't let a man come before my children again. I won't. I—"

Her monologue was interrupted by Connie pulling her in for a hug. Maeve pressed her face into her friend's shirt, and she was surprised to find it damp when she pulled back. Only then did she realize she was crying.

"Honey," Connie said, her voice thick with emotion. "All that guilt that's weighing you down…you have to let it go. You have never once let those children down. Yes, bad things have happened on your watch, but when they have, you've taken action immediately. When things with Jason got bad enough, you took the kids and left. As soon as you found out Andy was in the hospital, you were on your way here. Shit happens in life, but it's how we respond to it that matters."

"But that's the thing," Maeve argued. "I never should have had to respond, because those things never should have happened in the first place. I should have gotten the kids out earlier, knowing Jason would only get worse. And last night, I should have had my phone near me, but I was too preoccupied being selfish with Fletcher."

Connie took her by the shoulders then, giving her a little shake as if that would reset her thinking. "You are not, nor have you ever been, selfish," she said. "You have been the most amazing mother to those two children, but you also deserve a life outside of them. You deserve happiness, and I saw you getting that with Fletcher. You were happier with him than I think I've ever seen you. And not that this should be the selling point—because, like I said, you deserve something that's just for you—but seeing you in a healthy relationship, seeing you taking time for yourself, seeing you rebuild your life…that's all so good for the kids. You're so worried about letting them down, but if you push Fletcher away because of some misguided guilt, the only person you'll be letting down is yourself."

Maeve's head collapsed into her hands, her palms covering her tear-filled eyes. She faintly registered Connie's hand rubbing up and down her back in an attempt to soothe her. After a few minutes, she caught her breath and sat up straight, wiping her eyes with the arm of her shirt.

"I let him see my scars last night," she said, unprompted.

Connie's eyes grew wide. "Wow. That's huge for you. Did you tell him how you got them?"

Maeve shook her head, half embarrassed, half disgusted with herself for lying to him. "No, I told him a cup of hot coffee spilled off a shelf and onto me."

Connie nodded understandingly. "Well, maybe that would be a good step forward. Tell Fletcher the truth. Let him in all the way. Let him see why you are the way you are, and he can decide whether he wants to stay or not. But don't you go pushing him away preemptively."

Maeve sniffled, looking around for something to wipe her nose with. Connie followed her gaze to the box of tissues on the nurse's station and gestured for her to stay seated. As Connie hurried over and plucked a few tissues from the box, Maeve imagined what would happen if she told Fletcher everything. The whole ugly truth. Would he look at her differently? Would that pity that she so feared finally show on his handsome face? Would he be willing to stay with her? Or would she scare him away?

Connie returned with a small mountain of tissues and placed them on Maeve's lap. After blowing her nose thoroughly, she met her friend's concerned gaze.

"I don't know if I can do that," Maeve admitted. "I don't know what I'd do if he rejected me."

Connie placed her palm on Maeve's knee again. "I don't think that's going to happen. But even if it did, you'd get through it. You'll have to be brave. But that's okay, because you're the bravest person I know."

Those heartfelt words brought a fresh set of tears to Maeve's eyes, which she attempted to hold back by biting her lip and breathing in and out slowly through her nose. Only a couple of tears escaped, which were easily brushed away by Connie's thumb.

"Think about it," Connie said. "If you want to stay with Fletcher, like I think you deserve to, you'll have to be honest with him."

"I know," Maeve replied.

"And you have to be honest with yourself. You have to recognize that it's not selfish to do something that makes you a happier person and, in turn, a better mother. This is *your* life, Mae. You have to live it."

Twenty-four hours later, Andy was home and resting on the couch, armed with a little bell that he was instructed to ring when he needed something. Much to Allie's dismay, she did *not* get a bell of her own to ring for her every whim, though she *had* discovered that she could ring Andy's bell and someone would come running, unable to decipher who the bell-ringer was.

Connie had come over bright and early, her arms full of grocery bags containing all of Andy's favorite junk foods and the ingredients for chicken soup, which she was currently stirring at the stove. They hadn't talked any more about Maeve's complicated love life, but just having her best friend there to offer silent support was helping ease the tension wringing her gut.

She was set to go over to Fletcher's in a few minutes to pick up her abandoned suitcase. She hadn't wanted him to come around the house, knowing he would go into full care-taker mode, and she wouldn't be able to deny him when he was doing sweet things for her and her family. This way, she could see him, feel out where he was at, and decide what she did or didn't want to divulge.

Maeve still wasn't fully convinced that it wasn't too soon into her new life for romance. When someone first gets sober, they tell them not to date for at least a full year. Perhaps she should follow that guideline. Maybe she and Fletcher *had* moved too quickly. Maybe they could try to be friends for a while, then date again. So many maybes…

"That smells sooo good," Allie declared as she took a huge whiff of Connie's soup.

"Want a taste?" Connie asked, grabbing a fresh spoon from the drawer and filling it with soup. "You'll have to blow on it first."

Connie held the full spoon over the sink while Allie blew on the soup, then slurped it down.

"Mmm," she hummed. "Andy, I think this soup will make you all better."

The poor kid had been experiencing abdominal cramping this morning, a side effect the doctors assured her was normal. Maeve had been watching him closely, nonetheless.

"Maybe I should stay here to make sure he's really okay," she said to Connie.

Connie whacked her spoon against the side of the pot, producing a tinny sound. "No, you should not. He'll be just fine, and like Allie said, this soup is going to make him all better."

A sigh slipped from Maeve's mouth.

"Look," Connie said. "I know you're nervous about talking to him, but it's the only way forward."

"I could just take the kids and move again. Maybe we could go south this time—somewhere near a beach," Maeve joked.

Allie's head popped from behind the kitchen table. *Shit.* Maeve thought she had joined Andy on the couch.

"We're moving again?"

The alarm in her question had Maeve's heart skipping a beat. There she went, being a crappy mom again. She brushed away that thought, remembering Connie's assurances.

"No, sweetheart. I was just joking. We're not going anywhere."

Allie's shoulders relaxed, and she went back to whatever she was doing behind the table.

Connie gave Maeve a pointed look. "Not permanently. But you're supposed to be on your way somewhere right now."

She checked the time on her cell phone. Connie was right —it was time for the reckoning.

29

Fletcher watched through the window as Maeve pulled up in front of his apartment building. Part of him had worried she wouldn't show, but then again, he also knew how stubborn she could be. Of course she showed. She emerged from her vehicle in a flash of red hair and cobalt blue. The blue tunic she wore over her leggings accounted for the second pop of color. Marching up the walkway in her black flats, she looked vaguely like a very fashionable soldier heading into battle.

When the doorbell rang, Fletcher forced himself to count to ten before answering it, not wanting to give away how eager he'd been for her arrival.

"Hi," he said as the door opened, and Maeve appeared. She looked as gorgeous as ever, though he would have preferred her to be wearing a warm smile or even her signature sassy smirk. Instead, her lips were twisted into a grimace.

"Hi." She met his gaze in a strained way, as if she was forcing herself to do so. Her eyes darted around the entryway. "My suitcase?"

"It's in here." He gestured back to the living room. He'd

strategically placed her suitcase in the far corner so she would have to enter the apartment in order to retrieve it. "Come in."

Maeve did so hesitantly, as if she hadn't been there before. As if she hadn't been bare and vulnerable within these four walls. As if she wasn't the best thing that had ever entered this space.

"Thank you," she said politely as he shut the door behind her.

"Can I get you something to drink?" Fletcher asked as he stepped into the kitchen. Maeve eyed the half-full glass he'd been drinking from.

"What are you having?"

The corner of his mouth hitched up in a wry grin. "Water."

Warmth bloomed in her cheeks. "No, I'm fine. I'm really just here for my suitcase."

"Let's talk, Maeve, please," he said, desperate to patch things up. He'd worried about her all day and night yesterday. A million times, he'd had to hold himself back from texting her, calling her, getting into his car and driving to her. She had clearly needed space, but she was here now, and he was sick of holding back. "I don't like how we left things."

She blew out a breath and leaned uneasily against his counter. "Me either. I'm sorry I got mad at you. It wasn't your fault that we were away when Andy got sick."

A small sense of relief surged through him, but she was leaving out one important point. "It wasn't your fault either," Fletcher said. "You didn't do anything wrong. You're a great mom."

Her eyes grew shiny, and her lip wobbled. "Maybe I will take some water after all," she said as she turned her back on him to grab a glass from the cabinet. She was clearly stalling, trying to buy time to hide her emotions, but he would allow it because getting a glass of water would seem to indicate that she was willing to stick around awhile.

Halfway to the fridge, Maeve tripped on the leg of one of the stools at the island and stumbled. The glass fell to the floor and shattered, sending shards scattering across the wood floor. The color drained from Maeve's face, and the tears that had been swimming in her eyes began to fall. She swiftly knelt before the largest hunks of glass, sweeping them into her palms.

"Stop," Fletcher said, worried the glass would cut her skin. "You'll hurt yourself. I'll take care of it." He took a few steps until he was standing before her and reached out his hand to help her up.

She immediately shrank back from his outstretched hand. He snapped it back as if he'd touched his finger to a hot stove. Tears rolled down her cheeks as she gazed up at him. "I'm sorry," she said in a broken whisper before returning her gaze to the floor. "It was my fault. I'll clean it up." Her hands shook as she continued to gather the broken glass.

"Maeve," he murmured, kneeling down in front of her. "It's not your fault you tripped." He noticed a thin line of blood beginning to form on one of her palms. "Please stop," he said, gently encasing her hands with his. A sob tore from her chest, shaking her entire body. She didn't stop shaking as he guided her to stand, abandoning the mess of glass on the floor.

She was practically vibrating with…something. Was it fear? It wouldn't make any sense for Maeve to be afraid of him. Fletcher couldn't fathom why she'd had such a strong reaction to the accident, other than that she was already emotionally distraught from Andy's ordeal.

He grabbed a paper towel to press against her bleeding palm, planning to lead her to the sink to clean her up. But her shudders and sobs threatened to rip his heart out, so he wrapped his arms around her instead.

"Sweetheart," he murmured, pulling her into his embrace. "I've got you."

She wept into his chest, soaking his shirt with her tears. Though he didn't understand her reaction, he realized that she needed a moment just to feel whatever she was feeling. When her crying tapered into nothing more than the occasional sniffle, he pulled back and wiped away the moisture beneath her eyes with his thumbs.

"Hi," he said softly. "Why don't we take care of this cut, and then we can talk?"

She gave him a half-nod, half-shrug and allowed him to shepherd her over to the sink. He used the utmost care as he washed her hand and dried it with a clean paper towel, then placed a bandage across the open skin. They didn't speak as Fletcher patched her up, only the sounds of their breathing filling the room. Hers was still heavy and uneven from her crying jag. His was shallow from the adrenaline rush of seeing her so upset and from the resulting primal urge to care for her.

When Maeve's cut was taken care of, he led her over to the couch and sat her down, then took a seat beside her. Her expression was startlingly blank—hollow and listless. He'd never seen that look on her face before, and it terrified him.

"Let's start with this," he said. "Why do you think that everything is your fault?"

She took a breath that ended in a hiccup. After another deep inhale, she tried to speak. "Because…" Her voice broke on the single word, and she sat in silence for a moment before trying again. "Because Jason always made me feel like everything was."

The sentence hung in the air like a rancid smell. Of course all of this hearkened back to her shitty ex. Fletcher didn't know why he hadn't thought of that explanation before. Maeve had never said much about him, other than that he wasn't in the picture any longer.

"Well, he was an asshole," Fletcher said, drawing out a small half-smile from Maeve. More of a mere slanting of one corner of her lips, but he would take it.

"You don't know the half of it," she said as she picked at the corner of the blanket laying over the back of the couch.

"Tell me, then."

Maeve sighed heavily and dropped the blanket from her grasp, bringing her hands to clasp over one knee instead. "Jason was…not a nice guy."

"We've established that," Fletcher replied, hoping his impatience wasn't shining through too much. "What did he do?"

She fidgeted in her seat. "He seemed like a good guy at first. On our first date, he brought me to the fanciest restaurant in town and told me to order anything I wanted. I later learned that he'd worked overtime for a month to be able to pay for it. He was always doing thoughtful things like that. He bought me flowers once a week and a necklace on our six-month anniversary. I thought he was too good to be true, and it turned out he was." Maeve was staring at the far wall as she said the next part. "He didn't hit me for the first time until we'd been together for a year."

Fletcher's breath caught, a small gasp escaping him. She didn't seem to notice his reaction, though, and simply went on with her story.

"It didn't happen all that often at first—a slap here or there when I forgot to pick up milk or didn't clean the bathroom well enough. And he would always apologize and try to make up for it afterward, bombarding me with praise and gifts and excuses for his behavior." Maeve's leg began bouncing. "By the time I realized I was in a bad situation, I was pregnant with Allie." She shook her head as if in disbelief. "He started treating me like a queen the moment he found out I was pregnant. In fact, the combined eighteen months of my pregnancies were the only stretches of time during our marriage that he *didn't* hit me. I guess I let those periods lull me into complacency."

Fletcher grasped for something intelligent to say, something comforting or helpful or insightful, but nothing came. His mind was filled with haunting images and blistering rage. Maeve—his Maeve—had been in a ten-year-long abusive relationship. He thought back to all the times she'd seemed jumpy or apprehensive around him and wondered if it all stemmed from fucking Jason. He wanted to kill the bastard.

"Things got worse a couple of years after Andy was born," she went on. "Having two kids around gave Jason a whole slew of new things to be mad at me for. I waited too long to change the baby's diaper, and it smelled; the baby was crying too loudly, and I should have been able to stop it; I forgot to pick up more diapers at the store…" She ticked off the offenses on her fingers. "I couldn't do anything right. Everything was always my fault, and he punished me for every single little thing for years. Does that answer your question?"

Fletcher's mouth flapped open, and he snapped it shut. "Sweetheart…" He couldn't come up with an adequate response. She was still gazing at the wall. "It explains…a lot," he muttered.

That got her attention. Maeve turned to him, brows drawn together. "What does that mean?"

He scooted an inch toward her, needing to be closer but not wanting to scare her. "It means that I understand why you were so resistant to a relationship now. Why you're so protective of the kids. Did he… Did he ever hurt them?" Fletcher asked, unsure whether he even wanted to know the answer.

Maeve shook her head fiercely. "No. No, he never touched the kids. I made sure of it. But…" She paused, rolling her eyes toward the ceiling as she seemed to gather the courage to say what came next. "A few months ago, we were fighting. It was late at night, and the kids were both in bed—or so I thought. Jason and I were in the kitchen, and things got heated. Andy had come downstairs to get a glass of water, and he saw Jason slap me. He was so scared and confused. Jason, of course, tried to backtrack everything and tell Andy that we were just pretending, that everything was fine. Once we got him back down to bed, Jason hit me again for not hearing Andy coming. I knew then that I had to leave."

Fletcher fisted his hands in his lap as he resisted the urge to go punch a wall. "*Fuck*," he growled.

Tears sprang back into Maeve's eyes. "It wasn't the worst he'd ever hurt me physically, but in a way, it *was* the worst because Andy had witnessed it. I couldn't let my kids see their father doing something like that, or their mother letting it happen, so I finally left."

Thank God. Fletcher didn't know all that much about abusive relationships, but he understood that it often took many tries for someone to leave their abuser.

"What was the worst he ever hurt you?" Fletcher asked in a low voice, needing to know, needing to understand the worst of it.

Maeve hesitated, her gaze assessing, as if determining whether or not he was fit to receive the information. That couldn't be good. When he just continued to watch her, she relented.

"It was a few years back. I was making penne alla vodka for dinner—Jason's favorite—but it turned out I had forgotten to buy the pasta for it. Jason had just come home from a long day of work when I discovered my mistake. The water was almost boiling on the stove, but there was no pasta to put in it. Jason was pissed, and he…he grabbed the pot of water and threw it at me."

Fletcher gasped in realization. "Your burn?"

Maeve nodded miserably, bringing one hand to her scarred shoulder. "He freaked out as soon as he realized what he'd done. He knew I would have to go to the emergency room, and he knew they would ask questions. So, he forced me to make up the story about the hot cup of coffee. But everything else I told you about it was true. It was a second-degree scald burn that took a few months to heal with wrapping and antibiotics."

Fletcher's chest ached. Not only had she had to go through the trauma of being burned, but it had happened at the hands of her very own husband.

"What else have you been keeping from me?" he asked quietly, knowing there had to have been more. One didn't have a past like she did without a whole hoard of secrets.

Maeve tugged her lip between her teeth, seeming undecided.

"Tell me," he insisted.

She sighed, resigned. "This is going to sound bad," she said. "But my name's not really Maeve."

Fletcher's slack-jawed, open-mouthed expression would have been comical in any other situation. Maeve couldn't blame him for being so shocked—it was a big bomb to drop—but in all honesty, she didn't feel like it was that big of a deal. Her fresh start had included a fresh name, and the one she'd chosen was only a slight extension of her real one.

"What?" he sputtered.

"I've been using the name Maeve since we moved so Jason couldn't track us by looking up my real name."

"Back up," Fletcher said, waving his hands in front of him. "What *is* your real name?"

Gathering her patience, she spoke in as calm a voice as possible. "My given name is Mae."

His head tilted to the side in confusion. "The one time I called you that...you got upset."

"Because hearing you use that name triggered me," she explained. "I've done my best to erase Mae Sullivan from existence, and when that name left your lips…for a split second, I thought you'd figured me out. I quickly realized that wasn't possible, but it was a terrifying moment."

Fletcher nodded as he processed her explanation. "Walsh is fake, too, then?" he said a moment later. His tone wasn't accusatory, just curious.

"Walsh was my grandmother's maiden name."

He scratched at his chin. "I thought when we first met you said it was O'Shaughnessy."

"That's my mother's maiden name. Jason might think to use that if he went searching for me, but he never knew my grandmother's maiden name."

"Do you think Jason is looking for you?"

The question turned Maeve's stomach as she thought back to her ex-husband's most recent text. *Where are you? Tell me or I'll come find you.* She hadn't received any new messages in weeks now, and she wasn't sure whether to take that as a good sign or not. Had he given up? Or was he indeed searching for her?

Maeve gulped down the fear that tasted like acid in her throat. "I know he is."

Fletcher's gaze blazed into hers. "How?"

She chewed on the tip of her fingernail. "Because he's been sending me text messages from fake numbers, telling me so."

Fletcher's still-fisted hands curled even tighter, turning his knuckles white before he abruptly released his fingers to flex his hands. "Shit."

"Yes."

He blew out a breath and wiped his hands over his face. "I really wish you'd told me about this earlier. My brother is an ex-cop and current private security provider. He could help."

"I don't think we need anything like that," Maeve said, picturing a hulking bodyguard following her around everywhere she went. "Connie works in domestic violence support.

That's how we met. She helped us get away from Jason and across the country, and she set me up here. She has lots of resources. I think she has us covered pretty well."

Fletcher studied her for a moment. "That's good to hear." He scrubbed his hands over his face again. "God, I can't believe you went through all that, and I never knew."

He sounded so forlorn and guilty that Maeve couldn't help but place a hand on his thigh. Fletcher looked down at the point of contact, then back up at her. "Have I ever…" He hesitated, his face falling. "Fuck." He pushed a hand through his hair, making it stick up at odd angles. "*Fuck!*" he repeated with vigor.

"Fletch?" Maeve grabbed onto his arm. "What's wrong?"

"Jesus *fuck*, Maeve, I slapped your ass the other night!" he cried out.

Two things struck her in that moment. First, he'd still used her chosen name, even though he'd learned her real one. It showed some sort of acceptance—that he knew she was a different person now and treated her as such. Second, he thought he had hurt or triggered her during their night together. That was the opposite of the truth, and it was unacceptable that he might have been harboring guilt over what he'd done.

"Baby," she said, grabbing his hands. "It's okay. I wanted that. I told you so."

"I…I never would have done that if I'd known about your past," he said. "I am so, so sorry, Maeve."

"Don't be," she insisted.

"But… He hit you… I hit you."

"It's nowhere near the same," Maeve argued, desperate to make this sweet man understand that he hadn't done anything to harm her.

"How is that possible?" he asked.

"Because you left me in control," she said. "If I had told you to stop, you would have. That was *empowering*. I *chose* to allow you to do that because it felt *good*. That's why it's completely different. You…what you do…how you do it… It's perfect. You're perfect."

Thoughts of just how perfect he had been to her had tears filling her eyes. Patient, kind, caring, sweet, determined, and sometimes flirtatious, family-man Fletcher.

"Then, why are you crying?" he asked as he brushed away a tear from her cheek.

"Because," she said softly, "when I went into that bar the first night we met, I wanted a taste of who I'd been before Jason. I wanted to recreate myself, but I also wanted to get back to myself. I wanted someone to make me feel as beautiful as I felt before. And you… You made me feel even more beautiful than before."

Fletcher pulled her into his chest as tears slipped down onto his shirt. "You are so beautiful, inside and out," he whispered into her ear, eliciting even more tears. "And I'm not perfect, but I do think we're perfect together." He placed a kiss on her forehead. "Thank you for telling me everything."

Maeve, unable to speak through her silent tears, simply cuddled further into his chest in response. They stayed on the couch, wrapped in each other's arms, for long minutes before Fletcher eventually broke the silence with a question.

"What about the kids?"

"Hmm? What about them?"

"Are Andy and Allie their real names?"

Maeve tapped her fingers on Fletcher's chest. "Their real nicknames, yes. But legally, Anderson is Andrew and Alina is Allison. Luckily, they both have nicknames that could be associated with a few different first names. I couldn't bear to force them to learn new ones."

Fletcher covered her hand with his, stilling it. "You've had to make so many hard decisions."

She shrugged. "I had no other choice."

"I won't ask you to make any decisions today," he said. "I

won't ask you where we stand, or if you're ready to commit to me. But Maeve…I want that. I want you. I need you to know that."

She burrowed into his t-shirt, unable to get close enough to him. "I know."

30

———

True to his word, Fletcher hadn't asked Maeve to make any decisions about their relationship. He also hadn't asked her to stay, despite how badly he wanted to spend more time with her, because he knew she had to get home to Andy, and he respected her role as a mother.

To his satisfaction, she had agreed to let him talk to Beau about looking into Jason and whether or not he was really searching for them. If he was, they would get an official restraining order so that if he did get near her or the kids, he would go to jail. Beau would also be able to help arrange added protection for them if needed.

Though Fletcher's head was spinning in light of the new information from Maeve about who she really was and what she'd been through, he was relieved that she'd finally let him all the way in. Not only that, but she had accepted him as a source of support rather than insisting on handling everything herself. He was glad Maeve had leaned on Connie and the organization she worked with, but the more people who were looking out for her and the kids, the better.

She proved her newfound ability to ask for help when she called him the next week with a request.

"What's up?" Fletcher asked, his cell tucked between his ear and shoulder as he sorted through mail on the kitchen island.

Maeve's sigh rushed out of her. "While we were out at Andy's follow-up appointment this morning, someone vandalized the garage door. Connie was at work, so she didn't see who did it."

Fletcher dropped the letter he was holding to get a better grip on the phone. "What do you mean *vandalized?*"

"Someone spray painted a giant red *X* over the whole door. Probably just some wayward neighborhood kid, but it's going to be a bitch to clean off. I was hoping you could come over and help me."

"Of course," Fletcher said, but he couldn't shake the skepticism that crept over him. "That's unusual for such a quiet neighborhood, don't you think?"

"I guess," Maeve replied. "Maybe it was one of the PTA moms getting revenge for my absence at the latest fundraiser. I was *not* about to sit above a dunk tank and let little kids throw balls at a target to try and send me to my demise."

That coaxed a soft chuckle from him. He'd attended the fundraiser but had miraculously gotten away without being asked to go in the dunk tank. "Nah, you're probably right about it being an act of teenage rebellion. I'll grab some supplies and be over there soon."

"Thanks, Fletch," she said. After a short pause, she added, "I've missed you."

They hadn't seen each other face to face since the night the floodgates had opened and Maeve had told him everything about her past. She had been busy caring for Andy, and he had been busy distracting himself to keep from driving over there, grabbing her, and never letting her go. They'd texted and talked on the phone a few times, but he was determined not to push her too much.

Fletcher knew Maeve needed space to process Andy's

emergency, as well as the fact that she had finally let him in. It sounded like only he and Connie knew the full extent of what she had gone through in her marriage, and it must have taken a lot out of her to open up to him the way she had. He was dying for some sort of confirmation that they were in a good place—a *let's make this thing official* or, even better, an *I love you*—but the fact that she was turning to him for help was enough for now.

"I've missed you, too, sweetheart," he said. "I'll see you soon."

After hanging up, he gathered what he needed. A quick Google search told him that graffiti could typically be removed with household cleaners like dish soap or laundry detergent mixed with water then applied to the paint with a nylon brush. He had a couple of unopened nylon dish brushes stashed under the sink, so he grabbed those as well as various cleaners and headed over to the house.

As soon as he pulled into the driveway, Allie greeted him with her usual enthusiasm, practically bouncing into his lap in the driver's seat as soon as he opened the door.

"Somebody painted on our garage," she said. "Mommy says paint is only for paper."

Fletcher gently placed the girl on the ground as he got out of the car. "Mommy's right. Whoever did this was definitely not a nice person. But don't worry, we'll have it cleaned up soon."

He grabbed his bag of supplies and waved to Andy, who was sitting on the porch with Connie. "Feeling better, bud?" he called.

Andy gave him a big smile and a thumbs-up. "The doctor says I can eat anything I want now. We're getting hamburgers for dinner tonight!"

"That's great news," Fletcher said, amused, as always, by the kid's love of food. He turned to Maeve, who stood in front of the garage, scrubbing fruitlessly at the graffiti with a sponge.

"Help," she whined, sticking her lower lip out in a pout.

"Come here," he said, wrapping her in his arms and removing the sponge from her hand in the process. She took the opportunity to return his hug, her arms snaking around his waist as she laid her cheek against his chest. They stood there just like that for a moment, no words passing between them. Just holding each other. Fletcher breathed in her subtle rose scent as he dropped a kiss in her hair. He waited until Maeve loosened her hold to break the embrace.

"I don't think you're going to get very far with that sponge," he said as he handed her a brush and took the other for himself. "Let's try using these and see what happens."

Twenty minutes later, all that remained of the graffiti was a very light-pink *X*. Google had been right about detergent doing the trick, but red on white was a tricky combination. All it would take to make the mark fully go away was a fresh coat of white paint on the garage door, which Fletcher could easily take care of the next day. They collected up the dirty brushes and bucket of detergent-and-water solution and headed inside to dispose of it all.

Maeve seemed relieved to have that task out of the way. She'd been through so much in just the past couple of weeks between Andy's surgery and her worries about Jason. She really hadn't needed one more thing to fret over.

"Are the kids okay by themselves out there?" Fletcher asked as the front door closed behind him. Connie had taken off to the grocery story to get the burger ingredients, and Allie and Andy were playing on the porch.

"They'll be fine outside by themselves for a few minutes," Maeve said. "They know not to leave the yard."

"Good," Fletcher replied, placing the bucket he held on the ground and backing Maeve up against the wall of the foyer, "because I've been dying to do this since the second I arrived."

He leaned in close and cupped her cheek in one hand but didn't kiss her right away, still a little unsure of where they stood. They hadn't done more than hug and cuddle since they'd been on Nantucket for the wedding. Luckily, Maeve made it quite clear by pressing up on her tiptoes to claim Fletcher's lips with hers. Her hands came to his chest, sliding slowly downward as she devoured his mouth. When she reached his waist, she tucked her fingers into his belt and pulled him in closer.

Satisfied that she had clearly been missing him as much as he had been missing her, Fletcher grabbed her ass, gave it a firm squeeze, and hoisted her up off her feet. Her legs automatically wrapped around his waist, and the friction of their pelvises pressed together had a low moan spilling from his throat. She ground against him, eliciting another moan, and he pressed his face into her neck.

"Maeve," he mumbled into her soft skin, using his nose to draw a line across her neck before finding a spot to deposit a lingering kiss. "Your kids are right on the other side of this door."

She paused her grinding and sighed. "I know."

Fletcher leaned back to catch her gaze. "Thank you for asking me to come over today."

Maeve leaned in to kiss the tip of his nose. "Thank you for coming." She unwrapped her legs from around his waist and stood, smoothing the wrinkles from his shirt with her palms. "Hopefully, next time you come over, we can have some time alone together."

"That would be nice," he said, fixing some chunks of her hair that had gotten disheveled. "But I'll take you however I can get you."

She grinned up at him and snuck in one more quick kiss before Allie came barging in the door, announcing that

Connie was home. They all headed outside to help her carry in the groceries, and Fletcher stayed into the evening to help prepare and eat the burgers.

Overall, any tension that had formed since the events following the wedding had dissipated. Fletcher felt more connected to Maeve than ever, and everything seemed to have leveled out. That false sense of security was one of the reasons why the call he got one morning the next week was so incredibly jarring.

31

"Fletch?" came Maeve's broken voice. She sounded like she had after finding the injured baby bird—distraught and destroyed.

"What's going on?" he asked, instantly on high alert. He'd been sitting at his kitchen island, enjoying a cup of coffee as he daydreamed about his upcoming summer vacation. School would end for the year in just a few days, and then he'd have a lighter schedule for the months of July and August. There was a lot he hoped to fit into that time, most of it involving one-on-one time with Maeve.

Her panting breaths sounded over the line. "I…it's… Jason," she choked out. "He…he…took them."

Fletcher leapt from his stool. "What? He took what?" he demanded.

"He took…the kids," Maeve replied, the last two words almost drowned out by her shrill wail.

Fletcher's heart froze. "Oh shit," he breathed into the phone.

Maeve's only response was a sob, the mournful sound slicing through his chest like a knife. From everything she had told him, the kids weren't necessarily in danger with Jason, but the thought of that bastard laying a hand—even a loving one—on either of those children had Fletcher's gut turning inside out.

Snap out of it, he commanded himself. Maeve needed him right now.

"I'll be there in five minutes," he barked, slipping his feet into a pair of sandals and grabbing his keys as he spoke. He barreled through the front door, practically sprinting across the driveway to his car, then pausing once seated in the driver's side. The sound of Maeve's crying over the line shredded him to his core.

"Sweetheart," he said softly. "I'm coming. We'll figure this out together. Hang tight, okay?"

She continued to sob into the phone, but he thought he made out the muffled sound of an affirmative *mhmm.*

"Okay," he said as he started the car. "I'll be right there, baby. I—" He cut himself off from letting the three words he wanted to say fly off his tongue. "I'll be there soon," he finished. Hanging up so he could drive as quickly as humanly possible without any distractions, he screeched into Maeve's driveway just three minutes later. The front door was ajar, and as he slipped through it, Fletcher was greeted by the sight of Connie comforting a hysterical Maeve.

Connie glanced over as he entered, relief spilling over her features. "Hi, Fletcher," she said, drawing Maeve's attention to him. Her green eyes were filled with tears, the skin around them red and puffy. She was clutching a teddy bear that Fletcher recognized as Andy's.

"Hi." He hurried to Maeve's side, immediately drawing her into his embrace. Her crying intensified as soon as his arms were around her, but she melted into them, allowing him to soothe her. Eventually, she sank into his lap, her head on his chest, and continued crying quietly. Fletcher looked at Connie over her head.

"Have you called the police?"

"Yes," Connie replied. "I called them while she was calling you. They should be here any second."

As if on cue, a couple of cruisers rolled up and parked behind Fletcher's car in the driveway.

"I'm going to call my brother." He pulled his phone from his pocket carefully, so as not to jostle the woman in his lap. "It's not that I don't trust the police, I just…"

Connie's lips pressed together as if trying to suppress a smile. "Don't trust the police," she said, finishing off his sentence.

He shrugged. "I'd feel better if Beau was in on this, too."

Connie nodded and got up to greet the officers at the door. Fletcher sent an SOS call to Beau, who promised to be there within fifteen minutes. Considering he lived at least twenty minutes away, it was clear that he was taking this as seriously as Fletcher was. He wasn't sure he'd ever loved his baby brother more than he did in that moment.

Once the officers were settled in Maeve's living room, she sat up beside Fletcher to give them the information they needed: what the kids had been wearing, what type of car Jason had been driving, what he looked like. The questions went on and on. Maeve explained that the kids had been playing out in the yard while she finished washing the breakfast dishes. She had been looking out the window every couple of minutes to check on them, and the last time she did, they were being ushered into a blue minivan by their father.

She went on to explain how they'd fled from Jason months ago, and she chronicled his abuse over the years. She told them about the text messages she'd been receiving from him lately at different numbers and expressed how they felt threatening to her. The officers took lots of notes as Maeve spoke, in clear pain as she recounted the entirety of her relationship with Jason. Fletcher was glad she had already gotten it out to him and wasn't having to divulge all the gory details to him for the first time along with the cops.

Once they'd gathered all the information they needed, a couple of officers got to work setting up a robocall with the description of the missing children and the minivan to go out to everyone living within ten miles of Maeve's home. Some others devised a plan to set up roadblocks so they could check vehicles, and one officer copied all the data from Maeve's phone to see if they could trace any of the fake numbers Jason had been using.

Peeve was absolutely distraught, leery of all the unknown people in the house, but clearly wanting to comfort Maeve. He vacillated between rubbing his face all over her body and hiding beneath the couch. At one point, he ran off and came back with one of Allie's socks dangling from his mouth, as if it was his way of asking *where is she?*

Beau arrived in thirteen minutes, barging into the house through the still-open front door and taking in the scene of police officers, Maeve, Fletcher, Connie, and Peeve, who was now glued to Maeve's chest. Beau plopped himself on the floor in the midst of the fray and tugged his laptop from its case.

"Where are we?" he asked as he opened the laptop.

"The police are setting up roadblocks and robocalls," Fletcher said. "They're also trying to trace the fake numbers Jason was using to see if any of them lead back to Massachusetts."

"Have you heard anything from him since this morning?"

Maeve shook her head. "I haven't heard from him in weeks. I just kept blocking the numbers he texted me from. I hoped he had given up. But then…"

"Uh, actually, ma'am…" the officer copying the data off her phone said, holding it up so everyone could see she'd received a text from an unknown number. Maeve shot off the couch and grabbed for her phone. The officer instructed her to open the text as he looked on.

Her hands began to shake as she read the message aloud.

X marks the spot. They're better off with me, anyway, Mae. I can't believe you let my kid end up in the hospital. You always were a shitty mother.

Fletcher's hands clenched into fists. That *fucking* bastard. He kidnapped his own children, and he had the audacity to call *her* a shitty parent? At least that explained the vandalism earlier in the week. Fletcher knew it'd been far too out of character for the neighborhood. He should've realized something wasn't right and insisted on getting Maeve and her kids protection immediately. But now wasn't the time for guilt or blame. He could beat himself up later.

Now, it was time to comfort his woman.

Maeve handed her phone back to the officer before crumpling back onto the couch. Fletcher unclenched his hands and caught her just before her head whacked against the back of the couch. He arranged her into a sitting position and sat beside her, one arm around her for support. Peeve had situated himself on the top of the couch, as if poised to protect her.

Maeve's face was ghostly pale, her eyes wild. "That must be how he found us. We had to use Andy's real name at the hospital. I had been so careful, but…"

"You were frazzled. It's okay, Maeve," Fletcher said. "It's impossible to keep up the level of vigilance you had been since you moved here."

She bowed her head. "He's right. I *am* a shitty mother. How could I let this happen?"

Reaching over, Fletcher took her face in his hands. "Look at me, Maeve." When she ignored him, he physically brought her gaze to his. "Look. At. Me." Her eyes reluctantly found his. "You are a fantastic mother. It's Jason who's the shitty parent. You're doing all the right things. Look around." He directed her gaze around toward the flurry of activity throughout the house. There were officers everywhere—talking on phones, typing on computers, conferring with one another. Beau had moved himself to the kitchen and was typing away at his laptop, no doubt doing his own due diligence. Connie was eagerly attending to everyone, handing out glasses of water and snacks.

When Maeve's gaze landed back on him, he continued. "That text was Jason poking at your insecurities. Don't let him win. He's doing everything he can to get under your skin, and he's using Allie and Andy as pawns to get back at you. He knew taking them was the one thing he could do that would hurt you the most."

She sniffled, not outright agreeing with him, but not refuting his point either.

"We're going to get them back," he said. "And we're going to get Jason thrown in jail for this."

She sniffled again and nodded, tucking herself into his side where she remained for the next few hours. The morning passed in a whirlwind of people, questions, crying, and the arrival of Beau's ex-police partner, Diego, before they went off together to do God-knows-what.

Fletcher managed to coax Maeve into eating some crackers with peanut butter on them for lunch, but other than that, she mostly sat and wallowed. All the extra people in the house slowly departed throughout the afternoon to attend to their various tasks. By evening, Maeve was a complete wreck.

"What is taking so long?" she wailed.

Fletcher rubbed her upper arm. "These things take time. But he couldn't have gotten that far."

"Then why haven't they found them yet?"

He scooted closer to where she still sat on the couch, hoping to offer some comfort or reassurance, but as soon as their thighs touched, she sprang up and began to pace the length of the living room.

"This is killing me," she said after her second lap. "I can't stand all this waiting around."

"Maybe we should go to bed. Try to get some sleep, and see where we're at in the morning," he suggested.

She threw her arms up in the air. "There's no way I'll be able to sleep tonight."

He bit back a sigh. "I know your adrenaline's been pumping like mad all day, but your body is exhausted. You need to sleep. Or at least rest in your bed."

She paused by the window, arms crossed as she gazed out of it. "Are you staying?"

He stood, joining her by the window but not touching her. "Of course I am," he said. "I wouldn't be anywhere else. I won't leave until the kids are back, and maybe not even then."

Maeve's lip wobbled as her eyes remained somewhere outside the window. "There's something I haven't told you."

Fletcher's pulse sped to a gallop. Had she left something out of her account? Was it something pertinent to the kidnapping? Should he be calling an officer back here?

"What's that?" he asked in a deceptively calm voice.

Her arms remained crossed, her gaze averted. "I can't have any more kids."

The blunt statement left him perplexed. Why was she choosing this moment to tell him she couldn't have more kids? Was she saying she couldn't lose Allie and Andy because she had no way to replace them? That didn't seem likely. Was she telling him it was a medical problem? He knew that, at thirty-five, she was heading away from prime childbearing years. That didn't make having more babies impossible, though.

"Science has come a long way…" he began, grasping for any modicum of reassurance he could offer.

Maeve finally turned to face him, her lips curving into a snide smile he'd never seen her wear before. "No. What I should have said is, I don't *want* any more kids. After what I've been through with Jason…all the guilt, and the worry, and the fear…I won't bring any more children into this life. I won't have any more kids with anyone—no matter how much they may want them."

At that, Fletcher finally saw the conversation for what it was: one final attempt to push him away. She knew he'd always wanted a family, and this was her way of warning him off. She was rightfully wary of getting into another serious relationship, and she was laying all her cards on the table in an attempt to protect herself from future heartbreak.

She had to know he wouldn't scare that easily. Fletcher waited in silence until Maeve finally turned to face him, her green eyes piercing his. He cleared his throat. "It's true that I've always wanted kids."

As soon as the words left his mouth, she began turning back toward the window, closing herself off, but he reached out and placed a hand lightly on her shoulder, drawing her attention back to him. "But something has become very clear to me over the past few months. You…your kids…you're special. I've always had this vague idea in my mind of what I wanted my future family to look like, but as I got to know you and your family, I realized that your family *was* it."

Maeve sucked in a breath, her eyes widening to the size of quarters.

Fletcher squeezed her shoulder. "The love the three of you have for one another is everything I've ever dreamed of. The fierce way you protect them makes my chest ache. And the way they look at you, like you're their own personal super-hero…" He paused to collect himself as tears pricked at his eyes. "*That's* what I want."

A sundry of emotions danced across her features, and he brushed some hair off her face so there was nothing blocking his view.

"I don't just want kids, Maeve," he said. "I want *your* kids."

She heaved a huge, sad sigh as she leaned forward to rest her forehead against his chest. "Me too."

32

T he next morning, at 6:07 a.m., Maeve received the call. Jason had been found at a nearby motel with both children. They were reportedly unharmed, Jason had been arrested, and the kids were headed back home in a cruiser.

Maeve had barely slept, despite being tucked into the familiar safety of Fletcher's embrace. Intermittent crying jags had peppered the night. She checked her phone every hour even though she had set the ringer to the highest volume so she wouldn't risk missing a call. It was, without question, the worst night of her life.

They hurriedly dressed before heading downstairs to the front porch to wait for the cruiser. Maeve didn't realize she'd been chewing on her lip until Fletcher gently tugged it from her teeth with his thumb.

"Try to relax," he said gently. "If you're upset, the kids will be, too."

"Do you think they're scared?" she asked, peering as far as she could down the street but not yet seeing any cars coming.

"I don't know," Fletcher replied. "They're probably more confused. From what you told me, they didn't have a lot of reason to be scared of Jason, but they haven't seen him in a while, so they're probably wondering why he came and got them from your house unannounced."

Maeve nodded. That made sense. Other than Andy seeing Jason hit her once, the kids didn't know anything about his abuse. When she had left with them, she'd kept her explanations vague, only explaining that Jason wasn't able to be a daddy anymore, and they would be better off without him.

The cruiser pulled up at the end of the driveway a few minutes later. The first thing Maeve saw was little Andy waving to her through the tinted window. The sight immediately brought tears to her eyes, but she quickly choked them back, remembering Fletcher's words.

An officer stepped out from the driver's side and opened the back doors, releasing Allie and Andy into the driveway. Maeve ran to them, pulling them both in tight and whispering in their ears how much she loved them and how happy she was to see them.

The kids didn't seem to share her intense emotions about the reconciliation.

"Mommy, we got to ride in a real police car!" Andy exclaimed when Maeve released them.

"And we saw Daddy," Allie added, wrinkling her nose. "It was kind of weird."

Maeve swallowed the lump in her throat, reining in her emotions. "Wow," she said. "You two have been busy."

The officer rounded the car and headed their way. Maeve turned to find that Connie had joined them outside, so she instructed the kids to go with her while she talked with the officer. As she stood to face him, Fletcher caught her hand in his, uniting them as a team. She sent him a small, grateful grin.

"They appear to be totally unharmed," the officer said, pointing to the kids now sitting on the porch with Connie.

"But if anything should come up, please don't hesitate to call us."

"Thank you so much," Maeve said. "And Jason?"

"He's in lock-up now," the officer assured her. "He'll be held without bail until his trial. I'd guess he'll probably get at least a year of jail time, but in the meantime, we'll award you full custody and also get restraining orders against him for you and both of your kids. He should never bother you again, ma'am."

Her knees immediately went weak with relief. She would have toppled if not for Fletcher wrapping an arm securely around her waist.

Jason was locked up, and when he got out, he wouldn't be able to get near them again. Even if he tried, she now had resources to protect her family. Rumor had it that Beau and Diego were the ones who'd actually tracked Jason to that motel, and then the police had gone in and arrested him. She had no doubt they would do everything in their power to keep Jason from ever getting near her kids again.

"Thank you," Maeve said again, unable to express to the officer how grateful she was to have her kids back.

"It was our pleasure, ma'am," he replied. "It's always nice when cases wind up like this one."

A shiver raced up her spine at the thought of the cases that *didn't* go as well as this one had, but she had to remind herself that this wasn't one of them. Jason was gone, and her kids were back. It was the best she could have asked for.

Hand in hand, Fletcher led her up the driveway to the porch where they joined the kids and Connie. Suddenly, it felt like a normal morning, with the five of them crowding around the kitchen table, eating sugar-laden cereal. Connie—ever the spoiler—was picking the marshmallows from her bowl and inserting them into Andy's when he wasn't looking. Allie was cracking up at something Fletcher had said, and he was indulging her with an expression of faux seriousness.

The scene tugged at Maeve's heartstrings because, no matter how unconventional it may have been, this was her family now. The chapter of her life in which Jason played a starring role was officially closed. She could finally move on and have a true fresh start. She could get a job using her real name. Or she could legally change her name. The options were endless now that she was in control of her own life.

She could get re-married.

The thought swung into her mind like a baseball bat going seventy miles per hour. She would need to officially divorce Jason, which shouldn't be hard, considering she had a restraining order against him. It would take time for marriage to become an option legally and emotionally for her as well. But it would eventually be an option.

Fletcher had been open about the fact that he wanted her, and despite the massive amount of shocking information she'd shared with him over the past few days, that still seemed to be the case. And it wasn't just her he wanted. It was her family. It was the package deal that she didn't come without. He didn't want her *despite* her having children. He wanted her *because* of her children and the family dynamic they had created together.

Maeve couldn't imagine a better scenario for her next partner.

After breakfast, the kids zoned out in front of the television, watching that same wacky show from the hospital that made Maeve's brain twitch. They were exhausted—apparently Jason had let them stay up late into the night, eating junk food and watching movies at the motel—and quickly conked out on the couch. She took advantage of their impromptu nap by leading Fletcher up to her bedroom where they could talk without fear of waking the kids.

"What a day," she said as she stretched out on the bed beside him. Fletcher lay on his back, cradling his hands behind his head. When she scooted next to him, he wrapped one arm around her shoulders and pulled her in close before glancing at the watch on his other hand.

"And it's only 8:30 a.m.," he joked.

She smiled and patted his chest. "Thank you for being here through this whole thing."

He took her hand in his, lacing their fingers together. "You're welcome. There's no place I'd rather have been."

"Really? Because I'd rather have been anywhere else," she said, trying for humor.

"No," he replied seriously. "I mean, there's no place I'd rather be but beside you, supporting you."

She squeezed his hand. "That means a lot to me."

"Maeve…" Fletcher trailed off, then loosened his fingers from hers. Dread momentarily overtook her as she wondered why he was pulling away, until he began fiddling with her Claddagh ring, and she was sidetracked by curiosity. He managed to slide the ring off her finger and held it up, light glinting off the golden band and details.

"What are you doing?" she whispered.

He toyed with the ring in his hands for a few moments before catching her gaze. "I've tried really hard not to pressure you," he began. "And I don't want to do, or say, or ask anything that would scare you. But *Jesus*, Maeve. After everything we've been through…I need you to know that I love you." His voice cracked on the words. Emotions welled in her own throat, but where she would have expected unease and apprehension at hearing those significant words, she only felt joy and relief.

"I love you, too, Fletch," she said, the words spilling so naturally from her lips, as if there was no other possible response.

His eyebrows jumped as if he hadn't been expecting her to say it back. Then, a wide, splitting grin overtook his face. Looking toward the ring, he flipped it 180 degrees and held it to hover just in front of her fingertip. The heart was facing inward now, which would indicate that the wearer was in a relationship.

"I want everything with you, Maeve," he said. "But I think I've proven to you that I can be a very patient man. There's a big part of me that wants to be asking you a very different question right now"—her heartbeat began racing at that—"but I know you're not ready for that yet. So, I'm asking you this instead: Maeve, will you be my girlfriend?"

With a small grin, she took his hand and guided the ring onto her finger with a breathless, "Yes." She examined the ring from this new angle, deciding that it just looked right.

Despite all her attempts to push him away, Fletcher had proven to be very patient indeed. He'd been there with her through the ordeals of the past few weeks, giving her as much support as she would accept. He had demonstrated, over and over again, just how different he was from Jason, despite her automatic assumption that all men were out to hurt her. She appreciated him respecting that she wasn't yet ready to move straight into another marriage, but she needed him to know that she wanted everything with him, too.

"Hey, Fletcher?" she said, regaining his attention from the ring he'd also been admiring. "Just so you know, when you do ask me to marry you, I'll say yes."

EPILOGUE

6 MONTHS LATER

"Can I put the star on?" Andy asked, pointing to the top of the six-foot-tall Christmas tree they were decorating in the corner of Maeve's living room. Thank God the old house had high ceilings. When they'd gone to pick out the tree, they had used Fletcher's height as their guide, not thinking about the fact that he was the tallest of the bunch.

"No, *I* want to put the star on top!" Allie cried. She tried to cross her arms, but the giant red pom-pom that created Rudolph's nose on the ugly Christmas sweater she wore got in the way. That seemed to annoy her even more, and she batted at the pom-pom as if it was an adversary.

"How about you do it together?" Fletcher suggested, shooting Maeve a sidelong glance. She nodded in his periphery, an unspoken message passing between them. That had become a common occurrence in the past few months as they hit their groove co-parenting Allie and Andy. Fletcher was careful to defer to Maeve, hyper-aware of his role as her boyfriend and not the children's father, but more often than not, she looked to him for advice and guidance.

He couldn't quantify how proud that made him. Dropping

into a father-adjacent role had been the most natural thing in the world. More and more every day, he felt like he was exactly where he belonged.

Without a word passing between them, Fletcher lifted Allie up by her waist while Maeve lifted the slightly smaller Andy. Each child took one side of the star and carefully balanced it atop the tree.

"Perfect!" Maeve announced as they set the kids back down on the floor.

"I agree," Connie said, coming up behind them with a plate of sugar cookies. She had recently broken out her holiday head scarves, and today's was dotted with penguins riding on sleds. "But I think you need a few more ornaments on the tree, too."

Fletcher sent her a conspiratorial grin. He'd filled Connie in on his plan for the day, asking her to be there because he knew how important she was to Maeve, and he wanted all of her most important people to be there.

Connie returned a sneaky smile that almost made him wonder if she was keeping more secrets than just his, but nothing could be bigger than what he had planned.

"I have some special ornaments for the three of you," Fletcher said, turning to Maeve and her kids as he held up a small, brown, paper bag.

"Ooh!" Allie squealed, always receptive to the idea of presents. "Can we see?"

"Of course." Fletcher pulled hers out first—a ballerina with a glittery tutu to represent her newest hobby. Maeve had enrolled Allie in ballet classes at the start of the new school year, and she had taken to it like a natural. The outlandish costumes she got to wear and the attention she got from adults when she showed off her moves were major factors in her enjoyment, too.

Allie's eyes flew open wide. "She's beautiful!" She grabbed

the ornament and went off to find the perfect spot to put it on the tree.

"Remember, not too low, or Peeve will knock it off, and it might break," Maeve warned. The cat had initially been terrified of the tree but had slowly warmed up to it over the past few days that it had been in the house. He quite enjoyed batting at the branches and, even more so, any ornaments he could reach.

The kids didn't know it yet, but they would be getting a second cat for Christmas—a recent rescue from the shelter where Maeve now worked. They took in mostly senior or disabled animals that may otherwise be put down, and the week before, they had received a cat who used a wheelchair strapped to its waist in lieu of its paralyzed back legs. The creature had instantly stolen Maeve's heart, and she'd immediately come home and asked Fletcher what he thought about adopting it. Honestly, he was shocked it had taken so long for her to ask to bring one of the shelter animals home. One look in her pleading eyes, and he'd been a goner.

"Andy," he said, pulling out an ornament of the Lego-man version of his current favorite superhero. "This one's for you."

"Cool!" Andy exclaimed as he took the ornament. He treated Fletcher to a wide grin that showed off his two recently lost front teeth. They had already gotten many laughs out of playing *"All I Want for Christmas is My Two Front Teeth"* while Andy showed off his smile. The little boy trailed after Allie to put his ornament on the tree.

"And this one"—Fletcher pulled out what looked like a simple green ball ornament with flecks of gold on it—"is for you, my love." He held it up, allowing the ball to twirl in his grasp. The shiny material it was made of caught the light, making the golden flecks sparkle.

"It's beautiful," Maeve said, her expression softening into one of pure adoration.

Fletcher's chest tightened at the love in her gaze. "The color reminded me of your eyes."

She took a step forward to place a kiss on his lips. "I love it. I love you."

A grin spread over his lips. "I love you, too." He placed the ornament in the palm of her hand. "It actually opens if you unscrew it. Try it out."

She inspected the ornament for a moment before twisting it open to reveal that the bottom half was actually a velvet ring holder. Her lips parted on a gasp as she took in Fletcher's mother's ring nestled into the velvet folds. It was fairly simply —a gold band with a single round diamond in the center— but its elegance withstood the test of time.

Fletcher was down on one knee by the time she looked back up. Connie had stealthily rounded up the kids off to the side to watch.

"Maeve." He reached for her left hand. "You've worn your Claddagh ring facing inward for six months now, representing that your heart is taken by me. But the truth is that *my* heart has been taken by *you* for much longer than that."

Maeve covered her mouth with her right hand as tears visibly formed in her eyes.

"I have never been more pleased or more proud to belong to someone. You have shown me what true love is, and it's a love I would fight for every day of my life. I've told you time and time again that I can be patient, but sweetheart, I'm dying to make you my wife." Fletcher took the ring from the ornament and held it up between them. "Maeve, will you marry me?"

Tears streamed down her cheeks as she looked from the ring to Fletcher.

"Say yes, Mommy," Allie whispered-yelled from off to the side.

Maeve choked out a laugh. "Yes, Fletcher, I'll marry you. I would be proud to marry you."

Relief sliced through him, closely chased by elation. This was easily the best day of his life. He delicately slid the Claddagh ring from Maeve's finger, replacing it with the engagement ring and admiring the gold against her skin. Seeing the ring that had long ago been tucked into his sock drawer—along with all his hopes and dreams of a happily ever after—resting on Maeve's finger had his heart bursting with joy.

He stood and pulled her in for a kiss that lasted long enough to have Connie clearing her throat. Fletcher pulled back with a chuckle and looked toward their audience of three. "She said yes!"

The kids clapped and hooted. Allie ran over to see her mother's new jewelry while Andy tugged at Fletcher's sleeve. He knelt down until the boy could whisper in his ear.

"Does this mean you're going to be our new dad?"

Fletcher glanced at Maeve for help, but she was busy showing off her ring to Allie and Connie. He turned back to Andy, confident he knew how she would want him to explain things.

"It means I'm going to be your step-dad. You can keep calling me Fletcher, or you can call me Dad if that feels right to you. Allie can make her own choice, too. It's all up to you guys."

Andy nodded, his expression that of someone thinking hard. "Okay. I think I'll still call you Fletcher, for now at least."

Fletcher's lips curled into a grin at the boy's serious tone. "I think that sounds like an excellent plan." He ruffled the boy's hair and stood back up.

Maeve looked over as he stood. "I have something for you, too," she said, grabbing a bag of her own. "It's not an ornament, even though it kind of looks like one." She fished out a red ribbon with something shiny dangling from the bottom of it and handed it to Fletcher.

"A key?" he asked as he turned it around in his fingers.

"To the house." Maeve gestured around her. "I want you to move in, Fletch. I wanted you to before I knew we were getting engaged. You've been here more than you've been at your apartment for the past few months. I want us to live here all together. As a family."

He slipped the key into his pocket and enveloped Maeve in his arms. "Yes, I'll move in with you," he whispered, pressing a kiss below her ear. "But we might have to paint the bedroom walls two different colors like we did in Allie and Andy's room. I'm not so sure about the green you've got in there now."

Maeve pulled back with a laugh. "We can do whatever you want as long as you promise to sleep in that bed with me every night."

Fletcher raised a brow. "Just sleep?"

Maeve pursed her lips. "Okay…and other things." She put her left hand on his chest, admiring her new ring. "Wait until the school moms get a load of this."

He couldn't help but chuckle. "They were never any competition. No one was. It was always going to be you, Maeve."

She gazed up at him, love radiating from her expression. "And now it's always going to be us. Together. Forever."

He pressed a kiss on her forehead. "Forever."

WANT MORE?

Gain access to a bonus scene when you sign up for my newsletter! Visit my website www.mollymccarthybooks.com for more details.

If you enjoyed this book, I hope you'll recommend it to a friend and consider leaving it a review on Goodreads, Amazon, Instagram, or another platform. Thank you!

ACKNOWLEDGMENTS

Writing the acknowledgements for this book feels bittersweet, as it is the final book in my very first series (I can hardly believe I'm saying that!). While I'll be moving on to new characters and worlds, the McNally men will always hold a special place in my heart. I've learned so much from writing their stories, and I'm so grateful for what they have taught me.

Thank you to my editor, Jenn; my cover designer, Wilette; and my trusty beta readers, Alyssa and Laura. You all have been with me through all three books and have truly helped make them the best they could possibly be.

Thank you to my friends and family who have supported me without fail in both big and small ways throughout this process. Special shout-out to my mom, who always reads my work despite romance not being her genre of choice. I'm sorry you didn't like the spanking scene—but I'm not sorry that I kept it in ;)

And thank you to my internet friends who have taught me, supported me, and inspired me endlessly. Another special shoutout to the Bookstagrammers and Booktokers for the work they do to support us indie authors. It means the world, and it truly does make a difference.

Finally, thank YOU for reading!

ABOUT THE AUTHOR

Molly McCarthy is an avid romance reader and writer living just outside Boston, MA. She can often be found typing away in a café, drinking a latte, and dreaming of happily ever afters. Keep up with Molly on Instagram @mollymccarthybooks.

facebook.com/mollymccarthybooks

twitter.com/mollykmccarthyy

instagram.com/mollymccarthybooks

ALSO BY MOLLY MCCARTHY

Beauty In The Details (Jack & Natalie's story)

A New Beau (Beau & Emma's story)